I AM THE CAGE

Allison Sweet Grant

DUTTON BOOKS

DUTTON BOOKS
An imprint of Penguin Random House LLC
1745 Broadway, New York, New York 10019

First published in the United States of America by Dutton Books,
an imprint of Penguin Random House LLC, 2025

Visit us online at PenguinRandomHouse.com.

Library of Congress Cataloging-in-Publication Data is available.

ISBN 9780593616918

1   3   5   7   9   10   8   6   4   2

Printed in the United States of America

BVG

Edited by Julie Strauss-Gabel
Design by Anna Booth
Text set in Adobe Garamond Pro

To Kayo—
For not leaving
until you had to leave.

Hi.
My name is Elisabeth.
That's what I call myself now.
What I mean is, that's who I am now.
That's who I am.

1

MOST PEOPLE don't like coming home to an empty house, but it's the best part of my day. Leaving it is the hardest.

The walk to the store is long and cold, and I wrap my arms around myself. It's early and the fresh-laid powder is untouched. It snowed overnight just enough to make everything beautiful but not so much to make everyone miserable. The sky is a tranquil washed-out blue, and the streets are coated in a blanket of stillness. Icicles drip beneath snow-lined branches. The sun, so brilliant against the snow I have to shield my eyes, forms the shadow that is my only companion on my way to work.

Each step I take leaves a crunching footprint behind me. Approaching the end of the street, I pass the only house that could be considered my neighbor, though there's a huge plot of land that stretches between us, barren except for a small oasis of trees. The town's sheriff, Sheriff Harmon, lives there, though we've never met. I've seen his headlights, like tiny fireflies in the distance, pulling into his driveway late at night and pulling out again early in the morning. But catching glimpses of his police car from my window has been the extent of our interaction. As for anyone else who might be living nearby, they're all strangers to me.

I come to the end of the street and turn left at the stop sign onto the single-lane highway. Here, the narrow road has already been plowed, so I find a stretch of exposed pavement and quicken my pace. There's not much to see—a few large warehouses in the distance, a run-down barn and a decaying fence, vast expanses of snow-covered fields. It doesn't really turn pretty until I get closer to Main Street.

I turn left again at the corner and pass a small specialty market. Across the street is a two-story gallery with thickly framed watercolors and colorful beaded necklaces hanging in the window. I pass the flower shop with its latticed storefront and its lights already on. Steam rises out of an exhaust pipe above the little diner at the end of the block, and I can smell the flour in the air. There's a bakery with what must be decrepit fondant-covered boxes piled high in the front display, not having changed at all since I arrived in this town. There's a used bookstore, its aisles so narrow and jammed with books it feels like a life-sized maze. I've ventured inside a handful of times but refuse to visit too often. I don't want the owner to start referring to me as a regular. I walk by one of the many souvenir shops, which really aren't any different from the shop where I work, but which my boss, Mr. Ito, insists on calling convenience stores. I turn right on Cottage Row another block down and cut across the empty street.

I pull the key from the inside pocket of my parka and let myself in with a ding of the bell. I lock the door behind me and flip the switch, watching each row of fluorescent lights come to life in succession, like stadium spectators doing the wave. There's a small storage room in the back where Mr. Ito keeps all of the business's paperwork, and I hang my coat on a hook on the wall. It's just before eight o'clock. On Saturdays, the store opens at ten. I sit down in the office chair behind Mr. Ito's desk. And I wait.

Mr. Terry Ito and I are the establishment's only two employees. The wooden sign above the front window reads THE TREASURE BOX, but we just call it the store. I wandered in the week I moved to Fish Creek, a small town near the northernmost point of a serrated peninsula off the east coast of Wisconsin. I was looking for basic necessities—you know, like scented stationery and dream catchers. Mr. Ito was alone behind the counter and let me saunter around uninterrupted until I approached him to pay for my selections. He rang up my beeswax candles on an old-fashioned cash register, silently but with a smile. I paid the fifteen dollars I owed in cash. I was about to exit the shop when I stopped and turned to him. I knew I'd have to find a job eventually, and this looked like as good a place as any, so I asked if he was hiring. It turned out he had grown up in Fish Creek and moved away to raise a family but had returned after becoming a widower. He bought the store to keep himself busy, and he'd been running it alone for the past ten years since his wife's death. But now that he was getting older, he thought taking on some help wasn't a bad idea. I didn't disagree.

I started coming in a few days a week, doing inventory and straightening shelves. Mr. Ito lets me go about *my* business at *his* business without much interference. He likes to sit at the register and read the local newspaper, and if there's nothing for me to do, I keep myself busy sampling perfumes and testing candles and deciding on a daily basis which ones I like best. Fish Creek is a pretty small town. Although it gets plenty of tourists in the warmer months, the little bell on our shop door doesn't ring too often. Most of the time it's just Mr. Ito and me.

Mr. Ito pays me a pretty decent wage, considering I really don't do anything. It's not hard to order more stock when we run low on something (usually it's the lavender soap, which Mr. Ito says is favored by the more finicky families in town) or to dust the wicker rocking chairs lining the back of the store. I like Mr. Ito a lot, though I don't tell him so. Better not to become too invested. Better not to become too close. Mr. Ito's kind of like a houseplant—he adds life to the space but doesn't demand a lot of attention. He generally sticks to his side of the store, and I generally stick to mine. There are days when we say hello in the morning and goodbye when we close up and not another word in between. I think that's okay with both of us. I think he just likes having someone there.

And although he's never said so, I think he knows that for me this arrangement is not just okay—it's ideal. Because I can tell myself I'm not a weirdo—I have a job in town. And I'm not a burden—I'm nineteen and a contributing member of society. And I can tell myself I'm not paranoid, because I nod and wave as I pass people going to and from work every day. I'm just an introvert. A loner. A solitary person. And I can tell myself that everything is fine. There's nothing wrong with spending my days decluttering the dank corners of an empty souvenir shop. There's nothing wrong with spending every night alone in my little cabin. There's nothing wrong with making myself a little dinner, listening to a little music, reading a little book, and wishing for a little peace. And never letting anything out and never letting anyone in. And doing it all over again the next day.

I am fine.

2

_____

THE SHOP DOOR SWINGS OPEN and a gust of cold air rushes through, jingling the wind chimes in the window. I recognize the two women, chatty locals, though I don't know their names. I've seen them in the store a few times before. They tend to dawdle, comb through the shelves, and make messes of my neatly arranged displays, though in the end they always leave with the same item or two as usual. Today, the shorter one with the curly red hair makes her way to the small kitchen section to examine the novelty coffee mugs. Her friend, a poufy brunette, wanders halfway across the store to grope a set of whittled animal figurines. She spends a few minutes inspecting the bears in particular, turning them over to check if they're anatomically correct. They're not, and she appears disappointed. She then strolls over to the snow globes, grouped neatly by size on just-dusted glass shelves, and gives each one a hearty shake. Watching her dirty them with her fingerprints reminds me that Mr. Ito asked if I could select one as a gift for his wife's great-niece. I make a mental note.

Despite their distance, the two women continue to gossip and yammer on at each other as if they're side by side. When the redhead's done browsing, just as expected, she makes her way over to the soaps, chooses two lavender-scented bars, and brings them to me at the counter.

"That's sixteen eighty," I say, punching the items into the register.

She digs through her purse for the cash, pulling a tiny wallet out of an enormous handbag. "I hear we're in for a storm later today," she says.

"Mm-hmm," I reply, though I thought the storm was over.

Her friend comes up behind her empty-handed. "Hope this winter's not going to be a repeat of last year. I don't think my nerves can take it."

The redhead agrees and pulls out a few bills and some change. She looks at me, expectantly. They both do.

An ordinary person would think they're just being friendly. Striking up conversation, shooting the breeze, whatever. But that's not me. I look at them, their vacant faces, their air-pumped hairdos, their kohl-rimmed eyes scanning me up and down. Assessing. Judging. I internally recoil. I don't want to chitchat. I don't want to get to know you, and believe me, you don't want to get to know me. This is a transaction, not a conversation.

I give them a polite, closed-lip smile and place the soaps in a small bag before handing the redhead her receipt.

"Love these," she says, bringing the bag up to her nose.

Of course you do. "Thanks for coming in."

I spend the next thirty minutes putting everything back just the way it should be. The soaps arranged in a spiral pattern in their wicker baskets, the wooden animal figurines arranged by species and family, the coffee mugs stacked by color and type. When I get to the snow globes, I decide it's a mess that cannot be salvaged, and I take them all off the shelves to start fresh. I pause when I get to my favorite one, a medium-sized piece with a carved wooden base. The glass globe houses a blooming ceramic rose, butter yellow with faintly greening tips, with snow that is not snow, but silver glitter. I set this one aside.

Mr. Ito makes it in around noon with small chunks of ice stuck to the toes of his boots. I've been occupying myself with the window display, arranging little wooden bowls by size. They're handmade, so they're not perfectly round, and I'm vacillating between which bowl wins the title of largest—the deepest one or the widest. I weigh them both with my hands.

"Morning, Elisabeth. Did you have a hard time getting in?" he asks.

"Good morning, Mr. Ito. Nope. The walk was a little slippery, but everything's fine."

"Good," he says. "Could've been a lot worse."

"Mm-hmm," I reply, crowning the deepest bowl the winner and setting it in its rightful spot at the top of the display.

"Any customers this morning?" he asks.

"Just one," I say. "Lavender soap."

Mr. Ito smiles a small, knowing smile and disappears to hang his coat on the hook beside mine. When he emerges, the slush on his boots has melted, and only a thin wet sheen remains. He stumbles a little as he walks slowly from the back room, picking at a loose thread on his sweater.

"Toes bothering you today, Mr. Ito?"

"Oh, no, not at all. I guess they're just numb from the cold."

Mr. Ito is a small man with shoulders rounded from the dim confines of widowhood and gouty toes. But he doesn't want to trouble me any more than I want to trouble him. He smiles widely and shuffles to the counter with a newspaper tucked under his arm. He places it beside the snow globe that I've left there for him and takes a seat on the stool, propping his boots against the tilted stacks of *Ornithologist Monthly* collecting beneath the register. Mr. Ito hides his nose in the crisp folds of his newspaper. I hide myself in the thick haze of the incense racks.

I am okay.

3

MR. ITO AND I walk out of the store at four o'clock in the afternoon. We close early in the winter, before it gets dark. He locks the door behind us and tips his brown tweed hat at me.

"Have a good evening, Elisabeth."

"See you on Monday, Mr. Ito."

Mr. Ito walks east. I walk south.

I follow Cottage Row out of the touristy part of town and along the bay. I like to take this route home in the evenings, rather than the highway, because of the way the setting sun glistens off the water. It takes a lot longer, but it's worth it. Today the walk is particularly peaceful—the fallen leaves poking through the cloak of snow beneath the forest to my left. The low, white horizon where the vanilla sand meets the glassy bay to my right. The ice-slicked picnic benches frozen in time.

Passing the path to the little pocket of sand known as Sunset Beach Park, I watch the sun sink lower and lower in the sky and try to enjoy the duality of the sun's heat and the wind's chill simultaneously caressing my face. I gaze at the big houses to my right, picturesque beneath crystal canopies, with evergreen wreaths decorating their arched doors. The breeze picks up, shaking the branches above my head and blowing loose hairs across my vision. I don't mind; my feet are dry inside my boots, my hands are warm inside my gloves, and I have my fur-trimmed hood pulled up over my head.

Still, I wrap my arms tightly around myself. It has nothing to do with the weather.

I follow the road where the forest forces it closer to the water's edge. Something catches my eye ahead of me—flashing lights reflected off the snow. I stop, frozen on the icy road. Something is wrong. My brain immediately tugs at me, tells me to turn around, to walk back to Main Street and follow the highway home. But I'm almost halfway and the sun is setting quickly—if I double back now, it'll be dark before I make it there.

Tentatively, I continue on. Beyond the bend in the road I see the source of the red flashes of light. It's a police car—the sheriff's cruiser, in fact—blocking off a gigantic tree branch that has fallen in the middle of the road. I watch the sheriff's back as he finishes taping off the dicey area. Although I know I'm quiet, he turns around as I approach.

Having only seen his car come and go in the distance, I've never gotten a good look at the sheriff before. He's young, younger than a sheriff should be, as the word *sheriff* itself implies salt-and-pepper hair and a tobacco-stained smile. He appears to be in his midtwenties, tall, with thick brown hair cut short and pushed back off his face. He has dark eyes, set deep beneath equally dark brows, and a weekend's worth of stubble covers a square jaw. His khaki-colored uniform jacket, complete with a metallic star on the chest, is zipped up to his neck, allowing just the curve of a navy collared shirt to peek through. I know instantly I want nothing to do with him.

He clears his throat. "Excuse me, miss. You can't be here—it's not safe."

I stop again, this time at those words, as long, icy fingers slide slowly around my throat—*it's not safe*. My brain pauses—I don't understand—it *is* safe here in Fish Creek. I've gone to great lengths to keep it that way. He stands motionless—watching me with confused, querying eyes. Then I realize he simply means that I'm not allowed to walk here, that it's not safe because of the fallen branches.

The clutch around my neck begins to relax. I'm able to breathe again.

"I know," I say as nonchalantly as I can, in an attempt to cover up my misplaced alarm. I start moving again, but keep my distance, walking in a wide circle around the debris.

He looks at me questioningly as I tread carefully on the road. "You live across the field from me, don't you?"

I discreetly jut out my jaw. "Mm-hmm," I say.

He looks sheepishly at the snow-covered ground. "I'm sorry we haven't met yet. I mean, I'm sorry I haven't come by . . . to introduce myself or something."

"That's okay," I say. That's really okay.

He takes a few steps in my direction. "Well, can I give you a lift home? I'm done here until the cleanup crew can make it over. They're still working on a bit of minor damage from overnight."

"Um, thanks, but I'm good," I say, stepping away from him as he steps toward me. It's an awkward dance, and he watches me with curiosity as I maintain the distance between us. I complete the half circle around the perimeter of the fallen branch and start to turn away from the sheriff.

"Wait," he calls after me. "Please."

I stop again, out of impatience rather than obedience. I turn back around to look at him.

"What's your name?" he asks softly.

"Elisabeth," I reply.

"Elisabeth." He smiles the name. "I'm Noah. I've been a terrible neighbor. Please, let me be a good sheriff. Please let me give you a ride home."

I feel that tug again. The one where my brain says *no no no no no. Not safe.* My mind runs in circles as I consider his request. He's the sheriff, so it should be safe. But then, *he's the sheriff,* so that makes him definitely not safe. And then: *Is this kid really even the sheriff?* I can't make up my mind.

A strong gust of wind blows in from the bay and weaves its way through the edge of the forest. The trees above us rattle and sway, and a branch not much smaller than the one already fallen hurls itself to the ground between him and me. It cracks in half on the icy pavement; shards of bark fly in all directions.

I take a small jump back from the debris. My eyes and the sheriff's meet. Definitely not safe.

My mind is made up for me.

4

I LIKE TO KEEP LISTS. They help me remember things. They help me feel safe. Here's a list of all the people I don't trust. It's deceptively short—don't be fooled.

> Doctors.
>
> People studying to become doctors.
>
> Healthcare "professionals" of any kind.
>
> Anyone who likes to keep information about other people. (Here's where the deception comes into play. If you think about it, this encompasses a lot of people.)
>
> Anyone who wants to get to know me. (See also parentheses above.)

As I see it, the sheriff fits firmly into the last two buckets.

But again, I don't see that I have much of a choice, so I begrudgingly slide into the back seat of the sheriff's car. "Sorry," he says, holding the door. "Civilians aren't allowed in the front seat while on duty." I shake my head, dismissing it, as if it makes no difference to me. But I feel uneasy as I climb in and he shuts the heavy door beside me.

I look around the confined space—I've never been in a police car before. The leather seats are brown and worn with deep cracks stretching across them. The window next to me appears denser than usual, wavy somehow, and the door handle is absent from the space beneath it. A partition sits in front of me—shiny silver metal rods formed into the shape of a chain-link fence—separating the front and back seats. It's anchored at the corners by thick metal bolts.

A familiar fear moves through me.

My breath comes quickly; my heart starts to race. I lace my fingers through the steel grid just inches from my face. The metal is cold and slightly yielding as it creaks beneath my tensing palms—just like I remember. Just like I knew it would be.

I regret my decision immediately. I want out.

"So, how long has it been exactly since you moved to Fish Creek?" the sheriff asks after sliding into the driver's seat and starting the engine, oblivious to the panic percolating in the back seat.

Everything's okay. Everything's okay. "Um, about eight months," I say, clearing my throat.

"Right," he replies. "I remember Jonathan saying that you had moved in. Your landlord?" he clarifies, his eyes meeting mine in the rearview mirror.

The air feels thicker, heavy on my tongue. My throat shrinks to the size of a straw. I nod my reply.

"He's my brother, you know."

"Mm-hmm," I reply. The back seat of the car gets smaller and smaller. The metal partition before me gets bigger and bigger. "I think . . . I think he might have mentioned that," I squeak out.

He looks my way again in the mirror. "You okay?" he asks.

"Mm-hmm," I manage, and nod again as the sound sloshes around in my head. I vaguely sense him backing the car away from the fallen branches and turning north onto Cottage Row. I should've gone back this way myself. I should have gone back.

I glance out my fuzzy window and try to focus on the sun as it nears the horizon across the bay. It's an enormous ball of fire in the sky, scorching every little rise it touches on the water's rippling surface. Fire and water, coexisting happily for a brief moment in time. I weave my fingers together, bring my joined hands up to my lips, and exhale slowly over my knuckles. I attempt to unfurl my rigid body as much as I can.

I can feel the sheriff's eyes watching me in the mirror. To him, it probably looks like I'm just warming my hands with my breath. A perfectly normal thing for a perfectly normal person to do on a cold day. I keep my eyes from his, and I don't say anything to make him think otherwise.

We make our way through the downtown area, the streetlamps coming on as dusk settles in. A few brave people linger on the street, bundled up against the cold, locking up their shops or grabbing last-minute items from the market or the bakery at the end of the road.

Just then, big, fluffy cotton balls fall out of the sky and plop onto the windshield like pom-poms. In a matter of seconds, thousands follow, and we are surrounded by glittery, downy puffballs drifting slowly, like dandelion heads, to the ground.

I'm momentarily distracted from the panic sitting at the base of my skull and behind my eyes. This is what it's like to be inside a snow globe. "It's so beautiful," I say. And this time, when I take a breath, I feel myself relax a little.

The flakes pick up and quickly coat the road in a virgin layer of snow. "Whoa, it's getting slippery again," the sheriff says as the car skids a little. "I hear it's really supposed to accumulate overnight. We might get up to a foot or so."

"Oh, I didn't realize," I say, taking another purposeful breath, letting the clean, earthy scent of snow fill my lungs. "I thought last night was it."

"No, that was just the opening act. Tonight's going to be a lot worse."

The sheriff pulls onto my street—our street, I guess. Reaching what I know is my driveway hidden beneath a thin layer of white, he puts the car into park. I watch him through the warped glass as he approaches my door to release me from the back seat. He opens it, and I breathe in the evening air. I breathe in the stillness. I breathe in the calm.

"Listen," he says, and then he stops himself. Then he opens his mouth as if he's going to continue and then closes it once more. I raise an eyebrow at him, and he tries again. "I'll be home tonight. If the storm gets bad, if anything's wrong, just knock on my door, okay? Don't worry about the time."

Not going to happen. "Thanks," I say, climbing as quickly as I can out of the car. "But I'll be all right."

"Nice to finally meet you, Elisabeth," he says, his gaze following me while I walk the short path to my front door.

"Thanks for the ride home, Sheriff Harmon," I call, glad to be away from him.

"No problem at all. And it's Noah."

I unlock my door and push it open. I give a little wave goodbye to the sheriff still lingering on the driveway, as if to say, *Okay, then, you can go now.* I close the door as he backs slowly away from my house. I lock it behind me and exhale.

You might say I'm a bit agoraphobic. That's okay with me. I'm home, and there's no place else I'd rather be. I like the way my cabin feels, especially at dusk—the light making everything sharper and duller all at once. Then the evening comes in, settling over me like a cloud, soft and majestic. I take a slow, deep breath, letting my lungs expand almost to the point of pain. I blow it out and let my breath sweep away the dust of the day. I am home.

I am safe.

5

THEN

"NERVOUS?"

Mom stood behind me, pulling the thick strands of my hair through blunt, whisker-like bristles. The mirror sat in front of me, clear, harsh, exposing.

"No."

She brushed my shoulder—accidentally, I'm sure—with the back of her hand as she set the hairbrush on the vanity. I watched her in the mirror, elbows jutting out like chicken wings, as she gathered my hair into one hand and twisted the black elastic band around it three times before splitting the bulk of the ponytail in two, fisting the sections, and yanking them apart to pull it taut. It felt like a tourniquet.

"You look nervous," she said, placing her hands on my shoulders and meeting my eyes. Deliberate. Mom rarely touched me. When our bodies did come into contact, it was purposeful, and brief.

It wasn't that she didn't want to. It wasn't that she didn't love me. But her ambivalence held her back.

I glanced at my face in the mirror—a sharp contrast to the one behind it. Hers tan, painted, pretty in an obvious and pleasing way. Mine pale, plain, awkward—exuding the jumbled ungainliness of prepubescence. I cursed the mirror for betraying me and attempted to rearrange the features on my face. "I'm not," I said again as defiantly as I could.

"Good." She exhaled, looking straight through me. Through the imperfections of today and to the promise of tomorrow. "There's nothing to be nervous about."

But the mirror knew me better than my own mother knew me. Perhaps better than I knew myself. Then again, maybe she was just appeasing me.

Perhaps I was appeasing myself.

6

SHERIFF HARMON wasn't joking about the storm.

Outside my cabin the snow falls in a heavy, opaque curtain. The house vibrates with silence, with a creeping finality of being sealed inside. An unwanted thought pops into my head—my cabin as a little tomb. The warm wood paneling. The plush, comfy furniture. The ease with which I can lock myself in and nothing else. Those little touches that give it that cabin-y feel. Right now, they remind me of a coffin.

Upstairs, I change out of the clothes I wore to work. Then I search my bookshelves, overflowing with my favorite stories, for the threadbare paperback with the orange binding.

I find the book easily—at eye level along the edge of the bookcase—carry it downstairs with me, and set it near the sofa. I check the log holder next to my fireplace. It's about half full. I chew on my lip, wondering how long the sixteen or so logs will last me if the electricity goes out. I decide better to be safe than sorry and grab my boots from the front closet. I lace my feet into them before unlocking the bolt and stepping out behind the house. My eyes prickle at the cold. I make my way to the spare firewood rack that Jonathan always keeps full, uncover it, and pile as many logs as I can carry in my arms. I take them back inside and place them into the log holder beside the fireplace and then make one more trip, remembering to cover the rack back up with the tarp. Once the log holder is nearly full, I lock the back door with numb fingers, and I look for the matches.

I keep them on the mantel above the fireplace in a long, painted wooden box. It was a gift from my friend, Kacey. She made it for me in a woodworking class in school. She painted it a deep red, with a white teardrop-shaped border and a delicate pink, white, and green floral design adorned with tiny, iridescent pearls. While her craftsmanship is lacking, it's beautiful, and she made it for me.

That was back when I used to see Kacey nearly every day. Back when I knew everything that was going on in her life. Back when she knew everything going on in mine. Back when I used to answer her calls and not just listen to her messages. I flip the small box over in my hands and run my fingertips over the name shallowly carved into the wood—*Elisabeth*.

"I'm Kacey. What's your name?" a rail-thin girl with big gray eyes and cascading black hair asked. She had just moved to the Chicago area and was new to school.

"Justine," I replied.

She pulled a red Ring Pop from the pocket of her jeans and shoved it into her mouth. We weren't supposed to have candy in class. "Hmm. You don't look like a Justine. Do you feel like a Justine?" she asked.

"I don't know," I said shyly. I'd never thought about it before.

We caught sight of the teacher making his way around the corner. Kacey turned her back to him—she'd only been there a few days, but she knew the rules. Quickly she stuffed the saliva-slick candy back into her pocket.

My eyes grew wide. I loved that.

"*What's your middle name?*" *she asked.*

"*It's Elisabeth,*" *I said.*

"*Of course,*" *she said, her now-bright ruby lips stretched tightly across her face.* "*I'm going to call you Elisabeth. That's who you really are.*"

Up until eight months ago, Kacey had been the only one to ever call me that.

After removing a match, I place the box back on the mantel. At the time she made it, this wasn't what it was for. She told me it was a jewelry box. We didn't know then where I'd be now.

Using the fire poker, I rearrange the logs in the fireplace. I add two fresh logs to the top. Once I have the fire going, I cross my legs and sit before the hearth. I listen to the almost imperceptible exhale of the warming air, the crackling of the wood, the fluttering of the embers. I feel a blush rise on my face and the cold fade from my fingers. I sit there, quietly. Peacefully. Comfortably. I sit there knowing that I am where I'm meant to be.

I stare into the fire for a long while. I watch the flames go from orange to blue and then orange again. The sweetness of the burning wood stings my nostrils. Eventually, sweat begins to form beneath my hoodie, and I push myself up and head to the kitchen to make myself some pasta and vegetables for dinner.

I stand at the counter of my mint-green tiled kitchen, stirring occasionally, waiting for my food to cook. I glide my fingers over the buttons on the answering machine, pause momentarily, and press down. "Hey, Elisabeth," Kacey begins, but I stop it right there. I don't want to hear what she has to say. I *know* what she has to say. I just wanted to hear her voice. I turn my attention to the window, the faintest outline of the forest canopy sawtoothed against the last light of day. Like a mountain on fire far in the distance. I wait for it every evening.

I wonder if I'll ever talk to Kacey again.

I wonder what the sheriff's doing next door.

I sit down at the table. It's not like me to wonder these things.

After I've eaten, I make myself a large cup of peppermint tea before turning off the lights in the kitchen. I carry the tea to the sofa, where I tuck my legs beneath me and cover them with the old moss-colored afghan that hangs off the back of the couch.

I sip my tea. I open my book. Time slips away from me.

The storm is outside. I am inside. I am fine.

———

The house groans with the weight of the storm. I look up to watch the shadows cut across the ceiling. Branches like long skinny arms detached from their bodies reaching over me. They drape me with a blanket, warm like toast right out of the toaster and just as stiff.

Are you comfortable?

Are you crying?

Can you please count backward from ten?

7

I THOUGHT the power might have gone out sometime during the night, but to my great relief, it's still on. The alarm clock by my bed says 8:12 a.m. I check the thermostat behind the door—the heat has kept up with the setting. I brush my teeth and my hair, and I head downstairs.

The wind has waned in the light of day, but the snow continues to drift softly, falling like feathers from a pillow fight in heaven. It's reached at least a foot and a half high, rising up to the top stair at the base of my small porch. The tree limbs bend low under the weight of the snow. Icicles hang from the gutters like a banner of daggers and frame the top of my view.

I get the fire going, sit down, lean back into the cushions, and turn on the TV. Every station has been interrupted by emergency weather services. A large map fills the screen with ugly-looking clusters of precipitation moving angrily across the space in multiple shades of blue.

A woman's voice is on a loop, screechy, abrasive, and punctuated with mild alarm. ". . . all of Door County has been hit with over a foot, and it doesn't seem to be stopping anytime soon. A winter-weather alert remains in effect until noon tomorrow, at which point the snow totals could be well over two to three feet . . ." She's briefly interrupted by a beeping sound indicating a red ticker flashing across the bottom of the screen: *Green Bay Blizzard '99!* She continues, ". . . expecting gusts off the bay and drifts that could significantly affect travel and safety. Prepare to be homebound, as we're expecting power outages and . . ."

I turn the volume up slightly and take my mug from where I left it on the end table last night. I put the kettle on and ruffle the yellowing leaves of the tiny terra-cotta-potted ivy that sits in the foggy ray of light cutting through my kitchen. The dirt is gray and dry like cookie crumbs, and I know I'll have to replace it again soon.

A loud, intrusive beeping filters in from the other room. Then, and just for a split second, there's a flash of light. Or the absence of light. I'm not really sure. Then I hear a loud boom.

Then it's quiet.

I no longer hear the beeping. I no longer hear the weatherperson.

I wander with my mug in hand, slowly into the living room. The TV screen is black. I turn back into the kitchen and cross to the far wall by the sink. I lift the phone and place the receiver to my ear. Dead.

It's okay. Everything is okay. I have plenty of firewood. I have plenty of food. I have blankets and flashlights and batteries.

I am an adult. I am self-sufficient.

I am safe.

I just wish I had gotten to listen to Kacey's voice again.

I am not trapped.

The snow piles higher as the hands on the clock stretch from one number to the next. It's reached the top of the porch and is starting to creep a few inches up the side of the front door. And when I look out the window, all I see is white. White ground, white sky, white indecipherable lumps in between. A bumpy white ocean stretching on and on. Not a house in front of me. Not a car on the road. Not a person in sight.

But I am not trapped.

I've been trapped before. This is not trapped.

8

THEN

"NO REASON to be feeling nervous," Mom said again as she sat next to me in the hard, leather chairs.

I stared out the solitary window of the scheduler's office, and so did she. It was looking like an early winter, and already a thin sheet of snow had covered the ground. The cold air seeped in around the window edges. I hid my hands inside my sleeves and wrapped my sweatshirt tighter around myself.

I pulled my eyes from the window and glanced around the small room. The walls were covered in photos of children standing in their underwear with metal contraptions attached to their arms and legs. Some looked to be as young as four or five years old, and some were clearly teenagers, all with thick black bars covering their eyes to disguise their faces. Each photo had a handwritten diagnosis scrawled beneath it. I searched the walls until I found one that said FIBULAR HEMIMELIA AND CONGENITAL SHORT FEMUR. Like me.

I'd heard the explanation more times than I could count. Something's wrong with my leg. Some of the bone is missing, and the part that's there isn't growing right; it's three inches too short.

I heard it at home, my ear pressed firmly against closed bedroom doors as Mom recounted it to persons unknown on the other end of the phone. I'd heard it at the doctors' office, interrupted with *hmm*s and *I see*s as someone with a clipboard frantically attempted to scribble it down.

I'd heard it, but it was never explained *to* me. It was an explanation *for* me.

And this little office party was the culmination of those calls, those scribbles.

I felt sick as I looked around the room, because it was clear to me that although I might have heard it, I didn't fully understand it. Was this my future? Was I to become some faceless, skeletal form on display as if in a museum? Was I to be another piece in a collection of circus curiosities, or some macabre memento taped to the wall as in a madman's collection of souvenirs? My eyes skimmed the names scribbled beneath each diagnosis. Peter B., Charles V., Anneliese W. So many bodies, so many names, but no real people. Just unidentifiable specimens. They weren't kids; they were science projects. They were fetal pigs soaking in a bin of formaldehyde in the back of biology class. Things to be poked at. Things to be picked at. Things to be examined. I suddenly felt like I was the main attraction in the middle of an experimental theater. How had this tiny room somehow become even smaller?

I turned away from the pictures to the window again and began counting the cars as they pulled into the hospital's garage below us. They stopped briefly to roll down their windows and snatch tickets from the machine. *That's right, get your ticket. Get your ticket for the big show.* I counted 209 cars before I heard the doorknob turn.

"It's called an Ilizarov fixator," the scheduler said from behind us as she squeezed into the bomb shelter of an office after my presurgical appointment with Dr. S. "Sorry to keep you waiting." She had an enormous yellow bun on top of her head and long, glossy, hot-pink fingernails that gripped the thick stack of papers she handed to Mom. "Sign at the *X*s, please, Mrs. Amos."

She plopped down behind her desk with a grunt. "The guy who invented it, he was an orthopedic doctor who was inspired by the design of a horse-drawn carriage's harness," she said, her eyes lighting up as if she were talking about a spaceship. "See how the frame kind of holds everything together?" she said, pointing to textbook-like drawings in a tri-folded brochure. "It fixes you in place," she said. It took me a minute to realize she was referring to my bones.

This was how it was supposed to work: The doctors surgically break the bones in your affected limb. Fun. Then, in order to stabilize them, they drill through the bones (like, literally, with a hand drill) and intersect them with thick metal wires, or pins, at multiple points up and down the length of the bones. They then attach the ends of those pins to heavy rings of hardware that encircle the limb and attach the rings to one another with rods, creating an open, mechanical apparatus. The rods in between the rings are designed to slide into each other and are affixed with small rotary dials—clickers—that can be turned to increase the space between the rings. This effectively pulls the broken bones apart, little by little, lengthening the limb. Once the desired length is obtained, the fixator stays in place for a while, securing the bones and allowing new bone to grow and fill in the gaps. It is, essentially, a twenty-pound metal contraption that can't be taken off. Until, that is, a year or two later, long after you've realized what a ghastly experiment it really is, the device is removed and—voilà!—no more discrepancy. Your leg is just as long as the other one, no worse for the wear!

"Don't you worry about a thing," the office lady said, taking the freshly autographed paperwork from Mom and scanning it through thick frames sliding down her nose. There were no papers for me to sign. "Justine Elisabeth Amos. We'll have you fixed in no time."

Fixed. I looked to Mom. She appeared unaffected.

"It looks medieval," I said, trying my best to ignore her comment. "Will it hurt?"

Office Lady bunched her face up at my ridiculous question. "You'll have a PCA."

"What's that?" I asked.

"It's patient-controlled analgesic. It's a button that controls your pain medication. You're eleven, so you're old enough to push it when you need it. And then, when you go home, you'll have painkillers."

"So, it's going to hurt," I said. I had a feeling she wasn't giving me the whole truth. Just enough of it so that she couldn't be accused of lying, but not the whole truth.

"Well, it's better than amputation," she quipped. I felt the blood drain from my face. I didn't even know that was an option, but it felt like a threat.

"Besides," she continued, "Dr. S is the best."

"How do you know that?" I asked, a little snootier than before.

Her eyes flashed to mine. "There's no one else here who does it," she replied. By *here* she meant pretty much anywhere in the country.

"Well, if he's the only one, doesn't that also make him the worst?" I mumbled.

Mom yanked me up by my elbow to go.

The lady clenched her jaw and gave me a flat, tight-lipped smile. But it wasn't really a smile—it was a warning.

Suddenly I felt the undeniable urge to cry. It overtook me, like a pit bull bolting after a rabbit and I was holding the leash. But I couldn't look weak. I couldn't look scared. I bit my lip and scrunched up my face and pressed against the tears as hard as I could. Because it seemed to me that by crying, I'd be giving them more than just my tears—I would be giving my consent.

Only later, all alone, did I allow the tears to flow.

And then, I couldn't make them stop.

9

IN THE MIDWEST it's not a real winter without a record-breaking snowstorm and a major power outage. But this is my first snowstorm alone in Fish Creek.

I lace up my boots before I unlock the back door. It makes a wet, suctioning sound as I pull it away from its frame. The snow that was pressed against the closed door stays firmly in place, like a white concrete step leading out into a desolate void. I step out onto the snow and sink down. Little flurries fly into the air as I disrupt what has been so perfectly formed. Crumbled chunks of snow cover the tops of my boots.

I leave misshapen, sunken footprints behind me as I tromp out to the firewood stack. I remove the tarp from the wood and grab a few logs, then make a couple of trips carrying them to the side of the house. I stack them in a rustic, splintering deck box just outside the door. Inside, I leave my boots on a small rubber mat. A little puddle forms there.

As I put my things away in the closet, I think about what else I need to do. I've got wood—check. Flashlights—check. And I just recently went to the store. I head into the living room feeling confident and secure.

A small drawer is hidden in the TV stand in the living room. It doesn't have a handle or a pull on it—it has a secret lip beneath the trim at the top. I remove both the pen and the notebook and sit with them on the love seat. I open the notebook to a page near the front and look at the words neatly written there.

It kept you up in the night
like a fever—a weighty, oppressive cloak.
It seeped through you, through to your very
bones, like when you've been in a bath for too
long. It wrinkled and softened
the hardest parts of you. The parts you thought
were impenetrable—your smile, your light,
that special you-ness that is only you. All but your heart—
which hardened like days-old bread—
and then it went on a search for more.
You did not invite it in,
but you left the door ajar, and in it came.
A stealthy thief—it built a home in your crusty heart,
a bed in your brittle body.
It grabbed ahold of you because you could not
grab ahold of it.
You tell yourself it's the worst part of you. But
it is not a part of you at all. It's an intruder, an invader,
a terrible trespasser. It is a renter taking up
valuable space. It is a worm inside an apple.
Wriggling, writhing. Waiting for you to bite it out.

I lay the bookmark in the front and turn to a clean page at the back. I glance out the window and watch the snow. And watch the snow. And watch the snow. I tap, tap, tap the pen on the blank page again.

Tap, tap, tap. There's something there, something in the periphery. Don't look at it. Don't touch it. A snowflake on the tip of my tongue. It melts away, melts away. And it's gone.

The landscape is wild and messy outside, so naturally, I make an effort to tidy up inside. I start by making my bed, which I neglected to do after I awoke, and arrange the quilt to perfectly line up with the edges of the mattress. I smooth out the wrinkles and turn down the top hem. Each pillow receives a vigorous fluff. I dust around the bedroom, focusing on the nooks and crannies of my overstuffed bookcase, the window treatments, the baseboards, and the wicker rocking chair in the corner.

I think about how many other teenagers are voluntarily cleaning their already spotless homes at this very minute. Not very many, I'd bet. I sit down on my bed and blink away the hot, pitiful, disobedient tears that taunt me from inside my own eyes.

This is what I wanted. This is what I needed. This was my only choice. I knew it then. I know it now. I stand back up and force myself to finish the job.

My mind winds down along with the whir of the motor as I flip the switch on my handheld vacuum to OFF. I sit on the edge of my bed, feeling pathetic and pitiful, and take the nearby silver-framed photo of Kacey and me in my hands. I close my eyes and turn to my left before opening them again, and she is there beside me. She elbows me playfully in the ribs. I nudge her back. We smile at each other. "What are you doing?" she asks.

"Cleaning," I say.

She shakes her head and asks again. "What are you doing?"

I don't answer her. I stand up and place the picture frame gently on the nightstand. When I turn back to the bed again, Kacey's gone. I decide I'm done cleaning and head downstairs again to my spot on the sofa, where the only ghosts that await me are bound within the pages of my little orange book.

———

The shadows stretch across the white vastness outside my window as the afternoon draws on. I read; I settle my book on top of my chest and take a short nap; I read some more. I go to the kitchen and open the fridge to grab a diet soda before closing it quickly again. A loud, abrupt knock shakes the front door.

I check the peephole, but I can't identify a face beneath the oversized hood in the doorway. I hesitate to open it but then assure myself that no one with nefarious intentions would be out in this weather.

I unlock the door and yank it open to the abominable snowman. Nope, my mistake. It's Jonathan. He's wearing an enormous puffy jacket, thick snow pants, and heavy boots—a thin layer of powder coating him completely from waist to toe. I lean to the side and look behind him. He's carved a tunnel through the snow all the way from his red Jeep in the street to my front door. He lowers his hood and reveals a shock of blond hair curling up around his ears and at his nape. His blue eyes look like sapphires in the late afternoon sun.

Now that I've seen them both, I note that Jonathan and his brother look nothing alike.

"Lovely weather we're having, isn't it?" He jokes as a smile spreads across his face.

This is my home, but it's Jonathan's house. I'm just a renter. But Jonathan has never come over without calling first, and he's never entered the house without asking my permission. He assured me he'd be the ghostwriter of landlords when I first came to Fish Creek. It's one of the reasons I felt safe renting from him. "Hi, Jonathan. Do you want to come in?" I ask, hoping he'll say no, but stepping back into the foyer as to not appear rude.

"No, thanks, don't want to track in all this snow. I would've called, but . . . the phones, you know."

"Yeah. And thanks," I say, relieved, and I lean against the open door.

"I'll get someone over here to shovel as soon as I can after the snow stops falling. Have you used a lot of the firewood?"

"There's plenty left," I say. "I think I'm good for at least a week."

"Are you sure?" he asks. "I could check it."

"I'm sure." I nod. "Are the streets clear?"

He laughs a little, and clumps of snow slide off his jacket. "If you want to call it that. The plows are out, but they can't keep up. The snow's just falling too quickly." And then a look of concern crosses his face. "Are you planning to go out?"

"No," I say. "I was just curious. Do you know when the phone lines will be back up?"

"I don't, but probably not for a while. They're usually the last thing to be restored. They'll work on getting the power back on first," he says. "It could be a while, you know."

I nod and give him a small smile.

"All right, then," Jonathan says as he starts to back away from the door. He's a person of few words, kind of like me. Another reason why he felt safe from the beginning—he didn't ask too many questions. "Places to go, people to see. I'll check back soon, okay?"

I nod and wave goodbye.

He descends the porch steps and makes his way back into the tunnel of snow and toward his car. It's slow going, with his bulky layers and large chunks of snow caving in on either side of him. "Stay safe, Elisabeth," Jonathan calls as I close the door.

I will.

In the evening, I warm my leftover dinner over the fire in a pocket that I've fashioned out of aluminum foil. I tend to the fire. It seems to be burning through the logs quicker than it should, but what do I know? The daylight begins to fade, and I pull a few pillar candles out from my storage closet and place them around the living room. It's too dark to read, even by the candles, even with the fire, which glows with a fluctuating intensity under the veil of the dark room. I pull the afghan off the sofa, and I lay myself down on the wood floor alongside the large front window. I scoot my body as close to the glass as possible, parallel with the frosty pane.

I've done this before. I've lain beneath the window and watched the snowflakes pirouette in a flurry above me, looking ever so close but never close enough. I've lain beneath the window as my sisters played in the snow, my cheek pressed against the glass, my face stiff from the cool air seeping in around the edges. I watched the cotton confetti falling softly, cautiously, apologetically, as if to say, *Sorry, Justine.* I watched it drift lightly toward my face from a heaven that seemed so far above me. I closed my eyes and imagined the flakes' soft burn on my delicate skin, yet it never came. It was a strange middle place, not quite in and not quite out.

A kaleidoscope of memories dances before my eyes, shifting and transforming without ever coming into focus. A heavy thud. Paper crinkling beneath me. The glint of silver metal in the light. I remember the cold air blowing up my skirt. I remember the wind whipping my hair around my face. And I remember what frosty metal feels like in bone.

10

THEN

DAD WOKE ME UP while it was still pitch-black outside. We had stayed overnight at the hospital hotel. I groaned and got out of bed, washed up, and threw on the same sweatshirt I'd been wearing yesterday.

I stared back at myself in the mirror. *I am not ready for this.*

"Ready?" Dad called from outside the bathroom.

"Mm-hmm." I sighed and slid the door open. From the small table in the corner of the room, Mom directed a glance at my sweatshirt before looking away. "Our outsides are a reflection of our insides, Justine. Like the cover of a book. What does your outside say about you today?"

What she meant was if it's pretty on the outside, people don't care what's on the inside.

We checked in to the surgical department, where I was given a gown with drawings of little paper airplanes on it and a pair of scrub pants with the name of the hospital stamped carelessly all over them. After I changed, they led us to a small waiting room crammed with plastic folding chairs and a small kiddie table in the corner with construction paper and crayons stacked neatly on top.

They were supposed to take me in first thing, so I plopped down in one of the chairs, expecting to be called back soon. It was just after six a.m.

Nope, it was seven a.m.

It was eight a.m.

It was nine a.m. I was getting hungry.

It was ten a.m. Mom looked like she was ready to tear her hair out of her head.

It was eleven a.m. Dad got up and disappeared. I was suspicious he'd gone to the cafeteria.

It was noon. Dad was back, smelling like coffee and pastries. Traitor.

The Price Is Right was playing on a TV hanging in the corner near the ceiling. A woman had just won a white minivan, and she was jumping up and down like a maniac, screaming as if she had won a Corvette. A nurse dressed in blue scrubs poked her head into the waiting room.

"Miss Amos," she said.

It was one p.m.

They were ready for me.

11

IT'S MORNING. It's freezing. The thought of pulling my legs out from under the blanket is horrifying. I look around my bedroom. The windows are completely frosted over—a spiderweb of ice affixed to the glass, letting only phantom light creep through. The room feels wet in a misty, floaty sort of way.

I count to three and throw off the quilt, jump up, and dart to the closet. I change into a pair of leggings and pull a pair of sweats on top of them. I layer on three shirts, the top layer being the same hoodie I wore last night. It feels like too much and not enough at the same time.

I wander downstairs in my too-much/not-enough clothes. The fire is nearly out. I begrudgingly reach as little of my body as I must out and around the back door to bring more wood inside. I spend a good hour adding the logs, rearranging the logs, tending to the logs. My palms are rough and splintered, but I think I'm getting pretty good at building fires.

The house smells different than it did yesterday. A little bit metallic and smoky and empty. It smells like a room would smell if everything had been violently sucked out of it.

I putter around the house. I look out at the snow, still falling. The bottom third of the window is completely obscured by the packed, piled mounds. I pick up my book from the end table, but I don't feel like reading it right now. I don't feel like reading anything right now. I don't feel like anything right now. Sometimes this happens. Sometimes my thoughts become both itchy and fluid at the same time. I take an orange off the counter in the kitchen, and I use a knife to remove the peel in one long, curling ribbon.

"I've got Vanilla Bean, Orange Tang, or . . . ," she added with a small grimace, "something called Cotton Candy Carnival." She held the three tiny tubes of lip balm in front of my face. "What's your poison?"

Cotton Candy Carnival sounded interesting to me, but she obviously didn't think so. "Um, Orange Tang?" I replied. I angled my head to watch with curiosity as she coated the inside of the hard, translucent oxygen mask with the thick waxy substance.

I close my eyes and feel the inflated ring of plastic skin pressed against my own, inhale deeply, and recall the smell of citrus, sharp and bright just as the world became fuzzy and dark.

"Can you please count backward from ten?"

I can't think of anything else to do, so I pick up my book again.

───

In the afternoon, I throw my refrigerator door wide open, not caring if all the cold air escapes. There's really not much left to save anyway, I assure myself. I stand before it, willing something delicious to appear before my eyes. A big pot of chili, a bucket of fried chicken, a whole twelve-inch New York–style cheesecake. Alas, it does not.

I gather two slices of bread and two slices of cheese and wrap them in another little foil packet like I made the night before. I use kitchen tongs to hold it over the fire and make myself a grilled cheese sandwich. It's no cheesecake, but it's sustenance, and I wash it down with a cup of lukewarm chamomile tea.

Truth be told, notwithstanding the igloo encasing my home and the open-fire cooking, today is not that much different from any other day. The hours melt into one another. I find ways to keep myself busy. If I'm not at the store, I'm at home—safe and warm in my happy place. Drinking my tea. Reading my books. Writing in my little notebook. Looking out my little window. Living my little life.

I am okay.

It seems to me that more than three feet of snow has already accumulated outside. The tunnel to the front door created yesterday by Jonathan is completely gone now, just a strange wrinkle in the otherwise undisturbed wasteland of white surrounding me. I open the back door, sucking a cloud of pale, dusty speckles into the house, and maneuver the remainder of the transferred logs inside. I do my best not to let them touch too much snow and keep them as dry as possible.

For a brief moment, a wave of worry overcomes me. It's possible I'm not as prepared as I thought I was. What if I'm no better than that woman buying lavender soap at the store? What if I run out of food? What if the roof caves in from the weight of all the snow? What if I trip down the stairs, break my back, and die a slow, agonizing death while waiting for help that doesn't come until spring?

I close the back door, my hand scraping on the frozen metal frame as I pull it shut.

A memory flashes before my eyes, quick and fluttering—a white sheet flapping above me, a glint of metal beneath.

My brain freezes, blinks, and then begins to race. Images flicker behind my eyes like a strobe light—disorienting, blinding, making everything staccato and dreamlike.

My skin begins to itch with the first prickles of panic. I'm shivering and sweating and not sure which feels worse. I claw at my neck as the sensation creeps its way up to my face. My ears throb with a silence so loud it's abrasive, but it doesn't last long. They begin to fill with a thick, seeping substance, and everything within my head becomes slow and muted. I haven't moved, yet my heart starts to swell in my chest, and I have no doubt that it's about to explode. The room stretches out before me into one long, reverberating tunnel.

I feel my way to the floor and put my head in my hands. Slowly, slowly the jelly melts from my senses—receding back to wherever it is it came from. Once the room takes shape again, I crawl over to the drawer and pull out my notebook.

You're fine.

You're okay.

You're safe.

When I'm calm enough that the letters will be legible, I pick up the pen. Don't hold on to them—get them out. *Get them out of you.*

A fluttering white sheet,

The glint of metal beneath,

A jagged, rocky landscape as it

    settles over me.

A hollow ache,

A dreamlike state,

A heaviness that I cannot place.

Buttons and wires and beep, beep, beep,

"Quiet the noises, now, let her sleep."

A cold, wet pillow—it's mine to keep.

Someone whispering over me:

"This is not what I thought it was going to be."

This is not what I thought it was going to be.

I put my notebook down. Just as quickly as the memories came, they vanish—like footprints washed away by the sea.

These memories are the ones that bother me most. They hide from me, nearly forgotten, until something tiny, something meaningless, like the sudden touch of unyielding steel, stirs them from their secret places. Then they rush at me, a leftover, bitter, panicky wave that crashes down over my head, impossible to ignore, begging to be acknowledged, but totally ungraspable, like the tail of a long-forgotten film reel flapping as it spins around and around. They come and go without a moment's notice and toss me side to side and upside down and every which way, leaving me both completely overwhelmed and completely bereft.

And still, there's something else there, something right on the edge of the memory. Something that I turn away from. A little room beyond a door I dare not open. Something shrouded in the shadows. Something hidden behind a curtain. Something hard and cold and very, very wrong. Something playing hide-and-seek in the corners of my mind, waiting, crouching just out of sight.

12

EVENING FALLS, as it usually does, and the snow has not let up. The thermostat in the bedroom reads fifty-eight degrees. I turn on the water to wash my face, but I can barely hold my hands beneath the glacial stream long enough to complete the task. When I've finished, the power outage justifying an abbreviated routine, both my hands and my face are red from the cold.

Before lying down in front of the fire and burying myself in blankets, I stand at the window and gaze out at the expansive white nothing. A tiny sprite of a bird appears out of the nothingness and lands on the snowbank just on the other side of the glass. His body is the size of a kumquat, with brown and beige feathers and a beak as sharp as a diamond, and his tiny black eyes dart around like pinballs until they finally land on me. We look upon each other, the bird and I, in opposite worlds. Divided by an invisible barrier, touching but clearly separate. The light from my world penetrating the dark, the shadows from his world eclipsing mine.

He opens his beak with the precision of a protractor, and the slightest vibration can be seen at the apex of his throat. He's calling, but I hear no sound. We stand, staring at each other, curious, considering—until something within him is satisfied, or perhaps surrendered, and he turns from me and flutters away. Only pea-sized broomstick-like indentations tell the tale of where he's been. They disappear in the flurries almost as quickly as he does.

I feel a sense of sadness for this tiny, helpless thing lost in the storm. What must he think? What must he feel? All that he knows is now upside down—nothing is recognizable. How frightening it must be, to wake up to a world completely changed, and to no longer understand your place in it.

13

THEN

I AWOKE sometime in the middle of the night. I was in a dark room, some faraway rectangle of light casting shadows across a hard, metal bed. I couldn't move. Everything was heavy. Everything hurt.

The tears appeared out of nowhere—like dew on a windshield. Maybe they'd already been there, even as I slept. Maybe they were waiting for me.

Mom was in a recliner beside the bed. I didn't turn to look at her, my head no longer a head but a water balloon. I could hear her gentle snoring. Soft little sighs singing inches away from my screaming body.

I moved my arm in an attempt to wipe at a tear and froze as I felt the tug of an IV line taped to my skin. I tried again, dragging my arm up to my face, inadvertently disturbing the white sheet draped loosely across me. It rippled in a strange way—like it had caught on something. I moved again, a bit more forcefully this time, and the sheet fluttered gently above me. My eyes then caught on something, too—something shiny and ridged underneath.

14

I AM AWAKE before I open my eyes. I'm tired and stiff and feel the urge to stretch but refuse to uncurl my body from its pocket of warmth. Eventually, I uncover, uncoil, and listen for the hum of the furnace. I reach down and hover my palm above the nearby vent in the floor—hoping to catch any hint of airflow. Nothing.

Despite the thermostat reading fifty-two degrees, I spend a few hours rearranging the books on my bookshelf upstairs. I have them organized by genre, and then alphabetically by the author's surname. My fingers linger on some of my favorites before I pull them all off the shelves and stack them neatly on the floor. I spend some time thinking about how I'd like to recategorize them. I decide I want to stack them by color and carefully sort the stacks into new stacks based on the dominant color of each book's binding. Some of the books—the ones with multiple colors on their spines—give me trouble, and I really have to think hard about where they belong. In the end, the pile with black spines is by far the largest, whereas there are very few books with yellow or green covers. I decide that this discrepancy will make for a poor visual display, so I ditch the color idea altogether and regroup the books again—by genre, and then alphabetically by the author's surname. When I'm done, my bookshelf is exactly as it was before.

My eyes quickly touch upon the small pile of books in various stages of completion resting on my nightstand. And beside them, the silver picture frame. Me and Kacey, before I left. Before everything was different. My gaze hovers there, but only for a moment.

———

By noon, on this the third day since the beginning of the storm, I am admittedly feeling restless. It's not a sensation I'm used to. I like my little life of isolation. I like the simplicity, the predictability. Since coming to my cabin, I have not once felt lonely, not once felt bored. My books and my fire mountain and my mint-green tiled kitchen and my peace are all I need.

I like a quiet life. I'm good at a quiet life.

I sit with my feet to the fire and roll my pant legs up to feel the heat on my skin. I run my fingers over the scars, smooth white blemishes that mar my skin from my toes all the way to my hip. Some small and round, others long and jagged. I touch a small group of them near my ankle, shiny and dimpled, and remember how they got there. They were born out of a storm of a different kind.

It hurts to touch them. Not like it used to—not physically. That pain is long gone. It hurts to touch them and to think they will always be here. That they will always be a part of me. A part of me that I cannot hide, a part of me that I cannot erase. Cannot shed. No matter where I go. No matter what I do. No matter who I become, no matter what becomes of me. In the light, in darkness, at the bottom of some vast fiery gorge, in the farthest corners of the universe, when the wind flattens mountains to the sea. When I am nothing but debris and brittle bone, these scars will remain. Whether I want them to or not.

They're trauma tattoos—permeating and permanent. What has happened cannot be unhappened.

> 52 scars
> 209 cars
> One hundred dreams
> One thousand screams
> One million tears

15

THEN

DOCTORS AND NURSES AND TECHS. Lions and tigers and bears. And I was scared of them all. They came in; they went out; they came in; they went out. The hospital was one big carousel of people in white coats and squeaky shoes and stethoscopes snaked around their necks going around and around and around. It was dizzying and disorienting and I wanted to get off.

But within the carousel was another carousel going in the opposite direction. Like the cogs inside a grandfather clock, spinning back and forth and this way and that, and somehow you were supposed to know exactly what time it was. But on this ride there was no time, no distinction between day and night or up and down because it was all wrapped up in a big thick blanket called morphine. It was too big and too heavy and you were so deep within it that there was no way to find your way out even though you were dying to escape from underneath and take a frantic gulp of fresh air. The weight and the shadows made everything too difficult. Under the blanket that doctor could have been a lion or a tiger or a telephone booth.

But then, after an inexplicable amount of time crawling around in circles, the oppression of the morphine blanket began to dissipate, to cool, to fold back on itself, and day became day again and the cat in the corner turned back into a nurse and I began to sense something other than the blanket weighing me down. The weight became bulkier and more defined and it was achy and it was misery and it was no longer just a weight, now it was a jackhammer mangling my bones and steel teeth shredding my flesh. But I was stuck in that bed—*let me out, let me out!*—and I couldn't escape the incessant pounding. It got stronger and louder, and as much as it hurt, the hurt made everything crystal clear. The doctor was a doctor, the nurse was a nurse, my mom was my mom, and she was telling me to push the button, push the button, push the button. So I did, I pushed the button and waited for the blanket to come back up over me and make everything funny and backward again.

And around and around I went.

16

I'VE NOW used the last three logs in the log holder. I search through the storage closet until I find a pair of snow pants, drag them over my clothes, and retrieve my parka from the foyer. I zip it as high as it will go, pull my gloves on tight, and steel myself for the elements.

Flakes are still falling in clumps from the white stretch of sky above. I reach around and take the shovel that I've left by the back and begin digging myself a new trench in the direction of the spare firewood rack. The snow is heavy and wet; each shovelful feels like I'm lifting rocks. I keep my head down as I work, fighting with the snow that won't let up and the snow that's already fallen. Half of what I gather onto the shovel slides off and mocks me as I try to toss it aside.

My arms ache; my hands are cramping; most of my body is numb. When I finally make it to the firewood, I reach up to pull the tarp back. But wait—the tarp is not there. I look around in disbelief. A sense of dread settles over me. I don't know if I forgot to secure it, or if the wind completely dislodged it—but the tarp is nowhere to be seen. I start to become frantic. All four sides of the firewood pile are covered in snow, silver slivers of ice nestled in the crevices in the bark. I don't even bother trying to wipe it off. It's wet, and I know this wood won't burn.

Chastising myself, I turn around and make the slow, awkward trek back to the house empty-handed. I drag the shovel behind me in frustration. Once inside, I kick my sopping boots into the corner and slam the door. The loud crack echoes in the frigid space. "Shit!" I yell into the lifeless room. What am I going to do now?

The remainder of the afternoon is spent stewing in my own stupidity. Eventually, the last of the fire hisses at me. I adjust it with the fire poker. One of the logs slides to the bottom of the grate and sends up a flurry of sparks. Quickly I run my hand through my hair, making sure a stray spark didn't land there. I use the tongs to move the uncooperative log back on top of the others. It slips again, sending another wave of glowing embers toward my face. I give up on the logs. No matter how I arrange them, the fire remains weak.

I take a piece of newspaper and twist it into a fan. Attempting to coax something more out of the fire, I watch the newspaper burn to the point where my fingertips get hot and I have to let it drop. I say a little prayer for something magical to happen, for a secret special spark to send the fire roaring and reaching for the sky. But no. I give up on the newspaper, too.

The sun begins to set outside my living room window, and I carry myself to the kitchen to scrounge for dinner. I pull a potato out of its mini burlap sack. I wash it in the sink, my fingers screaming at the temperature of the water, and dry it with a paper towel. As I do this, I look out over the tops of the evergreens. The sun is not yet low enough to create the fire mountain—it just looks like an expansive mess of green and white.

I roll the potato in aluminum foil and twist each end until it looks like a giant piece of wrapped hard candy. I have no idea how long to hold it over the fire, so I just wait until the tin foil turns purple from the heat and the potato gives a little when I squeeze it with the tongs. It takes a long, long time. Once I unwrap it, put it onto a plate, and cut into it, I realize how undercooked it is. I eat it anyway.

I try to remember how long a person can go without eating. Is it three weeks? Four? I wonder how many disgusting potatoes I'll have the strength to force down my throat. I wonder when the dank scent of cold tea will turn me off from drinking altogether. I start to wonder about what happens to a body when it freezes.

I wonder how long it would take for me to shovel my way down to the road. Would I even make it that far? Would anyone even drive by to see me there? I wonder how long it would take for someone to find my body if I were buried beneath the snow.

I begin to feel my heart pounding in my chest. It gets stronger and stronger until I can feel it in my throat. Despite the dwindling fire, I am suddenly very hot. My hands tremble as I slough off my hoodie before sinking silently to the floor.

I am fine. I am okay.

I am fine. I am okay.

And then—maybe I'm not fine. Maybe I'm not okay.

Maybe I really am trapped.

Maybe I'm going to die.

17

THEN

I WANTED TO DIE.

The moon loomed impossibly large and white through the window to my side, casting streams of silver light into the dark room, and I wanted to die. Mom slept silently beneath it, covered with an afghan she'd brought from home and wearing a pair of hospital slipper-socks with the grippy soles that she stole from the supply closet when the nurses weren't looking, and I wanted to die. And the little blue box next to me, with its overflowing nest of wires and cords and flashing neon numbers, looking more like a bomb than a piece of medical equipment, chirped and pulsed at regular intervals, reminding me with annoying persistence that yes, yes, I was alive, I was alive!—but I wanted to die.

Not because of the pain, excruciating though it was. Not because of the warm pool of nausea that had dug a ravine from the base of my skull, nor the continuous cloud of tears casting shadows across my vision. But because of other things stirred up alongside them. Subtler things. Things I wasn't expecting. Things that I couldn't even see. Physical pain, as it turned out, wasn't a solo traveler—the body selfishly dragged an unsuspecting companion along for the ride. And where does the mind go when the body can't go anywhere at all? Far, far away. As far as it possibly can, I'd argue.

An animal trapped will gnaw off its limb to set itself free.

18

I DON'T DIE.

I take deep breaths in and out until the static impeding my vision clears. I pull myself back up and go to the window. Though the shadows stretch far across the yard, it's not dark yet. I attempt to formulate a plan while I scramble around the house.

I shut the mesh curtain and glass doors on what's left of the pathetic, puttering fire. I carry my discarded hoodie upstairs and put on a thick wool turtleneck sweater in its place. Back downstairs, I find a hat and tug it down over my ears. I stuff myself into a jacket and pull my hood up on top.

I don't want to go. I don't want to ask anyone for help. But I fear my only chance is to go and find Sheriff Harmon. If I don't go now, I won't go at all, and I'm not sure how long I'll last once the fire's completely out. But I'm also not sure if I can make it to his house. In my present situation, I figure this is either the smartest thing I can do or the dumbest.

I decide to leave through the back door—that way I can grab the shovel I've left behind the house and bypass any shrubs in the front that might hinder my journey. The path from this afternoon's trek to the spare firewood rack is not the neat tunnel I had left. It's caved in on both sides, making a little valley of crumbled snow at the base. I sidestep it completely, grabbing the shovel in my hands, and turn in the direction of the sheriff's house.

The squalls are cold and strong, and my cheeks burn. I start to dig at the waist-high mountain in front of me. Each shovelful is heavier than the last. My back starts to cramp, and my arms begin to quiver. I look behind me, and tears accumulate on the lower rims of my eyes. I have made devastatingly little progress.

I give up on shoveling and instead attempt to use the shovel as a walking stick. I dig my boots into the snow and begin to hoist myself up onto it step by step, creating a messy, uneven staircase. I spear the shovel into the depths in front of me and use the handle to pull myself along. Then I withdraw the shovel, drag my body through a few more inches of dense, wet weight, and plunge the shovel back down into the snow again.

I keep moving. The tip of my nose like an ice cube, my fingers so numb I'm sure I could snap them off. With each step, like quicksand, the snow threatens to swallow me up. I just keep going.

Tiny slivers of ice find their way beneath my hood to the exposed skin on the back of my neck. They collect there and settle onto the top hem of my sweater, a biting choker encircling my throat. Tiny puddles of water soak into my socks, leaving my feet stinging and wet.

I don't know how much time passes, but the sun begins to set behind the fire mountain to my left, and I sense the temperature dropping even further. My pace slows. Each step is a monumental effort. My hand is frozen into a permanent claw, like the bucket of an excavator. My legs don't even feel like they're attached to my body anymore. Every muscle in my body is constricted, spent, and screaming.

I continue on, placing one foot in front of the other until my body simply fails to do what I ask of it any longer. Completely exhausted and having exerted all my energy, my muscles turn into useless shreds of stretched fibers—pulled taffy, hanging loose and pale in the middle. The tiny beads of moisture that form along my hairline and throughout my scalp freeze as quickly as they form, leaving my head tight and prickly.

I look to my side and see the small island of trees separating the sheriff's land from mine. Only halfway there?! My hand cramps up and I drop the shovel. It sinks beneath the snow as if I'm watching it in slow motion. Mere seconds become hours as a resounding *NO!* echoes in my head. By now it's officially night, it's too dark, and I can't go after it—I know I'll never find it. I'm too tired, too weak. I won't come back up.

I need to stop. I need to rest. I crawl a few paces on my knees, roll over, and lie face up with my back to the smooth icy surface. I stare up at the stars, plentiful and twinkling in the moonless, inky black sky.

I take one shallow, barely there breath after another. I watch the sky as the world tilts. I watch the stars as they start to dim. I don't feel cold anymore. I don't feel anything, really. I close my eyes and watch the light radiating from the stars inside my head, glittering brilliantly just for me.

I wait for the stars to stop moving.

I'm ready for them to stop moving.

It's okay. It's okay.

I'm okay.

The world starts to fade away.

19

"MAYBE SHE SHOULDN'T COME," I said to Mom.

The hours ticked by before Kacey's arrival, and my mood became a tug-of-war of equal parts verve and vomit. The closer it got to when she was supposed to show up, the more vomit pulled ahead. What if she was scared? What if she was repulsed? What if she didn't want to be my friend anymore? Suddenly my anxiety declared itself the winner, and I looked to Mom for help.

"She's already on her way," she said.

The final agonal minutes passed as I stared out the window. Then I heard a quiet knock on the door.

Kacey's eyes found mine quickly in the far corner of the hospital room. I remained quiet as she disregarded the girl in the bed to my left and came to my side.

"I'll be back in a bit," Mom said, excusing herself.

"Elisabeth?" Kacey said. But I could barely look at her. I kept my head down.

"Elisabeth, it's okay." She came to my side and without hesitation encased me within her skinny arms. "I missed you so much," she said.

"I've missed you, too," I choked out.

"Of course you did!" she crooned with a confident little smile.

Kacey then took in the reality of what sat before her. She looked me up and down in a way that would have bothered me if anyone but her had done it. "Can I see it?" she asked.

I nodded and slowly removed the knitted blanket that I had draped across my lap and legs. It caught a little on the brace, and her eyes went immediately to it. And I waited for it. I waited for the shock, for a look of disgust.

But it didn't come.

"Ouch," she said simply.

I let out a small puff of a laugh, not realizing I had been holding my breath. "Yeah."

"This sucks."

I laughed. "Yeah."

"No, I mean, that is the most awful thing I've ever seen. In my entire life."

"Right?"

"You didn't tell me you were going to be half-robot! That's so cool. I mean, does it give you super robot strength or something?" she asked, sitting beside me and pulling a Hershey's Kiss from her backpack.

"Hardly. I can barely lift it."

She stuffed the candy in her mouth before offering me one. I shook my head. She poked my arm and shook her head back at me. "You're always so much trouble."

"I know," I said, giving her a weak smile. But really what I felt was relief. I should have known that I had nothing to worry about—that Kacey would act like this. Because she was amazing. She was my amazing friend Kacey. She was the kind of friend who brought an extra cookie to school because she knew your mom never packed dessert. She was the kind of friend who always remembered your birthday, your favorite color, your aversion to green peppers, and your love for all things Hello Kitty. She was the kind of friend who would take the inside seat on the bus, walk out of her way to walk together a little longer, and always pick you in gym class even if she knew it meant she'd likely lose. She was the kind of friend everyone needed but only a few lucky lucky lucky people had. And she was mine.

Kacey sighed, all joking now gone from her face. "You look tired."

"I am tired," I agreed.

"Well . . ." She scooched a chair as close to the bed as she could and then reached across me, dragging the blanket up to cover us both and bringing it all the way up over our heads. She leaned her head on my shoulder and used her arm to prop the blanket up like a tent, allowing the light from outside to shine like stars through the holes of the pattern. "Let's just take a nap, then."

A loud, intermittent beeping from my roommate's IV machine filled the room. Then one of my machines went off, too—a higher pitched beep in between the first, as if to say *me too, me too!* BEEP, beep, BEEP, beep. The girl in the bed next to mine started to cry. BEEP, beep, waiiil, BEEP, beep, waiiil. Then she started to scream. BEEP, beep, waiiil, SCREAM, BEEP, beep waiiil, SCREAM.

SCREAM, SCREAM, SCREAM, SCREAM, SCREAM.

I could feel my whole body starting to shake. A silent, solitary tear rolled down my face.

"I'm scared," I whispered to Kacey.

"I know," she whispered back. "But I'm here. I'll always be here, I promise. Pretend it's just you and me," Kacey said, snuggling me closer. I could smell the chocolate on her breath. "Pretend there's no one else here."

And I let the noises bleed together into one loud booming pulse, until it sank inside me and became indistinguishable from my own heartbeat.

And I gazed at the little speckles of light as they danced off of Kacey. I watched them bend and move and flicker like stardust as the world was falling apart outside our little tent. But under there, I knew Kacey would keep me safe. Under there, I knew nothing bad could happen, and I wrapped myself up as tightly as I could. I don't know how long we stayed under that blanket, but the light from those stars felt like the first light I had seen since my surgery. The first little piece of something that wasn't 100 percent horrible. And I wished I could stay under there forever, just looking at Kacey's stars.

20

TWINKLE, TWINKLE, little stars,

Connect the dots between my scars.

Sticks and stones and silver pins,

Map the heavens on my skin.

I see spots of light flickering above me. I feel the soft brush of a blanket against my face.

And then I hear a voice.

"Elisabeth?"

But I could have sworn it had just been a scream.

"Elisabeth?" the sheriff asks again. And the memory fades into the whipping wind. His hood-framed face comes into view upside down above my head. I sit up and spin around to face him. "Are you okay?" he asks. "What are you doing out here?"

It takes me a moment to find the words, dizzy from the sudden movement. "My fire went out," I try to say, but it comes out as a whisper. I try again. "I mean, I ran out of firewood, and my fire went out. I didn't know what else to do."

"Come on," he says. He grabs my glove-covered hand with his and pulls me up. We both sink into the snow, and he drags me forward a few hundred feet until we reach what I assume is the side door of his house. The little square patio appears neatly shoveled in the reflected light of a lantern.

Sheriff Harmon grabs the lantern, pushes the door open, and pulls me inside a warm, dark room. "Take your coat off," he orders. Disoriented, I follow his directions, peel off my wet gloves, and unzip my parka. He takes them from me and tosses them over a table in the corner on top of his own. "Boots," he says, pointing to my feet. I lean on the wall for support and use the toe of each foot to step out of the snow-encrusted boot of the other. Sopping-wet wool socks come with them and dangle limply from my feet. I roll them off and tuck them both down inside the boots. "No, don't do that," he says, and pulls them back out to lay them flat on the rug.

He takes one shaky hand and leads me from the small room into a dark hallway. I follow him—flickering shadows coming into view at the far end. The hallway opens up into a living area crowded with a giant leather sectional piled high with throw pillows. Heavy curtains cover windows on opposite sides of the room, and right in the middle on the far wall is a beautiful, blazing fire.

My body melts at the sight of it. I walk as close to the fire as I can and collapse before it. The warmth caresses my lips, my face, my hands. My eyes close as I let my muscles relax. The tip of my nose, the ridges of my ears, the breath in my lungs—everything starts to thaw.

The sheriff walks behind me and sets the lantern on a table. "How long were you out there?" he asks, sitting down on the floor beside me.

"I'm not sure."

"What were you doing?"

I'm not sure of that, either. "Trying to find you," I say hesitantly.

I hear him smile, though my eyes are still focused on the fire. He stands up and disappears for a few minutes, and I try to ignore the faint clanging noises coming from somewhere behind me. I push the sleeves of my sweater up my arms, rub my hands together, and rotate them to allow the heat to touch their every surface. I hold them there as my pruney fingertips begin to dry and smooth. I hold them there until they're so hot they almost blister.

The sheriff returns and sits down again holding two big green bowls in his hands. He passes one to me. It's filled to the brim with some kind of stew and a large, shiny spoon sunk halfway to the bottom. The bowl is hot against my skin.

"Thank you . . . Sheriff." It sounds so formal it's hard not to laugh.

He coughs on a spoonful of stew. "Please," he says. "It's Noah."

I don't want to call him Noah. I don't want to pretend to be friends. But I also don't want to be rude. I sidestep the awkwardness and begin mixing the thick, chunky contents of my bowl. "How did you make this?" I blow the steam from the rim and it swiftly returns. There's no way he could have warmed it up this much by the fire alone.

"I have a hot plate."

I look at him quizzically, noting the darkness of the room.

"A battery-powered hot plate," he clarifies.

"I didn't even know they made those," I said. I lift the spoon and taste the stew, anticipating something wonderful. But the dream quickly fades away. It's salty and metallic. But it's hot and edible, and it was really nice of him to share it with me. I'm in no position to be picky. "Thank you," I say again.

"Best I could do in the storm."

"Don't be sorry—I was eating raw potatoes," I say, and his smile wrinkles his nose.

"Are you feeling better, from the cold, I mean? You're not developing any frostbite, are you?" he half jokes, motioning to my toes.

"I'm fine," I quickly assure him.

"Are you sure? It looked like you might've been out there in the snow a really long time. You kind of looked like one of those mummies they unearth after being lost in the Alps for centuries. Are your feet okay?"

"They'll be okay," I say, ignoring his joke. Who knew law enforcement could have such a wry sense of humor? I rotate my feet in small circles in front of the flames.

"You sure? I could—" he says as he gestures toward my ankle.

"I'm sure," I say quickly, yanking my feet away before he even thinks of touching them. What is wrong with me? "Sorry," I murmur.

He smiles. "No reason to be sorry."

I look around his living room while we eat our stew. The fire casts a glow on everything in the room—two old ceramic lamps, a cabinet with brass fittings, and lots and lots of picture frames. In fact, from what I can see, all the walls are covered with family photos. Some black-and-white, some more modern. Many are of Noah and Jonathan, pictures from high school at formal dances and proms, glossy girls in strappy dresses with roses on their wrists and lust in their eyes, groups of kids huddled together, their white-picket-fence smiles wide for the camera. Some are of just the two of them—two little boys shoved awkwardly together, bucktoothed and shiny beneath the hot lights of a photographer's eighties backdrop—and some are with people I assume are their parents.

The house seems kind of outdated for a young guy. "Is this the house you and Jonathan grew up in?" I ask.

"It is. It was our parents' house."

"Where do they live now?" I ask, looking around again.

Noah shakes his head. "They passed away. It's just me here now."

"Oh. That's terrible," I say, immediately uncomfortable. Now it makes sense, and I feel bad that I asked.

Noah doesn't seem to mind, though. "Jonathan and I were both in high school. I was a sophomore; he was a senior. We were fortunate to be able to keep the house, and I've been here ever since."

I nod. "Guess you were lucky to have each other." I shrug, because I don't know what else to say. It feels a little weird—I don't know him, and I barely know Jonathan. It seems wrong to make an assumption about their relationship.

"We *were* lucky to have each other. And Cardinal. He really helped us out."

It would be impolite to ask who he's talking about, and honestly, I don't know if I care. So I just nod again. I realize right now that I'm an uninvited guest. My little adventure out in the snow was totally one-sided—I just barged into Noah's house, barged into his present and into his past. And now it seems like I'm making him talk about his dead family.

I know everyone has baggage. No one lives a Teflon-coated life. But I'm not here to bond with Noah over traumatic childhoods. I don't want to share sob stories. I don't want sympathy. And I don't want to give it to him, either.

I clear my throat. "So, um, do you happen to have any firewood that you could spare? I could carry a few logs back to my cabin and get out of your hair."

Noah's face looks as if I asked him to do long division. "You want to go back to your house?"

"I don't want to be an imposition," I say. "Not any more than I already have been. I just came to see if you had any extra wood."

"Elisabeth, you could have frozen out there in the snow if I hadn't randomly been outside at the exact moment to see you. The snow's way too deep, and it's still coming down. You really shouldn't go back out there." He's trying to take care of me. This is exactly what I don't want. I can take care of myself. Except, he did just save me from certain death. Maybe I should just assume he's being nice. Maybe *I* should just be nice.

"Don't you have, like, sheriff-y duties to do? People to help?"

"Yeah," he says, not breaking eye contact with me. "I'm doing them right now."

Aw, that's sweet—now, please stop. "I don't want to be any trouble," I say.

Noah waves his hand dismissively. "Come on, you've got to help me finish this five-star stew." He carries the half-eaten bowls to the kitchen and I pad along silently behind him. "You know, once the power's back up, I'm going to write a letter of appreciation to the Hungry-Man people. 'Salty Beef Stew Saves Sheriff and Neighbor from Snowstorm.'"

21

THEN

"SOMETHING SMELLS GOOD," the physical therapist said as she rose from the side of my hospital bed. I was just thinking that the children's unit had taken on a particularly putrid odor—lunch was about to be served. "I think that's enough for today, anyway. Tomorrow we'll try to get you down into the PT room." She smiled at me in a way that she had no business doing.

"But how will I do that?" I asked nervously as an orderly came into my room pushing a cart with the offending trays. "I can't walk."

"Don't worry. We'll take care of everything. We'll get you into a chair and wheel you down." She took a lunch tray from the cart, placed it on the little table next to my bed, and peeked under the lid. "Looks yummy. Do you want help with this?"

I exhaled a loud and absurdly long breath. I felt dejected. I wanted to wear my misery like a coat so everybody knew. "I don't need any help," I said rudely.

Just then, Dad walked into the room with my sisters behind him. They lingered uncomfortably by the door.

"I see that you don't—your family's here," she said, and clapped her hands together. "I'll leave you to it. See you tomorrow, Justine."

I was crestfallen. I knew that being in a wheelchair would be a part of this, at least temporarily, but it was hard to hear. And I hated the thought that Shauna and Hattie might have overheard her.

"Where's Mom?" Hattie asked, just as she came breezing through the door behind them.

"I was giving Justine some privacy with the physical therapist," she said. Not exactly. I had asked her to stay, but she'd declined. *You'll do better without me here.*

Mom crossed to my bedside and lifted the lid off my lunch. She smelled whatever was under the cover and made a face before setting it back down. Hattie and Shauna were still huddled together, half in and half out. "Come on in, girls," Mom called to them.

They plodded a few steps farther into the room. Shauna had a small bunch of balloons, and Hattie held tight to a stuffed gorilla covered in chocolate fur and with a little leather nose. One of its legs was wrapped up tightly in a toilet-paper bandage. Tentatively they came toward me.

"Oh God!" Shauna stopped. Then Hattie behind her. They froze in the middle of the room.

I looked down and realized the physical therapist hadn't re-covered me with the blanket before she left, and my leg and the brace were totally exposed. It was a gruesome sight. I was encased from toe to hip in titanium. The entry points of the pins were bloody and oozing. The blood mixed with the yellow iodine stains that had not yet faded from my surgery, leaving most of my skin a sickening shade of rust.

I looked at their faces and wanted to burst into tears. Shauna looked like she was going to puke—she was actually green. And Hattie, well, she was just too young to see something like that. She looked horrified. And for the first time I wondered just how much Mom and Dad had told *them* about what was going to happen to me. I hurried to cover myself with the blanket.

Mom saw their panicked faces and stepped in. "They haven't cleaned her up yet. Her skin is too sensitive. It looks worse than it is."

I dragged my narrowed eyes to Mom. Looks worse than it is? Really? Who does she think she's kidding? It looks awful because it *is* awful.

Hattie tried hard to compose herself and carefully walked over to hand me the gorilla. Her enormous eyes had trouble meeting mine. "I bandaged his leg for you."

"Thanks," I said quietly.

"Are you okay?" she asked, finally meeting my gaze.

I nodded right away. I didn't want her to worry; I didn't want her to feel scared. "I'm okay," I assured her.

She smiled a tight smile and moved back to sit in one of the chairs that Mom pulled out for them. Mom cleared her throat, signaling to Shauna that it was her turn, and she approached me, still emanating a shade of pea soup.

Shauna made a move to sit down on the bed beside me. Mom quickly stopped her. "No, no, you'll shake the bed. Sit over here, please, Shauna," she said, motioning to the chairs again. Shauna retreated and handed me the balloons from arm's length without saying anything— then immediately took her assigned seat.

We talked about nothing: the weather, what was going on at school, where they ate dinner last night. Shauna looked at the untouched tray beside me and asked me how the hospital food was. I shook my head. "Kind of like the food at school," I said, and she made a gagging noise in response. Hattie asked quietly about the other girls I was sharing the hospital room with. I motioned to the girl beside me.

"Her name's Oona," I told her. Shauna asked if she could turn on the TV. Mom said no.

Hattie pulled a deck of Uno cards out of her jacket pocket and asked if I wanted to play. I was beginning to feel sleepy, probably from the pain pump that I'd dosed myself with before their visit, on top of the dose I took before my session with the physical therapist. But I nodded and said okay.

"Maybe Oona would like to play, too," Hattie suggested quietly. "Get it? Oona, Uno . . ."

I shrugged and looked at Mom, who shook her head, dismissing the idea.

Dad moved my lunch tray from the C-shaped bedside table parallel to my bed and lowered it across me so that he, Mom, Shauna, and Hattie could all fit around. Hattie dealt us each seven cards from the deck, placed the remainder in a pile on the table, and flipped the top card up.

And we played. And played. And played. Uno was like, the longest game ever. Just when someone thought they were about to win, little Hattie screwed them over, her eyes wide with pride.

"Hattie! Stop!" Shauna demanded after Hattie had blocked her win twice.

"No way," said Hattie, "that's the point of the game. Duh."

"You're awful," whispered Shauna.

"Um, I'm awesome," replied Hattie.

"Girls, stop bickering!" Mom whisper-yelled, sending them a stern look.

We'd been playing for nearly forty-five minutes when I interrupted. "Um, I need to use the bathroom."

"Okay, I'll call the nurse," Mom said with a strange sense of relief.

Pushing away from the table, Dad excused himself and muttered something about needing to make a phone call. The nurse arrived to help me, but neither Shauna nor Hattie moved to step to the other side of the curtain. I raised my eyebrows at Mom.

"Oh." Mom stood and motioned for them to get up, too. "Um, come on, girls, let's step away for a minute."

"Don't forget we're on my draw," Hattie said as she started to move around the curtain.

But Shauna lingered near the table, and Hattie caught her out of the corner of her eye. "Hey," Hattie said loudly, "she's going to stack the deck!"

Shauna looked insulted at the accusation. "No, I am not! I don't need to cheat at your stupid card game."

"Girls," Mom said, hurrying them out. "Come on. Justine wants some privacy."

I sighed. I didn't realize I was asking for that much.

"Jeez," Shauna said. "What's the big deal? We're all girls here."

Mom pulled Hattie and Shauna away and left me with the nurse. "We'll just be outside," she called as she exited the room. Seriously? What was the matter with them? Could you please leave me a drop of dignity?

When I had finished and washed up, the nurse headed into the adjoining bathroom. The curtain was still drawn around the bed. And I wasn't sure why the desire came over me—I'm not a cheater. But for some reason, I just wanted to make Hattie happy. And, maybe, if I was being totally honest, I just wanted this game to be over. Quickly I reached across the table and looked through everyone's cards, rearranging the top few cards in the deck so that Hattie would draw what she needed to win.

Just as I was straightening the pile to hide my crime, I heard a small noise beside me. I turned and looked over at Oona—she was watching me through a break in the curtain. She had seen me cheat. I pulled my eyes away from her and bit my lip. The nurse exited the room and sent everyone back in. I waited for Oona to rat me out.

She didn't.

Shauna and Hattie took their seats again. "It smells like pee in here," Shauna whispered to herself, but I knew she knew I heard. "Awful."

Mom and Dad sat down, too, and the game resumed. Hattie drew on her turn, and a smile made of rainbows and sunshine spread across her little face.

"Awesome!" she nearly sang.

22

LATER, we stand at the sink and wash out the bowls. Actually, Noah washes out the bowls—I just stand at the sink. I look out the little window behind it, similar to the one in my kitchen. It's too dark to tell, but I wonder if he has a view of the fire mountain like I do.

The house is a ranch, small and with every corner in sight of the others. It's divided into thirds—the kitchen on the far left with the small entry area we came into earlier, the family room in the middle and two small bedrooms on the far right. An old, ornate game table sits in front of the picture window in the family room.

"Can you play?" Noah askes, catching me looking at the dusty black-and-white chess set arranged there. It looks like it hasn't been touched in years.

"Not really," I say.

We walk over to the table and Noah indicates for me to take a seat. He opens a large box beneath the table and shows me the other games he keeps in there. I sit, unenthusiastically, and scoot my chair up to the edge. I peek inside at the old checkers, Rummikub, and backgammon sets. "I don't really know how to play any of those," I say.

"Really? Not even checkers? Jonathan and I used to love playing checkers as kids."

I shake my head.

"How about Uno?" he asks, digging a deck out of the bottom of the box.

"Well," I say hesitantly. "It's been a long time."

"Not a problem," he says. He takes his seat across from me and pushes the chess pieces aside with a swoop of his arm. He rolls his sleeves up, slides the Uno cards from their box, and begins to shuffle them.

"You know, I'm not really sure—"

"Oh, come on," he says, and deals us each a hand. "We've got all night to fill."

I raise one eyebrow. What does that mean? Is he trying to be cute?

I exhale. *Relax, Justine.* He's just one of those flirty boys who makes everything sound like an invitation. He'd probably flirt with me if I were a seventy-year-old librarian. I'm stuck here. I might as well make the best of it. I try to remember the rules of the game. Match color or number, save your special cards until you need them, try to figure out what your opponent does and doesn't have. Can I use a Skip card if only two of us are playing? I can't remember. Noah motions for me to go first. I tentatively place a Skip card on the table in front of me. I watch Noah's face to see if I've made an error already.

He appears impassive and motions for me to go again.

I play a blue 5.

"So, what kind of kid doesn't know how to play checkers?" Noah asks nonchalantly.

A weird one. One whose childhood wasn't filled with fun and games, but obligations and obstacles. But I don't want to tell him that. "Well,

I'm sure I could figure it out." I shrug. "I was at an old hotel once," I continue, though not really sure why. "There was a huge checkerboard in the main hall, made out of fabric, sort of like a picnic blanket, and the pieces were the size of dinner plates."

"Typical northern ski-lodge lobby activity."

I look at him briefly and then look down at the table again. I feel like I've already said too much. "Mm-hmm."

Noah puts down a blue 7. It's my turn again, and I place a green 7 on the table. We go back and forth for a while, both of us having to draw extra cards, until the discard pile in front of us is a big, jumbled mess. Then Noah throws down a Draw 2 card.

"Hey," I say.

He smiles. I draw my two cards and search through my hand. It's my turn to call a color. I feel like Noah's been playing mostly greens and blues. "Yellow," I say.

Noah hesitates, like he doesn't want to do it, but then he throws down a Draw 4.

"Hey!" I say again, as if he's not playing fair. He is, of course.

"There's no such thing as nice in Uno," he says. "Every man for himself."

I pick my cards and Noah calls red. I put down a red 9. We each take a few more turns laying down cards. Noah's hand is shrinking more rapidly than mine, and he makes a big show of searching through the few cards he has left. Then he tosses down a red 7. I'm forced to draw until I can put down a red card of my own. On his next turn he plays another Draw 4, and before long I have more than a dozen cards in my hands while Noah's down to two.

"I didn't realize I was playing against some kind of Uno prodigy," I say.

"Nah, compared to you, anyone would look like an expert," he chides. He sets down his second-to-last card, a green 5, and silently mouths, *Uno*.

"You think so?" I say, and throw down the card I've been saving, my only Draw 4.

"You little sneak," he says, and begrudgingly takes four cards from the pile.

He's deliberately flirting with me. I deliberately don't smile.

We play a few more turns. Then Noah calls blue, and I lay down a blue Skip, followed by two more Skip cards and a yellow 3. Noah plays a yellow 6. I draw one card. Then I follow with a yellow Reverse, a red Reverse, and a red 8. Noah has nothing and is forced to draw five cards until he has one he can use. It's a red 4.

I look at my penultimate card. I look at Noah. I slowly place the red 9 on the pile. "Uno," I say.

The tables have totally turned, and Noah's game is in trouble now. I know he doesn't have any special cards—he would have used them already if he had.

"You hustled me," he says, looking through his hand, trying to decide what card to play to block my win. He lays down a green 9.

It wouldn't have mattered what card he chose—I have a Draw 4. "No," I say, smiling at my well-earned comeback and placing the winning card on the table. "I just know how to keep my cards close to my chest."

23

THEN

MOM DIPPED A SYRINGE into the bowl of warm water, drew it up, and watched me with guarded eyes. "Ready?" she asked.

No. I wasn't ready. I could never be ready for this. To be tortured at the hands of my mother in the name of care. I knew she wasn't ready, either, but now that we were home from the hospital—three weeks, or twenty-six episodes of *The Price Is Right*, later—I was her responsibility.

No longer Dr. S's, who had discharged me with a grand send-off: "No pain, no gain!" he'd said while giving my shoulder a crippling squeeze. "I'll see you for a checkup in a few weeks."

No longer the nurses'.

Just Mom's.

She and Dad had set me up in the den beside the kitchen. That way I didn't have to worry about climbing the stairs. They stuck a baby monitor by my head at night in case I needed them for anything. It stung, like alcohol on an open wound, and I promised myself I'd never use it.

It had been thirty minutes since I'd taken more painkillers and put aside the homework stacking up on the folding table beside the bed. A few math dittos and a new book from my favorite teacher, Ms. Conti.

"Let's get started," Mom said, shaking.

I was shaking, too, because each pin site—and there were about fifty of them—was covered with a little square sponge meant to keep the area clean and protected where the pin entered my leg. The pin sites had to be cleaned with antiseptic and the sponges changed every day. The problem was that because the wounds were so fresh, the sponges became bloody soon after they were changed and would then dry and stick to the wounds. Getting them off was a hell designed by the devil himself.

Once she finished cleaning the sponges between my toes and my knee, she moved to my outer thigh. If there was one part of this hellish process that was worse than the others, this was it. Because the skin by the thigh was looser, there was more flesh to move around the pins, and loosening the sponges there felt like being stabbed in my thigh over and over again with a thorny, wooden stick and then wiggling the stick around inside to make the puncture wound bigger.

An hour later the crusty sponges had all been replaced with clean ones. My inflamed, weepy body was screaming at me, but Mom was decidedly quiet. "Don't cry," she said, carefully patting the space on the bed in between where she and I sat. "We're all done."

Don't cry, don't cry, don't cry.

Every day. We had to do this every day. And every day I felt like I had never before wanted to fade away like I did in that very moment. I wanted to melt into the mattress and vaporize and never be seen or heard or touched again. Every day I muffled my moans. Every day I swallowed my screams. Every day I folded my fear into the back of my brain.

I went through this every day.

And Mom did, too.

24

"I'VE BEEN SLEEPING on the couch these last few nights," Noah says a little too casually. The fire licks fiercely, satiated by the dry logs he keeps piling on top every thirty minutes or so. The rhythmic flickering emits a calm, contemplative haze throughout the room. "You know, by the fire."

"Mm-hmm," I reply, unsure where this is going.

"I could sleep on the floor tonight."

In truth, I'd prefer if we slept in different rooms. But this is his house—*I've* inconvenienced *him*—and it doesn't feel right to ask. Besides, I'm sure there's no other fireplace. And, perhaps most compellingly, he's the sheriff. I should be able to trust him. I came here because I could trust him. I can trust him. At least, enough for one night.

I turn around to look at the huge sectional he and I are both leaning against. It would easily accommodate us both.

"I think we can fit."

"Oh, we can definitely both fit, but I don't want to make you uncomfortable."

"If you think about it," I say, "you're actually doing the opposite."

I'm rewarded with a rakish grin. "You know what I mean."

"I do. And, thanks. But it's fine—we can both fit."

Noah stands and removes a large navy sleeping bag from behind the couch. He then briefly disappears behind a door in the bedroom section of the house and emerges with another sleeping bag half in and half out of its sleeve.

"I'm sure Jonathan won't mind," he jokes, handing the awkward thing to me.

The laces keeping one end of the bag rolled in a coil give me trouble. The knot is tight and hard, as if it had been damp and then dried stuck together. Noah takes it back from me and pries the knot apart with his fingers. "This was probably last used during a muddy campout while we were in high school." He hands the sleeping bag back to me again and shrugs apologetically.

"No worries." I shake out the bag and lay it across the couch, placing the opening for my head up against the arm of the sofa. He does the same with his on the opposite side.

"I'll be right back." Noah grabs a flashlight off his mantel and vanishes into the bedroom area again. I hear water running and a door sliding on a metal track. He returns a few minutes later in different clothes—gray sweatpants and socks and a black oversized sweatshirt with a white T-shirt poking out at the collar.

"Do you need anything? A change of clothes?"

"I'm good," I say, not wanting to ask him for anything else—he's done so much already. "Just the bathroom?"

Noah directs me to the bathroom and pulls a few clean towels and a fresh mini tube of toothpaste out from a small linen closet. He hands me a flashlight, then leaves and shuts the door behind him. I remove my turtleneck sweater and sweatpants, leaving on the long-sleeve T-shirt and leggings I had layered underneath. I rinse my face with glacial water and use my finger to brush my teeth.

A clean pillow is waiting for me on the armrest when I return. Noah's already in his sleeping bag, zipped up to his chest, his head resting back on his elbow. Feeling more than a little awkward, I climb into my bag as well.

I ask Noah a question that's been bothering me since he drove me home the other night. "So, no offense or anything, but aren't you kind of young to be the sheriff?"

Noah gives me a boyish smile. "A common misconception," he says. "Let me guess, you're picturing *Dukes of Hazzard*, right?"

I shake my head. "Actually, I was kind of thinking . . . Robin Hood."

"Ouch," he says, and grits his teeth. "Bycockets?"

"What the heck is a bycocket?"

"You know, those little green hats with the feather."

"Oh," I said. "No."

"Well, what were you picturing, then?" he asks.

"Kevin Costner," I reply, adjusting my ponytail.

"I see. Well, that's acceptable," he says, smiling. "Therefore, I'll let you in on a secret. This isn't exactly where I had thought I'd end up. I was planning to go to school for criminal justice. But last year, I had just graduated from the academy when the prior sheriff retired. It's a small department, and no one else was eager for the job. It's tough working in a rural agency—limited resources and not a lot of room for specialization or promotion, you know. It's hard to retain officers for the few positions we have. Anyway, the community had given a lot to me and Jonathan when we were younger. It kind of felt like it was the right thing to do, you know, repay the favor."

"Yeah, that makes sense," I say, settling back onto my pillow.

"Besides," he says, raising his eyebrows. "A sheriff is just a cop who thinks he's in charge."

Hmm. "Details," I say.

"So, what do you like best about living in Fish Creek?" he asks, facing the fire. His profile is soft and shadowed in the dim room.

Anonymity. But I pretend to have to think about it for a moment. "The quiet."

Noah nods and clicks on his flashlight.

"What about you?" I ask, wholly out of politeness.

"The people," he says rather quickly. "I've lived here my whole life, and everybody knows everybody. Everybody cares about everybody. It's a lot like living in a sitcom." He laughs at himself. The reflection from the fire shines brightly in his eyes. "The community is just really special. I like that I can walk into the diner at noon and Veronica has a turkey club waiting for me without even calling ahead. I like that the guy at the service station knows my name and probably more about my car than I do. And I like that the librarian, Mrs. Duncan, is the same librarian who I borrowed books from when I was a kid, and that she sets aside new books that she thinks I'd like."

I can't keep my mouth from turning up at the librarian reference. "You like that?" I ask. "Everyone thinking your business is their business?"

Noah shrugs. "I like that I'm known here." He looks at me and lies back on his pillow. "But I guess that comes with the territory, living in a small town." His gaze holds mine. "Besides, I have nothing to hide."

I lie back on my pillow, too, and pull my eyes away from his to stare into the fire. It's kind of bewildering how two people can be in the same exact place and see completely different things. Fish Creek is a type of sanctuary for me, too, but for exactly the opposite reason. I can be a ghost here. I don't have to avoid certain roads so that I don't pass by buildings that hold bad memories. I don't have to wonder if I'm going to run into someone I'd rather forget.

"You'll see," he says, mistaking my silence for longing. "Give it some time, it'll become like that for you, too."

The thought unsettles me.

I pull my zipper up to my chin, snuggle down into the sleeping bag, and try not to dwell on what Noah said. I've worked too hard over the past eight months to arrange everything just how I like it. Keeping people at a distance is what I do. Keeping people at a distance is what I'll keep doing. Everything is fine.

Noah clicks off his flashlight.

The cold is outside. I am inside.

I am fine. I am okay.

I am safe.

25

THEN

CLICK, CLICK, CLICK, CLICK.

"Oh my God. Please stop." God is punishing me. This is all a big mistake. I'm not really supposed to be here.

"We just have to get through it, Justine." Mom sat back and took her hand off the brace. She gave me a minute. There's no way she could've imagined what this felt like for me. This was the part where she was literally stretching my bone. The point of the fixator was to keep the bone in place while it was simultaneously being stretched. The "clickers" were metal dials, spaced in three groups of four around the diameter of the brace in the locations where the bone was cut—one group near my ankle, one at my shin, and one above the knee. The twelve clickers worked together with the pins to pull the brace apart, sort of like how a telescope extended, and as the brace lengthened, so did my leg. Each set of clicks stretched my leg by one quarter of a millimeter. We did this four times a day. My leg was lengthened a millimeter each day.

It doesn't seem like a lot—a quarter of a millimeter each time. It's a tiny distance, really, smaller than a crumb, no wider than a strand of hair. My eyes could barely see it, a space so small. But my body could feel it.

Mom leaned down to start on the second set. *Click, click, click.* But on the fourth click she felt resistance. I started to tremble. It hurt in a way I couldn't explain, but my brain immediately knew whatever was happening was not natural. It was a deep, visceral repulsion.

She tried again and pushed harder, eventually turning the clicker with a small struggle. She paused again before the last set.

"What does it feel like?" she asked cautiously. Her eyes were glued to the floor as she ignored the wetness forming in mine.

I thought for a moment. "Like I'm on the rack."

"Funny," she said, though I knew she knew I wasn't joking.

"I wasn't joking," I said anyway, just in case.

"How do you even know what that is?" she asked.

"Shakespeare."

"Oh." She nodded. But I doubted she really got it. Mom didn't like the classics. *Past is past, there's no point in dwelling on it,* she'd always said.

I stared at her. I wondered if she thought I was exaggerating. *Look at me, look at me, look at me. Do you see me, Mom? Do you hear me? Do you understand what I'm saying to you? I'm comparing my situation to a medieval torture device. I'm talking torment and damnation. DO YOU HEAR ME?*

I continued to stare, but she didn't look me in the eyes. She was waiting for me to tell her I was ready to continue with the last set. She was waiting to get this over with. Eventually, I pulled my gaze away from her and looked up to the sky. This she saw.

"Please don't be rude, Justine."

I blew out a long breath. I wasn't trying to be rude. I was just trying to get through this. I knew Mom was just trying to get through this, too, but I'd also bet that she thought it would make me a better person in the end, like, *look at what you went through and you made it,* or some crap like that. I didn't really believe that, but what was the harm in her believing it if it helped her get through it? My heart broke a little with every click.

It was time to finish up the turns. She plastered on a smile.

And I wasn't sure, but it almost felt like, just maybe, she pushed a little harder than necessary.

Click, click, click, click. Break, break, break, break.

26

THEN

"YOU'RE SHAKING, JUSTINE."

Mom craned her neck and frowned at me from the front of the car. I was sitting behind her, my legs stretched across the back seat. The blanket that was covering my leg had fallen off with the movement of the drive. I didn't bother to pick it up.

"Yes, Mother, it's cold." Duh.

"You've got to keep it warm." She turned back to watch the road.

"Mom, there's no way to keep it warm." What did she expect me to do? My legs were bare and the air was freezing. The metal of the brace was so cold that it actually looked cloudy.

I couldn't wear pants because nothing would fit over the brace. Before my surgery, Mom had had a seamstress make me a few pairs of special sweatpants with snaps along the sides, but none of them ended up fitting right. So I was left wearing loose cotton skirts with elastic waistbands that I could shimmy up over the brace.

"Please put the blanket back on." She eyed me again through the foggy rearview mirror.

I blew out a long breath and kept my hands in my lap.

"Fine, Justine, do whatever you want," she grumbled when I didn't comply.

I closed my eyes and tried not to hear her. I rested my head against the window and felt the chill of it through my hair. I took a deep breath and imagined the cold creeping in—a white, glittery wisp that wrapped gracefully around me like a taffeta shawl and floated fluidly down to my leg. It entwined in and around my brace, leaving an icy frost on the metal frame. I pictured the frost creeping slowly from the exterior of the frame down to the pins, closer and closer to my leg. It tickled my skin as it passed into my bone, sending shivers straight through me. The frost then spread out across the length of my leg, encapsulating it from hip to toe, penetrating it and turning the entire thing to ice. All of a sudden, the brace evaporated, and my leg became one enormous silvery-blue icicle. Looking down at it, I saw my face reflected back to me as if in a mirror. Flat, cold, and hollow. I raised my fist above my head and slammed it down as hard as I could onto my reflection, watching the icicle and me break into a million tiny shattered pieces.

They met us outside the building at the curb in front of the entrance. Getting me out of the back of the car and into the wheelchair was a big deal, and they were there to help. God bless!

Why anyone decided that the middle of winter was a good time for me to become a convalescent was beyond me. The wind was blowing delicate flurries around the car, and the Good Samaritans couldn't decide whether to slide me out of the back seat headfirst or feetfirst. They had a whole discussion about it.

Come on, people. It's cold!

They decided to go with feetfirst, and I was maneuvered like a mannequin into the wheelchair. They wheeled me inside the foyer of the building while Mom parked the car.

"So, Justine, are you looking forward to starting physical therapy?"

"Oh, yeah. Super excited. Can't you tell?"

They both smiled politely and then looked away from me. I felt a little bad for being rude. No one said anything else until Mom returned.

The PT clinic was in the basement of a medical offices building. I shall henceforth and forever refer to this torture chamber as the Pit of Despair. I'd been in this building before for routine lab work, but never in the basement. It felt strange for there to be a clinic down here. It seemed like it should just hold empty gurneys and the ghosts of people who died here.

Mom stood at the desk filling out paperwork while one of the physical therapists took me into the "gym" and gave me a tour of the space.

In the center of the room was a huge table occupied by two gray-haired people doing leg exercises. Pieces of equipment were positioned around the room: stationary bikes, treadmills, and other machines I couldn't name. Large rubber bands in a rainbow of colors hung from pegs on the walls, along with knotted ropes and cords and weird devices. I saw no windows, and to compensate, the overhead lighting was objectionably bright. It was a dungeon with a disco ball to me.

"This is where you'll do stretching, and here's where we'll start to strengthen those muscles. This is some of the machinery you'll use. Not now, of course, but as you get stronger." The physical therapist wheeled me into another room in the back with three stainless steel tubs. "This is for hydrotherapy—you'll love it," she said.

Excuse me? I stared at the tubs. "I have to get in those?" She must be kidding.

"Well, not now, but soon. The water helps to loosen your muscles and the jets help with circulation. Most people like it a lot."

This looked like the absolute last thing I wanted to be doing. The tubs didn't look like Jacuzzis—they looked like miniature dunk tanks that you'd find at a county fair—I could just picture her rooted there throwing fastballs at my head. I could barely stand being touched, but a tub with jets? No way. I loathed the idea of getting into one of them, of these people seeing me wet and vulnerable.

"I'll pass," I said, and quickly looked away from the tubs.

"You don't get to pass."

My head snapped back to glare at her, and I recoiled as much as possible in the confined space of my wheelchair. *Oh, really? Who do you think you are?* I glared at her with all the hate-fire I could muster. She stared back at me. *Don't look away, don't look away!*

"But how can I get a bathing suit on?" I seethed. "It won't fit over my leg!"

"You can wear shorts, or a really long T-shirt. Don't worry," she said, as if my concerns were meaningless and she knew everything. "We'll figure it out."

I decided this therapist was now my enemy. I stole a glance at her name tag. GRETCHEN. It suited her. She reminded me of the secretary I'd met back at the hospital before my surgery. Something in her voice was mean. Are there people who like to see kids in pain?

Gretchen wheeled me back up to the front and Mom stood to shake her hand. *Don't do it, Mom. Don't do it.* As their hands touched, I swear Gretchen's eyes swept over to me in a silent show of victory.

I looked around the waiting area. I was the youngest person in the PT office by at least thirty years. This was not where I belonged.

All I wanted to do was run away. But I couldn't run.

I couldn't even stand.

God is punishing me.

This is all a big mistake.

I'm not really supposed to be here.

27

I WAKE IN THE MORNING before Noah does. His sleeping bag and sweatshirt are rumpled. His dark hair is a mess—matted in some places, sticking straight up in others. His eyelids are lavender above a brush of thick, black lashes. He looks young. He looks peaceful. I turn away from him.

"Morning," he says quietly.

I turn back around and give him a quick, weak smile. This feels intimate. Too intimate. "Morning," I say.

He sits up, the sleeping bag falling in a heap at his waist. He looks embarrassed. "Most people don't see the sheriff like this," he says, pushing up his sleeves and running a hand through his hair.

I nod in agreement. "The illusion is shattered."

He smiles a shy smile and unzips the sleeping bag all the way to his feet. He climbs off the couch and kneels down in front of the fire, adjusting it with a fire poker.

"How many times did you have to get up to keep it going through the night?" I ask.

"Just a few."

"Thanks for doing that," I say. I hope I didn't drool in my sleep.

The snow seems to have finally stopped, and the view out of Noah's window looks like the sky has turned upside down. Rolling hills that look like clouds stretch as far as I can see. The sky is gray above it, recovering from the massive effort of the storm.

Noah uses his hot plate to warm up two cups of instant coffee and two bowls of instant oatmeal.

"Now that there's a break in the snow, I should really try to shovel the driveway. I'm sure it's going to be a busy day." I feel relieved. The thought of being stuck in here all day with him makes me uncomfortable.

"Can I help?" I ask, mostly out of politeness.

"Not necessary."

"I know, but I'd like to. Do you have an extra shovel?" It feels like he's done too much for me, and I want to even it out. I don't want to owe him anything.

Remarkably, Noah somehow finds the shovel that I lost in the snow the night before. It seemed like an impossible task in the maze of the storm, yet I watch him dig it up and bound back over to me with barely any trouble. We start by digging out his front porch and laying salt on the steps. We then shovel our way over to his detached garage and get started on the driveway. I start shoveling a line down the left side from the top, and he starts at the bottom right and works his way up. Every few minutes we meet in the middle and he makes some kind of joke.

"Fancy meeting you here," he says on the first pass.

"Excuse me, might I interest you in purchasing a case or two of Thin Mints?" he says on the next.

And then: "Definitely having regrets about chasing away that snowblower salesman last week."

I wonder if this dumb kind of humor is a prerequisite to being the sheriff. Or maybe he's just trying to make me smile.

We're drained and breathless by the time we finally finish. We rest our backs against the mounds of shoveled snow that reach far above my waist. "You know," he says, "you could have worked a little faster. I'm paying you by the hour."

"I'll send you my bill," I say, glad to see he considers this a professional interaction, despite the disheveled state in which we saw each other this morning.

"I'm impressed," he says, gesturing to my half of the driveway. "I wasn't sure you'd be much help, but you turned out all right."

Noah's words touch a nerve, but I don't let him see it. I've heard those words before. I've felt those words before.

We work up the strength to go back inside. Our cheeks are rosy from the wind and our hair is covered in icy crystals. Noah reaches a hand up to brush the snow from my hair. I quickly back away and do it myself. He laughs a little and adds another log to the fire before going into the kitchen to make us each another cup of coffee.

"This must be driving you crazy, the power being down for so long," Noah says.

"Why would you think that?" I ask, sounding more defensive than I intended.

"Well, I imagine it must be driving most people crazy. No TV, no internet, no phone, no food. Having to just *be* with yourself for an extended period of time. Now, me, I'm an excellent person to be stuck with. But most people get sick of themselves when they spend enough time together," he says, smiling.

I twirl my spoon in my coffee. "I like being alone," I say simply.

He nods. "You're not in school?"

I shrug. "I follow some online syllabi." Occasionally.

"Taking a gap year?" he asks, trying to figure me out.

No. "Something like that," I say.

"Are you always this obtuse?" he says jokingly, trying to hide the genuine curiosity behind it.

Deliberately. "Often so," I say with a knowing smile.

Noah cocks his head to the side and narrows his eyes at me. "Are you on the run? In the witness protection program? I could help with that, you know—I *am* the sheriff."

"Why is it whenever someone doesn't spill their guts and share their entire life story, someone teases that they're in the witness protection program? I mean, how many people do you think are actually in the witness protection program? Probably not a lot." Noah looks at me quizzically. "No," I acquiesce. "Nothing like that." I consider how much I should say. I like Noah, but he's exactly the type of person I try to avoid—warm, personable, interested. The kind of person who wants to get to know you. And I don't want anyone to get to know me. "I'm just kind of a loner."

He's the kind of person who wants you to trust him. And I don't want to trust anyone. Even the sheriff. Noah remains quiet, and I feel the awkwardness creep in. "I'm just better off on my own," I add, to fill the silence.

"Except for last night," he says. "You weren't better off on your own last night."

"True," I admit, with great difficulty.

"You needed help," he states.

"Mm-hmm."

"You needed me to rescue you from the snow and thaw you by the fire."

"Mm-hmm," I say again, feeding his ego.

"You needed me and my Hungry-Man stew."

All right, now he's just being dramatic. I shake my head in denial and hide my smile in my coffee cup.

He rocks back in his chair and takes a large swallow from his own mug before lowering it empty to the table. "Yup," he says to himself, while stroking his stomach. "It's good to live next to the sheriff."

28

HATTIE PATTED HER STOMACH with her small hands and chortled in a deep voice, "Can't wait to dig into some of that turkey."

"Well, you're going to have to," Shauna retorted, crossing her arms over her chest. "We have to get Justine out of the car first."

Thanksgiving had always been my favorite holiday. It made me think of fallen acorns and foil-wrapped caramels, gleaming silver and creamy china placed perfectly on a white linen tablecloth. It made me think of clouds of flour filling the air and my lungs as Mom pounded out pies in the kitchen.

But this year was different. Mom delegated her usual role as hostess to Nana, who was more than happy to take up the responsibility. And instead of helping with the place settings or pressing fork-crimps into the pie crusts, I sat in the back of the car in my grandparents' driveway listening to Mom and Dad argue about the best way to get me and my wheelchair through the narrow front door.

"Sorry, Justine," Hattie said, giving me a weak smile before sliding out of the car and leaving me behind. "The smell is calling to me!"

"You can't smell anything from out here, dummy," Shauna said loudly, exiting the car behind Hattie without a glance in my direction.

"I'm imagining the smell, and it's calling to me!" I heard Hattie's voice cut through the cold air.

Eventually, Dad decided it would be easiest to just carry me. Mom balanced a pie in one hand and hauled the wheelchair out of the trunk with the other. "Better not indulge too much, James. You won't be able to carry her back," Mom joked, dragging the wheelchair in the snow. The wind was chilly, and I felt it blow up my skirt as Dad tried to shelter me from the snow flurries on the way to Nana and Papa's front porch. I could feel my heart hammering beneath my puffy winter jacket, and it made the trip from the car to the door feel even longer than it was. When we finally got there, Papa looked at me hesitantly as he held the door open. My brace banged into the aluminum screen twice as Dad tried his best to squeeze past.

When our dysfunctional group finally made it inside, I could see that we were the last to arrive. Shauna and Hattie were already in the thick of things, and all my cousins' eyes turned toward me. Hands paused midair; mouths hung open. They raked me over with obvious, yet predictable, shock and curiosity before turning obediently away.

I kept my head down, because there was nowhere else to put it, as Dad brought me farther into the house. Nana relieved Mom of the pie she carried, and Mom placed the wheelchair in the periphery of the living room where everyone was gathered. Nana led Mom into the kitchen as she brought the pie to her nose. "Too much nutmeg, Iris."

I settled back into my wheelchair, and for a few minutes everything was as close to normal as I could have expected. My youngest cousins were playing on the floor, trying to build card castles by digging the foundation cards into the plush carpet. Nana was going on about how she forgot to make the turkey and so we'd all have to eat

McDonald's—an old joke she was delighted to resurrect this year. Aunt Gwenni and Aunt Carole busied themselves running back and forth between the kitchen and the dining room with dishes. Papa, Dad, and my uncles couldn't have looked more at home in their designated spots on the couch. Nana's fire crackling in the corner and the steady hum of the Bears game in the background served as the soundtrack to what was a familiar routine.

I started to relax a little. Maybe it was going to be okay.

But then, as we were about to sit down at the table for dinner— "Justine, I have you set up over here." Nana motioned to Papa's big La-Z-Boy recliner in the far corner of the room.

"What?"

"Well, I know you can't fit easily at the table, so I'm going to put you here."

She had placed a couple of ratty old towels on the seat of the leather recliner about twenty-five feet from the table. I looked at her questioningly. "So that you don't rip the seat," she said with a grin, proud that she had thought of it.

My heart sank. Literally. I felt it fall from the cavity of my chest and bounce onto the floor in front of me. It rolled gently to a stop near the now-collapsed card castles, loose carpet fibers sticking to the matted, muscly mass. And there it sat, in the space between us.

Could she be kidding? Hattie sent me a look of pity from her seat at the far end of the table. But looking around, it was clear that no one else was bothered by Nana's suggestion. I felt incredulous. Tears spilled over my lower lids as I resigned myself to my fate and tried to make my way over to the recliner. The wheelchair caught and got stuck in the deep carpet. Mom hurried over to help me.

"I can do it myself," I said, trying hard to keep the tears from my voice.

Could she tell how hurt I was? "I think you'll be more comfortable there, okay?" she said, glancing back at Nana, and I suddenly wondered if it had been her suggestion. I glared at her. *Et tu, Brute?*

I continued to push my way over. The closer I got to the chair, the farther I moved from everyone who was supposed to love me, supposed to embrace me. The rest of the able-bodied traitors gathered at the dining room table and took their seats. We were in the same room, but we might as well have been on different planets. I pivoted myself onto Nana's shabby towels as angry, humiliated tears cascaded onto my lap. I couldn't hide it—my outrage, my despair. I couldn't make myself look in their direction, and I didn't want anybody looking at me. I wanted to disappear.

"Don't worry, Justine," Nana called to me as they started passing dishes across the table. "I'll bring everything over to you."

And she did. She piled a plate high with turkey and stuffing and cornbread soufflé and brought it over just for me.

Only it didn't taste like Thanksgiving. It tasted like sorrow.

29

NOAH OPENS THE PASSENGER DOOR for me. "I'm not on duty . . . yet," he says, before placing a dozen or so dry logs into a mesh bag and loading them into the back of his police car.

I slide in, and he walks around the car, tossing my shovel into the trunk before relaxing into the driver's seat. Slowly, slowly, slowly, Noah backs out of his driveway and onto the street. Although it's obviously been plowed more than once, the snow is still deep and heavy and crunches beneath his tires. Jagged chunks of snow blow from the branches and fall onto the windshield like broken teeth.

I peek down at the stretch of leather between us and see an ID badge of some kind resting there, Noah's broad smile stretching across the hard plastic. Beneath the photo it says NOAH EISENHOWER HARMON and his date of birth. I do the math in my head. He's twenty-five.

"Your middle name is Eisenhower?" I ask.

Noah's head spins toward me. His eyes dart around and land on the badge, and he shuffles it beneath some loose papers as quickly as he can.

"Ah, that's classified police information, miss."

"Mm-hmm. Okay." I tease him.

"What?" he says defensively, his eyes trained on the road again. He's taking it very slowly. Too slowly. Does he not know how to drive in the snow? "It's presidential!"

I laugh. "Yeah. Totally." I nod my head in feigned agreement. Then I make peace with him. "It's not so bad."

Noah ignores me. He stares straight ahead, totally focused on the road. "Jonathan's is Garfield," he coughs out, throwing his brother under the bus, too.

Noah inches his way to my house, where the driveway is indistinguishable from the rest of the space around it. "Thanks for the lift," I say, ready to jump out and wave. But he parks the car along the road, takes the shovel from the trunk, and starts digging a narrow aisle up my yard to the front door. I follow behind him with the bag of wood.

"Hopefully they'll get the power back on today," Noah says when we reach my front door.

"Yeah, but I'll be fine," I reply.

"That should last you all day," he says, motioning to the wood, "and I'll bring over some more when I get home tonight."

"You don't have to," I say. "I'll be fine. Really."

"Perhaps we can have another candlelit dinner. I'm thinking chicken noodle . . ." He rubs his chin with his gloved hand, his mouth pulling up at the corners.

"Thank you, but it's—"

"Fine?" he interrupts me. "Elisabeth, I know you'll be fine," he says with sincerity. He raises his hand in a quick goodbye and walks backward down the steps. Then he turns away, leaving large, heavy footprints in the newly shoveled snow. Once he's halfway back to his car, he shouts, "I'm coming over anyway," into the frosty morning air.

30

THEN

SUFFOCATION IS A WEIRD WORD. It has two meanings that are the exact opposite of each other. The first is being deprived of something (usually air), while the second is being oppressed by something.

Type 1—deprivation: In this type of suffocation a person will say, "I can't breathe!" They're panicked. Maybe they're being relentlessly tickled and can't catch their breath. Maybe they're locked in a refrigerator or in an otherwise tiny room. There is a deficiency—there's something they need and they don't have access to it.

Type 2—oppression: In this type of suffocation a person will also cry out, "I can't breathe!" Maybe they've accidentally sucked in a handful of glitter and they're choking. Maybe they're at a petting zoo and the stench inside the goat barn has become too much to handle. The issue here is there is an excess—too much of something hazardous.

Type 1 suffocation is all about the absence of something good, while type 2 suffocation is about the abundance of something bad. Good and bad. Positive and negative. Right and wrong. It's not a subtle distinction. It's Newton's third law of oxymoronic definitions, and it all comes down to science, really.

Lying in bed at night, staring at the wheat-colored ceiling above me, I shook in my brace. My mind and body were in a state of constant rejection of an object that I couldn't get rid of. Something was in my body that didn't belong there. It was savage! It was literally *in my bones!* I couldn't get away from it; I couldn't pull it off. I'd been impaled. Enclosed in an iron lung—*Let me out, let me out, let me out! Get it off, get it off, get it off!* Clearly, type 2, oppression.

But apart from the pain and the bitterness that accompanied it—worse than the blinding, mind-numbing, excruciating pain—was the void it left behind. Once the panic settled, once the painkillers kicked in, once the Valium turned everything into a slow-motion dream sequence, an emptiness filled that wheat-colored room. An echo that reverberated off the nothingness. A vacancy that existed where there once was something sound. And somehow that void became bigger and more important than anything that could have ever filled it before. Case in point, type 1, deprivation.

My little den-room had become an oubliette—a place to be put—and I wasn't sure whether I wanted to be rescued or forgotten.

I was no doctor, but I was pretty sure I was suffering from an undiagnosed case of Suffocation, Mixed Type.

31

EVERYTHING INSIDE MY HOUSE is just as I left it. The mess of blankets strewn haphazardly over the sofa, the small puddle beginning to warp the softened wood near the back door. But before I can take care of these things, I must attend to the most egregious remnant of the deserted space—the frigid cold.

The fire, which I abandoned to die alone the night before, is just a drafty, dusty hole. I clean out the hearth, removing as much ash as I can, and place the grate back in its spot. I remove three logs from the bag that Noah gave me and arrange them on top. I add strips of newspaper in between the logs for extra kindling. I use the matches in Kacey's box on the mantel, and before long I've built a substantial, searing blaze that I feel proud of.

I sit by the fire and let my body soak up the heat. It happens imperceptibly, each molecule melting into another, but pretty soon I'm stifling hot, and I step away from the fire. I take my notebook out of its drawer, sit down a little farther from the flames, and open to the page where I last left the bookmark.

I start scribbling an intricate pattern of curlicues and swishes and hearts and stars along the bottom of the paper. I wonder what time Noah will be back. I think about the way he rolls his shirt sleeves, coyly leaving them about two inches below the elbow. I think about the way his mouth curves when he smiles, two tiny parentheses forming at the corners like they're encapsulating something special—not as a digression, but in emphasis. And then I catch myself. What the hell am I doing? Was I really about to start daydreaming about the sheriff? No way.

I need to put a stop to this immediately. I'm not here to find romance. I'm here because I need to be alone. Because I can't let people get too close. Because I can't let people know who I really am. Know *what* I really am. What's really wrong with me.

That's the only way I can feel safe.

And I know I'm right. I think about Noah's words—words that have hurt me before. *You turned out all right.*

Just thinking about them again makes my hands tremble. And the pain seeps to the surface like a thin sheen of sweat on a summer day.

I'm not all right, they say. There's something wrong, they say. There's something wrong, there's something wrong, there's something wrong—with me.

I can't let whatever this thing is with Noah go any further. I was in a dire situation. I mean, I could have frozen to death! I needed help, and he helped me. That's it. That's all it is. That's all it was. End of story. Everything's fine now. I don't need him anymore. I don't need anybody.

I don't need anybody.

Returning the notebook to the drawer, I lay the pen neatly on top. I brave the stairs, the temperature dropping with every step I take. In my bathroom, I turn on the water, not even bothering to turn the dial to the hot side. I reach up and adjust the showerhead, the cold, hard metal stinging my fingertips.

And a wisp of something—something stale and rancid—infiltrates my senses. Alarming, like a whiff of gas. It's fuzzy around the edges, staticky like an old record. Staticky, sticky, seeping. And then it's gone.

32

THEN

THE SMELL of freshly popped popcorn tickled my nostrils. Mom was playing cards in the kitchen with her girlfriends. Ladies whose silver bangles jingled lightly on their wrists as they peeked inconspicuously at the plate of chocolate truffles in the center of the table, but who would never dare reach out and take one. They played every week—they had been for years—but this was Mom's first time playing since I came home from the hospital.

I was sitting in my den bed adjacent to the kitchen, totally unfocused on the book in front of me, struggling because my leg was throbbing and I had to use the bathroom. I needed Mom's help getting up, but I didn't want to bother her. I could hear the ladies chatting and laughing, twaddling on about their husbands, their parents, their neighbors. But every once in a while they got real quiet, and I knew that was when they were talking about me.

But I didn't want to bother her. Because at this point, I could tell she was getting frustrated. That my situation was taking its toll. That *I* was taking a toll. And I didn't want to be a problem. I didn't want her to look at me like I was a problem.

Because she did sometimes look at me like I was the problem—like I was the pebble in her patent leather shoe.

At some point, after they'd been playing for about an hour, I couldn't hold it any longer. I tossed my book to the side.

"Mom," I finally called out, embarrassed. "I need to use the bathroom." She came into the den and helped me up. "I'm sorry to bother you."

"It's fine." And then: "What are you reading?"

"A play. Ms. Conti sent it for me."

"For class?" Mom asked.

"No. She just thought I'd like it."

Mom helped me with the walker, and as we passed the kitchen, one of her friends muttered, "She needs help in the bathroom? I mean, how many people can you fit in there!" She smirked and turned to the other ladies, expecting them all to laugh at her cleverness.

"Keep going," Mom said under her breath, and she tried to quicken my pace. My heart hurt. This was a woman who had known me my whole life. Why would she be so mean?

When we got into the bathroom, Mom shut the door behind us. I could tell she was angry, her eyes filled with tears. She stared into my eyes, like she wanted to say something. But she turned away from me and didn't say anything at all. She didn't stand up for me; she didn't comfort me; she just avoided my gaze.

Humiliation crashed over me, and I asked Mom to step outside the door. I didn't need her help. I didn't need anybody's help. I could do this all myself. I could.

She exited hesitantly and left me alone.

I stood there at the sink, tears dripping from my chin and mixing with the water as they spun and swirled and finally found their sweet escape down the drain. I stood there trying to wash myself clean of the indignity and shame. I washed and washed and washed.

It didn't budge.

Not long after the ladies left, I sent Hattie on a hunt through the kitchen for leftover goodies. She returned to the den with two small bowls of popcorn and a few chocolates piled on top. "They hardly touched anything," she said with a conspiratorial wink, and began walking away with her own bounty.

"Where's Shauna?" I called after her.

"Homework."

"And Mom?" I wasn't sure where she had disappeared to.

"She's crying in the kitchen."

Oh. Of course she was. I had been so overwrought with my own mortification I hadn't stopped to consider hers. What must she have told them to make it all more palatable? What must she have told them to make me seem less appalling? Surely this was shame weighing painfully upon her. The shame of having witnesses to the details of our dilemma. The shame of having such a damaged daughter. Or maybe the shame of feeling ashamed.

I started to cry then, too.

"Um, do you want me to get you some Tylenol or something?" Hattie asked.

"This isn't a headache!" I nearly shouted at her.

"I'm sorry," she said softly, before turning away. "I didn't understand."

Neither did I, Hattie.

Neither did I.

And the guilt quickly became another very heavy thing to hold.

33

I SHIVER through the fastest shower I've ever taken. Then I layer on warm clothes and brave the cold and wind to shovel a little bit around the exterior of the house. I move some of the wet logs from the back of the house to the front pergola in the hopes of them drying out.

Noah returns in the late afternoon with extra firewood and a few bags of groceries. I briefly debate not letting him in, but I don't want to be rude. Plus, he has food. Nothing to get all worked up over. He's just my neighbor. He's just the sheriff. I can keep this all very, very professional.

"Now, don't go getting too excited, but I brought plenty of that stew you love, along with a few other essentials." He pulls six cans of soup out of the bags.

I lift one of the cans and read the label. "You know, this isn't even Hungry-Man. It's Campbell's."

"It's Hungry-Man. That's what hungry men eat," he says with a hint of Neanderthal.

"Nowhere on this label does it say Hungry-Man. You're going to send a letter about the wrong product. To the wrong company. Does Hungry-Man even make stew?"

He furrows his brow at me and continues emptying the bags. There's a loaf of bread, peanut butter, a bunch of bananas, a box of instant oatmeal, and instant coffee.

"Where'd you get all this?" I ask.

"The shops are all still closed to lay folk like yourself, but I was able to get inside to make some deliveries to some of the older residents in town."

My mouth turns down. I think of Mr. Ito. I hope he's okay.

"Don't worry," he says, reading my mind. "I just brought what was extra." He digs into the bottom of the last bag and wiggles his eyebrows.

"What is it?" I ask.

Noah pulls out a bag of supersized marshmallows. "That was extra?" I say. "Seems like they'd be a hot commodity right now."

"You'd be wrong about that," he says. "Dentures and marshmallows do not mix."

I laugh and Noah helps me put away the new supplies.

We make peanut butter and jelly sandwiches with our combined ingredients and eat them in front of the fire. The sun begins to set outside the living room window, over the sparkling white landscape in the distance. Noah stands up and lights the candles spaced around the room. "It's very clean in here," he says. I notice him looking at my blank walls, empty and unrevealing compared to his.

I shouldn't like him being in my place. But strangely, it's not so bad.

"You're a little particular, aren't you?" he asks, taking his time looking around the space.

"What makes you say that?"

"Oh, nothing." Noah picks up my paperback book sitting on the end table. He opens the front cover.

118

"What's this?" he asks.

"Oh, well, it's this amazing new invention. I think they're calling it a book," I reply, though it's technically a play.

"Thanks for the clarification." He gives me a look of annoyance, but his eyes hold something that tells me he finds my annoyance adorable. I need to kill that as quickly as possible.

I exhale loudly. "It's called *The Tragical History of the Life and Death of Doctor Faustus*. Do you know it?" I ask him.

"No." He shakes his head. "Shakespeare?"

"No," I say, not elaborating any further.

"And . . ." He motions for me to continue, a smile curving at his lips.

"And . . . ," I say, trying to think of how to explain it. "Ever hear of a Faustian bargain?"

Noah shrugs his shoulders.

"It's about this guy, Dr. Faustus. He's a scholar, a scientist—but he's bored. He feels above it, like he's already learned everything and mastered everything. So he turns to mysticism, hoping to become like a god. But then the devil shows up and offers him a deal."

"Hmm." Noah pauses, considering. "It's about making a deal with the devil?"

"Well," I say, interlacing my fingers back and forth. "Yes and no. That's the plot—Faustus trusts someone that he shouldn't—but the story really is about much more. It's about predestination. And deception. And suffering," I add.

"Predestination?"

"Yeah, it's the idea that your whole life is preplanned for you. That you really have no free will—even when you think you do. It's about the illusion of choice."

"And how many times have you read it?" Noah asks.

My eyes meet his hesitantly. "Am I that transparent?" I wonder out loud.

"No," he says, chuckling. "But it looks like it could fall apart in my hands. I can barely read the cover." He picks at the fraying jacket and lays it back on the table. "It sounds interesting, though. Are we destined to sin, or do we choose to?"

"Right," I say.

"And are we destined to suffer, or do we choose that, as well?" he muses.

"Another excellent question."

Noah points his chin in the direction of the book. "Why do you like it so much? To read it over and over again, I mean."

I think about my response. It feels really personal, but I guess I can give him a little. We're just talking about a book, after all. And, after all these years, I think he's the first person to ever ask me about it. "No matter how many times I read it, I don't know who the bad guy is—the devil, Dr. Faustus, neither, or both. What I like best about the story is, you don't really know who's to blame. Every time I read it, my opinion changes."

"Interesting," he says, crossing his legs dramatically and massaging a fake beard into a point. Then he tilts his head in contemplation and rests his chin over his steepled fingers. "What's worse?" he asks, a question designed for the universe before us. "Being deceived by others or being deceived by ourselves?"

34

THEN

IT WOULD BE INACCURATE to say I woke in the middle of the night. The reality was I hadn't fallen asleep at all.

Mom had finished cleaning my pin sites and changing the sponges again, just as she did every night. The nurses had told me that as time went on, the pin sites should bleed less, and the sponges wouldn't stick to my skin so badly. But it had been months, and that hadn't happened yet. As we continued turning the clickers daily, the moving pins stretched the wounds faster than the skin could heal, leaving open, oozing gashes in their wake.

Even though she premedicated me, there hadn't been a cleaning yet that didn't leave me in tears. It was actually physiologically inexplicable that my eyeballs hadn't run out of tears at this point. Still, I wasn't sure whether it was better for Mom to go slowly and try to be gentle, or rush through it to be done as quickly as possible. I guess I didn't really notice the difference either way—pain was pain, fast or slow.

God is punishing me. This is all a big mistake. I'm not really supposed to be here.

This is what I told myself hours later as I lay immobilized beneath my pastel-heart comforter. The tent my mother had adjusted for me above my foot—so that the weight of the blanket wouldn't touch my big toe—had collapsed, and the blanket now felt like a bowling ball. This made me angry—that the unbearable lightness of this ridiculous little-girl comforter could crush me and bring me to tears.

But even worse than the weight of the blanket on my toe was something we called the bar. The brace on my leg could be described as two separate braces—one on my lower leg and one on the upper—connected at the knee by two hinges that allowed it to bend. At night, under Dr. S's strict orders, Mom used a wrench and bolts to affix a metal bar about six inches long from the bottom of the upper portion of the brace to the top of the lower portion, essentially locking my knee in place.

She'd been doing it since the beginning. Dr. S had said it was to prevent my muscles from tightening up and not being able to straighten my leg all the way.

I'd said it was barbaric.

Once Mom put the bar on, there was no more wiggle room. And it served as a bridge between her resentment and mine.

So I lay awake, refusing to call for help, tears rolling down my cheeks out of frustration and desperation. Mulling over the taunting weight of the blanket. Mulling over the existential weight of my situation.

Why me? What did I do to deserve this? How long will this agony go on? God is punishing me.

This is all a big mistake.

I'm not really supposed to be here.

35

THAT STUFFED GORILLA in the corner—its hand just moved.

Don't be ridiculous.

Okay. No, wait. It did. It just moved. It just waved at me a little.

Sigh. Okay. Well, what do you want to do about it?

I should call for Mom.

And tell her what, exactly? That the gorilla moved all by itself? She'll think you're nuts.

No she won't.

You're going to wake her in the middle of the night to tell her a stuffed animal moved by itself?

Yes.

Don't do it.

Why not?

She'll think you're crazy, and she'll tell the doctors. Then you'll have two problems.

Oh. Okay. You're right. So what should I do?

About the gorilla?

Yeah.

I don't know. Wave back.

36

"IS THERE ANYONE you want to call?" Noah asks as the evening tiptoes on.

The wind has picked up again, and the house creaks and moans with every gust. "What do you mean?" We sit before the fire, roasting marshmallows on sticks that Noah brought in from the yard.

"Well, the phones have been out for a few days. Is there anyone you want to let know you're okay? I can connect you with my police radio—it doesn't work through the regular phone lines."

"Oh." I consider dialing in to my answering machine to listen to Kacey again, but I don't think that would be the best idea in front of Noah. "I think I'm good," I say, shaking my head. "I don't really have anyone I need to call."

"Yeah," he says, nodding his head and pulling his marshmallows away from the flames to check their doneness. They're a perfect medium brown. "I, ah, kind of gathered that."

I can tell he thinks I'm weird, and I suddenly feel the need to explain myself. "I'm not a hermit, or anything," I say defensively, holding my marshmallows over the fire a little longer. I like them well done.

"Okay," he replies, like that's a totally normal thing to say. "And I agree. You're too cute to be a hermit."

I chew on the inside of my cheek. I don't want to be rude—Noah's gone way out of his way for me. But I don't know how to explain why I am the way I am. I've worked really hard to not have to explain why I am the way I am. "I'm not a good person," I say very simply.

Noah freezes with his marshmallow stick in midair. "What?"

"I'm not," I say. "I'm not nice. I don't have a lot of friends."

Noah remains quiet for a few moments, his eyebrows knit together, presumably thinking about what I said. "I understand," he says.

I know he's waiting for me to say more, but I can't, so I just shrug.

"When my parents first died. I was kind of off for a while." He holds the stick up to his mouth and slides two marshmallows in. Then he drags it out slowly through pursed lips—it's almost completely clean. Noah takes the hand I have resting on my knee and gives it a little squeeze. "I get it."

I pull my hand back. *No, you don't.*

"That's the other thing—I don't really like, um, people touching me." Might as well get it all out now. "Sorry."

"You don't have to be sorry," Noah says.

"No? Don't you think it's weird? Aren't you, like, insulted, or something?"

"Should I be?"

"Most people are," I say.

Noah shrugs. "It's not really any of their business, right? I mean, I don't like to be . . . um . . . punched in the stomach. And every time someone tries to punch me in the stomach, I say, 'Hey, man, look. I don't want to be punched in the stomach, okay?' and usually people are pretty cool with that. Although, occasionally, some tough guy will get all up in my face and try to punch me in the stomach even though I've clearly just asked him not to, and then, you know, Bad Noah comes out. But for the most part it's no big deal. I don't go around apologizing for not wanting to be punched in the stomach."

I wonder how he knows that people touching me—it often *does* feel like being punched in the stomach. It's a sudden blow. A deep, vibrating assault.

I can't tell if Noah's ramblings are meant to be sarcastic or sweet, but something makes me think maybe both. He's looking at me with soft eyes. I know what he's doing. And it makes me think maybe he's a good guy. Because Noah doesn't seem like the kind of guy to put on airs. Despite the borderline-arrogant things he sometimes says, he doesn't actually come across as arrogant. Despite repeatedly telling me how impressive he is, he isn't trying to impress me.

"Are you done now?" I ask.

"What? Are you telling me you like being punched in the stomach?"

"Noah . . ."

He raises his eyebrows in surprise. "Wow, you must have a six-pack under all those layers. Do you, like, do lots of sit-ups or something?"

I roll my eyes and shake my head doubtfully.

"Just naturally tough then, I guess."

I'm quiet for a long time. I don't want to tell him that he's got me pegged all wrong. I'm not tough. I'm not strong. I've had the wind permanently knocked out of me and I'm perpetually gasping for air.

"Don't be sorry," he says again. "It's okay. It's okay to do what you have to do in order to survive," Noah says out of nowhere, compassion lacing each syllable.

But it sounds too much like charity to me. I keep my eyes in my lap. "Look," I say. "I'm okay. I'm not lonely. This is by choice." As if that makes everything all right.

"You don't need to explain yourself, Elisabeth. And you don't need to defend yourself. Whatever the reason is that you're here all alone—footnote, very Thoreau of you, by the way," he says, and then pauses before knitting his brows together, "and, also very Unabomber-y. Hmm." He wrinkles his forehead in contemplation. "Anyway . . ." He smirks as he shakes his smile away. "I'm just telling you that you don't have to answer to me. Or anybody. We all take detours in life. 'Cut is the branch that might have grown full straight.'"

My head snaps up. "Did you just quote *Faustus*?"

Noah shrugs.

"You *have* read it!" I'm officially impressed. "I'm impressed."

Noah shrugs again. "I'm impressive."

I snort. "Okay, Eisenhower." But then I think about the quote. I recognize it from the very end of the play. It's a line I've turned over in my mind many, many times. "Wait a minute. Are you suggesting I'm on my way to hell?"

Noah laughs. "Quite the contrary. Like I said, we all get off track. Everybody does. You can get back on anytime you like. Even without the threat of devils dragging you to your doom."

"But he didn't get back on track," I say, talking about Dr. Faustus.

"No, but he could have," Noah says. "I mean, that's what it's all about, right? It just takes courage."

Are we talking about the book, here?

Noah doesn't seem like the type to dispense unsolicited advice, and I am absolutely not the type to take it. But then again, I don't really know him, so I let it slide. "That's not always true. Sometimes the courageous thing *is* to take the detour. Sometimes the best thing you can do is get off the ride you're on and, I don't know, wait for your brain to recalibrate. People usually stay the course because it's what's easiest, because they *lack* courage."

The wind rattles at the windows like it's desperate to be let inside, and we both turn toward the noise.

"Do you lack courage?" Noah asks, meeting my eyes again.

"Yes," I say, without hesitation, surprising myself. I turn back to the fire. "I'm a coward."

"How are you a coward?" Noah asks.

"I ran from my demons, instead of facing them." I can't remember the last time I was so honest with someone. And Noah's essentially a stranger.

"Well, if you're going to run, it seems to me that demons are a pretty good thing to run from. Like you said, sometimes that's the brave choice."

Now I'm not sure. "Yeah, but I left someone good behind. Someone great, actually."

"And now you're alone," he says, nodding like he understands. I know he doesn't. He can't. But I let him believe he does. "You're a not-good, not-nice, not-lonely-but-all-alone coward," he taunts.

I look at him sharply. "You're joking, but it's true."

"Huh," he says. "Or perhaps you're . . . deceiving yourself?"

I let out a small huff of irritation. "Clever."

Noah doesn't respond but flashes a wide smile.

"You're alone, too," I say. Let's see how he likes it.

Noah shakes his head and meets my eyes. "I'm not alone. But I am sometimes lonely."

I nod, and the clattering windows settle. He must be thinking about his parents, and I am suddenly grateful to Jonathan. And for the first time in a long time I find myself wishing I had someone like that, too. I feel a small pang as I think about Hattie—and then an even bigger one as Kacey comes to mind. And then I find myself wishing I didn't wish it at all.

"Maybe it's both," Noah says. "Maybe it takes courage to stay, and courage to go."

And I have to agree with him. "Maybe it's both."

After a while the wind tires itself out and the bag of marshmallows grows empty. I turn to him and say, "So, tell me about Bad Noah."

37

THEN

"WANT TO PLAY QUESTIONS?" Kacey asked, sitting to the side of my den bed, her feet propped up near mine.

We were bored, and she was reverting to a game we hadn't played in years. "Do *you* want to play Questions?" I replied.

"How could you even wonder such a thing?" she smirked.

"Why wouldn't I?"

"Do you think you can beat me?"

"Why would you ever doubt it?" I shook my head and adjusted the pillow behind me.

"Hmm. Could it be because of that thing?"

"What thing?"

"Don't you know that thing I'm talking about?" she said, pointing to my head.

I shot her a confused look. "Um, do you mean my brain?"

"Are you referring to the empty space where your brain should be?" Kacey asked, slightly tongue-tied, but she managed to keep the game going.

Ha-ha. "Are you implying I'm an airhead?"

"Perhaps I'm calling you . . . a dreamer, no?"

"That does sound better, doesn't it?" I said.

Kacey laid her head back against her chair and looked up at the ceiling. Her eyes shut slowly and she remained quiet for a few moments. "Need any help with your assignments?" she asked, opening her eyes and sliding them over to the stack of work by my bed.

"I'm not so concerned with them, you know?" I replied.

Kacey raised an eyebrow. "That seems very unlike you, don't you think?"

I shrugged. "Yes, well, I'm becoming a whole new person. A mutineer. A guerrilla," I said, glancing at the stuffed gorilla in the far corner of the room. "I'm thinking I'll move to some remote cabin in the woods, change my name, and spend all my time reading and watching infomercials and eating grapes off the wallpaper. Want to join me?"

Kacey laughed and closed her eyes again. We were both quiet for a long time, and I wondered if she had fallen asleep. But then the slightest fissure marred her measured features. "Is that really your dream?" she asked. "To move away and leave everything behind?"

I'm not really supposed to be here.

Kacey's my best friend. I can tell her anything—but I can't tell her everything. And this feels like too serious a question—with too serious an answer. "Did I ever tell you about that dream I had about the 'More Than Words' guys?"

Kacey opened her eyes briefly to roll them at me. "Don't you have any dreams that aren't about ponytailed guitarists?"

"Well, not any good ones, right?" I laughed and rested my head back, too.

My eyes fell to the gorilla again and his bandaged leg. I sighed. And then, for no reason I could discern at all, I decided to tell Kacey just a little bit more. To let just a little bit of the worst part of me slip out. That worst part of me that I wished wasn't there, that I'd never admit was there, but was just a little bit . . . there. "What if I just didn't do this anymore? What if I just gave up for real?"

My words hung in the air between us, and it felt to me like a cloud of electricity had settled in the room. One wrong move and we could both go up in sparks.

Kacey turned to me slowly, with furrowed brows over suddenly clouded, gray eyes. "What do you mean?" she asked quietly.

This was what I didn't want. I didn't want to worry her. I didn't want to scare her. But it seemed that was exactly what I had done. I could tell by the way she was looking at me that she knew exactly what I had let slip.

Immediately regretful, I cleared my throat and tried to make it a little bit better. "Um, I mean, would it be so bad? If I decided not to be fixed anymore? If I decided I've had enough? If I decided nothing was wrong to begin with? If I decided to just say stop?"

It was stupid. I couldn't just say stop. She knew it; I knew it. But it was nice to pretend. And, most importantly, it seemed to set her mind at ease. "Well, can you do that?" she finally asked.

I was quiet for a long time, too. No, I couldn't do that. But it made me think about what I *could* do. "I don't know." I shrugged. I really didn't know.

"You lose," Kacey said kindly, head tilted to the side. It took me a moment to realize she was referring to the game.

The thing was, we both knew I'd lost much more than that.

38

NOAH AND I stay by the fire while the hands on the clock creep closer to tomorrow. I make instant coffee and he keeps the logs burning in the hearth. I find an old puzzle in my storage closet, and together we complete an image of a turquoise-and-yellow macaw surrounded by lush greenery.

Sometime after midnight, Noah stands up. The wind has been quiet now for a little while. "Think you'll have trouble keeping the fire going through the night?" he asks.

Oh. He's leaving? I'm not sure why, but I had just assumed he was going to stay. "Um, not at all," I reply, trying to play it cool, trying to keep the surprise and, strangely, the disappointment from my voice. But this is fine. This is okay. Obviously, this is what's best. There's no reason for him to stay. *Professional, Justine. Keep it professional.*

He takes his time pulling his boots and jacket back on and then walks over to the front door. "Noah . . . ," I begin weakly, not sure what it is I want to say, but feeling the need to say something.

He waits for me to continue, but I can't find the words. My mouth feels like glue. I just stand there like an idiot, like a kid holding up the line at the ice cream counter because she doesn't know what she wants.

"I'll be back tomorrow," he says, taking my hand like he tried to before and pressing it between his hands, gloved and warm.

I forget to flinch this time.

39

THEN

AFTER what seemed like an eternity at home, I had finally graduated from my wheelchair to crutches, and they let me return to school. But the crutches were tricky. The weight of my brace turned me into a pendulum; when I would swing my left leg through, I had to be very careful to stop the momentum so that I wouldn't fall forward. Combine this with the lopsided weight of my backpack slung over my shoulder and the slick, laminate public school flooring—it made for a perilous journey.

As I made my way down the hall for my first class back, I caught sight of Ms. Conti. With her long, strawberry-blond curls and silky billowing skirt, she looked like she belonged outside the steps of a Parisian café, smoking little cigarettes and leaving berry-colored lipstick stains on a mug full of something dark and creamy, not stuck here in between these cold cinder-block walls. "Justine," she crooned. "It's so good to have you back! You were missed."

"Thanks, Ms. Conti." I paused and rested on the pads of the crutches. "Um, I wanted to ask you. You didn't really send me any work to catch up on while I was gone."

"That's right," she said.

"Well, didn't you want me to do anything?"

"Did you read the book I sent you?" she asked.

"I did, but . . . anything else?"

She just shook her beautifully coiffed head.

"Um, aren't there, like, requirements, or something?"

"There are exceptions, Justine," Ms. Conti said, her blue eyes gentle. "You're an exception."

I bit my lip to hide its quivering. I didn't want to be an exception.

"I'll tell you what, Justine. Why don't you write me a poem?"

"A poem? About what?" I asked.

"About anything."

"Any poem?"

"Any poem," she said, and squeezed my shoulder before turning away, her heels clacking to the beat of my weary heart.

Well, I guess I could do that, I thought as kids zipped past me on both sides. But I should've been paying better attention. As I started to move again, my right crutch shot out from underneath me and went gliding along the floor. I fell forward onto my good leg and then my rib cage met the tile. The weight of my brace came crashing down onto the hard floor. It bounced once and then slammed back down again, a collision of steel and obliteration and bone. I was immediately paralyzed by the pain, like bolts of lightning shooting up both legs and throughout my entire body. A guttural noise ripped free of my chest. A noise I'd never heard before. A noise I didn't know I could make. I squeezed my eyes shut—*don't cry, don't cry, don't cry.* But it was no use. I began to shake. I couldn't contain the tears, hard as I tried. My backpack had spilled open in the fall, sending my Hello Kitty pencils rolling down the hallway.

Everyone in the hallway turned to stare. Some kids snickered, some looked around for help, but no one dared to touch me. The looks on their faces made me turn away. Concern? Pity? Horror? I didn't know which was worse. And though I was surrounded by onlookers and splayed out like a pig on a spit, in that moment, the hallway stretched to infinity, and I sat alone at the end of it with my knees to my chest and my arms wrapped tightly around them.

Finally, a teacher I didn't know stuck his head out of a nearby classroom. He came quickly to my side.

"Oh gosh. What can I do? Should I go get the nurse?"

I hoisted myself up. I wiped at my cheeks. I straightened my spine the best that I could. I shook my head and refused his help. Then I slung my backpack over my shoulder, gripped my crutches, and continued slowly down the hall, leaving my pencils and my dignity behind me.

40

THE HOUSE feels a little bit empty, like there are too many corners for just me alone. I like the quiet. I like the space. But all of a sudden it's like there's too much of it. And it's pretty obvious what's missing.

I don't think there's anything particularly wonderful about the sheriff. Okay, he is really funny and fun to be around. And our neighborly banter is spot on. And, I guess, he is pretty cute in an "it's such a curse being naturally tall, dark and handsome" sort of way. But anyone would think these things. It's not like we're a pair of star-crossed lovers or anything. He's a distraction. That. Is. All.

But for just a minute, I let myself wonder what it might be like if Noah weren't just a distraction. If I decided I didn't need to be alone, I didn't need to hide. If I decided to stop pretending to be a normal and functioning member of society and actually became a normal and functioning member of society. If I got to know the people in my new town. If I went to restaurants or book clubs or the farmers' market on Main Street. If I actually chose to strike up a conversation with a customer at The Treasure Box. Or if I chose to answer one of their many questions with any interest or sincerity. If I actually asked Mr. Ito about his life, rather than just wondering about it myself. If I stopped being so closed-minded, so egocentric, so selfish. If I stopped being such a coward.

I let myself wonder what would happen if I stopped lumping everyone together as villains. If I stopped expecting the worst of people. The worst of myself. If I stopped believing that everyone could hurt me, that everyone would hurt me, that everyone wanted to hurt me. For just a moment, I let myself wonder what would happen if I just gave someone a chance. If I just gave myself a chance.

I sit down on the sofa, and I open my notebook.

41

I SLEEP ON THE SOFA beneath a pile of blankets and wake throughout the night to maintain the fire. In the morning, I make myself a cup of lemon tea with water warmed from the fire, and I eat a few crackers dipped in grape jelly, as well as half a banana. It's Thursday, and it's going on five days without power.

Searching through the drawers in the kitchen, I find a bottle of craft glue. In the storage closet, I rip a large flap off one of the cardboard boxes. I use the cardboard to flip the puzzle that Noah and I completed last night upside down. I cut the cardboard to fit the puzzle, drizzle it with glue, and spread it around until it is evenly coated. I then press the glue side of the cardboard down onto the back of the puzzle and place a heavy book on top to let it dry.

Checking on my firewood out on the porch, I find that most of the snow has blown off, but it still feels damp. I go back inside and snuggle up on the couch. I spend most of the rest of the day reading from my worn paperback, its dog-eared corners like flower petals against my fingertips.

When the light finally begins to fade and I find myself squinting to make out the words, I close the book and put it on the end table. Just before swaddling myself in for the night, I hear a knock on the door. I check the peephole and let Noah inside, fumbling with the doorknob.

"Considering not letting me in?" He laughs.

"No," I say, and wipe my sweaty palms down my sides. He has a few sacks of firewood by his side. "You didn't need to bring all that. I've got wood drying out on the front porch."

"Drying out from this storm?" he asks, glancing at the wood piles behind him.

"Mm-hmm," I say, and take the bundles from him.

"You mean, that firewood there, with a little bit of snow on it?"

I look back and forth between Noah and the wood, not sure what it is he's getting at. "Yeah . . . ," I say.

"That firewood's perfectly fine. All you have to do is brush the snow off. It's not wet all the way through. And if it were wet all the way through, you wouldn't be able to dry it out just like that. It can take months. You wouldn't know just by feeling it."

"Oh," I say, and look down again at the logs he's brought over. "Good to know."

Noah simply nods and does his best to hide his smile. I appreciate him not rubbing it in.

I close the door as he kicks his boots on the mat to try to remove some of the snow. He then carries the wood over to the log holder by the hearth. "In any case, this should last you for a while." He adds a fresh log onto the fire, and I watch him as he works. Despite the freezing temperatures, despite the fire I already had burning, the whole room begins to fill with a different kind of warmth.

"Jonathan asked about you," he says. "I ran into him in town early this morning. He wondered if you had enough firewood. I told him I was bringing some over to you."

"The power's back up in town?" I ask, wondering when Mr. Ito would expect me to return to the store.

"No, I saw him on the corner as I was driving past—he was helping to clear the roads near another rental."

"Oh. That's really amazing of him," I say.

"He is kind of an amazing guy . . . when he's not being a dirtbag," Noah jokes affectionately. "Then again, amazingness runs in our family."

"Does it?" I ask.

"It does indeed," he replies, as he stands and gestures to the fire, his brown eyes reflecting its light. "Have you ever seen a more amazing fire?"

I glance at it out of the side of my eye. "It kind of looks the same as it did thirty minutes ago. You know, before you got here," I say wryly.

"Outrageous," he says, walking toward me, and I catch him taking note of the puzzle we completed yesterday, glued together and drying on the table. He doesn't mention it, though. "It was like an icebox before I got here. Now I'd say it's more of a bread box." He laughs a little at his own joke. "It's much, much warmer."

And as much as I don't want to admit it, he's right. I give him a small smile. "It is."

"It was an accident," Noah says, lounging on the floor beside me, our backs propped on pillows against the sofa and our feet facing the fire.

I don't say anything. I just stare into the flames and let him go on.

"Not a car accident. Something was wrong with the heater in the house. It was fall; the weather was starting to turn; Jonathan and I wanted to camp out in the backyard in our tent—it was something we did a lot as kids. Camping, hiking, Boy Scout stuff. Jonathan wanted to be a survival instructor. Anyway, that night, we thought it might be the last chance before it got too cold. Dad said it was already too cold for him. So he turned on the heat. Jonathan and I slept outside; Mom and Dad slept inside." Noah closes his eyes and rests his head back on the couch cushion. "They didn't wake up."

"Noah," I whisper, shaking my head in disbelief. "I don't even know what to say."

"When the police arrived, they ushered us out and wouldn't let us back in the house. They had to bring in special inspectors. Turned out the furnace was leaking carbon monoxide. There was an alarm in the house, but by the time it went off, they were already unconscious."

The first time Noah began telling me about his family, I had no real interest in learning more. But now I can't help but want to understand him better. "How old were you?" I ask.

"I was fifteen; Jonathan was seventeen."

"That's horrible," I say, almost to myself. "You said they let you stay here? You wanted to keep living in your house?" This seems so foreign to me. I try my best to avoid places with ghosts.

"Not at first. Even after they said it was safe, I didn't want to go back inside. I was scared and really mad at my parents for dying. As if they had a choice. The only person I would talk to was Jonathan. But then Cardinal convinced me to come back in—he made up some excuse about looking for paperwork for their estates—it was just a ruse. But once I stepped back inside the house, looking at their things, looking at all the pictures of them on the walls—it was like they were still here in a way. It was like, I could take care of the things they loved even though I couldn't take care of them. And I didn't want to leave."

It seems like he has more to say, so I wait for him to keep going.

"This was the only place we knew; we've lived here our whole lives. And everyone was so kind and compassionate after they died. People started coming by all the time, reminiscing about our parents, bringing us food, including us in their lives. Cardinal moved in for as long as Jonathan and I would let him stay. I made some new friends," Noah said, glancing at me. "Soon, it was like we had a new family, even though we had just lost ours. And there was no reason to go anywhere else."

"Is Cardinal a relative?" I ask.

"He was my dad's closest friend. They met on a local fishing expedition. Dad would always invite Mom, but she'd never want to go. So he'd end up bunking with a stranger, and that's how he met Cardinal. He was on his own, too; he didn't have any family around. They hit it off, and after that Dad stopped inviting Mom along with him. She was always grateful to Cardinal for that," he says with a smile. "And it just became a regular thing after that. Dad started bringing Cardinal over to the house, too. He taught us a lot about camping and fixing things and nature . . . Jonathan really loved it.

"Anyway, he really became like a second father to me and Jonathan, though the three of us don't really hang out together anymore. Jonathan still spends a lot of time with him, though." Noah scoots closer to me and scans the room again. "You don't have any photos around the house."

"I have one or two upstairs. Of me and my friend Kacey."

"Do you have any siblings?" he asks.

"Actually, I have two sisters," I say. "Shauna and Hattie."

"Older or younger?"

"I'm in the middle."

"But no photos?" He glances around the room and comes up empty. "Let me guess . . . Girls screaming. Hair pulling. Blackmail and back-stabbing over boyfriends. Diary stealing and pillow fights?"

"No, nothing like that." I laugh, wondering if he's serious. "Just your typical childhood drama."

"And where do you fall in all of that?" he asks inquisitively.

I focus on the fire, its flickering flames almost hypnotizing, and I think about my family. "Like I said, I'm in the middle."

42

THEN

IT WASN'T WARM. It wasn't even anywhere close to summer. For some reason Dad wanted to take us all to the Sleeping Bear Dunes for spring break. I eyed him suspiciously.

"Why?" I asked.

"We've got nothing else to do," he said.

"But you don't like camping. Or hiking. Or outside."

"That's not true. I like *outside*."

"Okay, whatever," I said, and tried again. "Just how am I going to hike?" I raised my eyebrows questioningly and gestured to my leg. "Ahem?"

"It's not real hiking. It's dunes. Besides," Dad said as he looked down and away from me, "your mother needs a break."

The national park was huge, with beaches, winding trails, and, of course, the dunes. Since that was what we had come to see, Dad decided we should attack the Dune Climb first. The brochure described it as relaxed and scenic, a nice introductory climb with breathtaking views of Lake Michigan. As we headed out of the hotel and made our way toward the dunes, it didn't look so bad. Pretty much like a beach but with waves in the sand instead of the water.

"I want to do the Heritage Trail," Shauna said, stopping in the middle of our path and waving one of the brochures at us.

Mom took it out of her hand and looked it over. "Shauna, that's a twenty-two-mile hike. Justine can't do that."

Oh please. I'm not the only one.

"But that's what *I* want to do," Shauna said.

"Well," Dad interjected. "Maybe Shauna and I could take a stab at the Heritage Trail, and you three can stay here on the dunes."

"That sounds good," Hattie said, trying to make everyone happy.

"No," Mom said, glaring at Dad. "This is a family vacation. We're not splitting up. Let's just do the dunes as we planned."

"But—" Shauna tried to say.

"Justine can only stay on the beach. We're staying on the beach."

Dad led the way, and we trekked about a quarter of a mile toward what I imagined was the horizon. Hattie skipped along by his side, while Shauna muttered behind them. At first, I was able to follow my family at a decent pace. *I can do this,* I thought. *It may take me some time, but I can do it.*

But then, as we went a little farther, the dunes grew steeper. And within a few more minutes, the hills of sand were so high that I couldn't see the water in front of me. My crutches grew heavy and started sinking into the sand, and I could barely keep up with the rest of them. Hattie yelled from up ahead, "Come on, Justine!"

But the farther I went, the hillier it became, and all of a sudden there were mountains of sand in front of me. There was no way I could climb them—I started to slide backward with each step I took. They might as well have been Mount Everest.

The feet of my crutches were buried at least six inches into the sand.

I didn't know what to do. I couldn't go any farther, but as I turned around and searched for the building we'd come from, I realized it was too far for me to go back. I couldn't see anyone in my family at all. So much for staying together.

I was stuck. I was alone.

I'd been worried about holding them back, but I had been left behind.

43

NOAH HAD THE RESOURCEFULNESS to toss his hot plate in the back of his police cruiser before coming over, and we share a can of soup and bread with peanut butter for dinner. After we eat, he suggests another game of cards. I shake my head.

"Scared I'll beat you this time?" he asks.

"Not scared, but not stupid. I'd rather not relinquish my title."

"Okay, well . . . do you play any instruments?" He looks around the candlelit living room.

"No," I half lie. I had to give it up when my Frankenstein fixture wouldn't fit beneath the piano bench.

"Can you sing?" he asks.

"Can you?"

"Moving on, then." He tilts his head and purses his mouth in concentration. "Paper football?"

"What's that?"

"You know, it's where you fold a piece of paper into a small triangle and then flick it across the table . . ." He forms his fingers into the shape of a field goal and then flicks his middle finger out from his thumb.

I give him a questionable look. "Are you making this up?" I ask.

"Oh, forget it," he says, smiling. "Don't you have *any* talents?" Noah asks, as he plops down dissatisfied on the rug beside me.

"If you're bored, you're free to go home," I say, but, oddly, I regret it the moment it escapes my mouth.

Noah doesn't seem fazed. "I'm never bored."

I sit there for a few moments, trying to think of something to do so that he won't want to leave, when an idea pops into my head. "Stay right there," I say, as I grab one of the burning candles and head to the storage closet. "I'm used to looking for things to fill the time." I find a few pieces of paper and a pair of scissors and I plop down beside Noah.

"Are you making snowflakes?" he asks.

"It seems kind of fitting," I say, folding a sheet against my knee and cutting careful triangles out of the corners and along the edges. I try to remember how Kacey and I used to do it.

"I'm counting on you girls to make the snowflakes really beautiful for the dance. Lots of glitter, lots of foil. Let's make this cafeteria sparkle!" Ms. Conti said.

"It'll take a lot more than some glitter to make this cafeteria beautiful," Kacey muttered to me under her breath.

I kicked her beneath the table with my good leg and said, "We'll do our best, Ms. Conti."

Ms. Conti's skirt brushed my knee as soft as peach skin as she walked away. I turned back to Kacey and caught her staring at me.

"Listen," Kacey started. "I've been thinking about what you said. You know, about running away to live on Gilligan's Island or whatever."

"Yeah," I laughed.

"I can help you," she said matter-of-factly.

What? *"What do you mean?" I asked, and paused mid glitter shake.*

"I mean, I don't want you to go. I don't think you should go. But if you really want to go, well, I can help you."

I was stunned. I knew I hadn't totally fooled her, but I hadn't imagined Kacey had taken my comment that seriously, let alone would try to help me. I wondered how much thought she'd given it. "Really?" I asked.

Kacey picked up the snowflake in front of her and began pressing on the creases. She turned to look at me. "Yeah. Obviously, we'll still be best friends and everything. But I understand why you'd want to leave. I mean, to tell you the truth, I'd probably want to leave, too."

I smile silently at the warm memory of Kacey. But my smile fades as guilt sets in, as I am reminded of the most wretched, pathetic parts of me.

I try to concentrate on the task before me. When I'm finished, I unfold the paper and reveal my masterpiece. Noah takes a piece and begins working on one of his own.

"That's a really intricate-looking snowflake," he says.

"I've had some practice." I shrug.

Noah takes his time, finishes up his own, and unfolds it. The jagged lines and floppy corners leave much to be desired. He looks at me questioningly.

"Ah, it's nice," I say, quickly looking down at the table.

"I know, I know, my artistic skills rival those of a toddler fisting a crayon," he says.

I look up at him and bite my lip a little. "I'm not going to disagree with you," I say.

Noah tosses his snowflake and the scissors onto the table in defeat. He leans back on his elbows. "I excel at other things," he says with a wink.

I don't respond.

"Your friend—Kacey? Does she come and visit you a lot?" he asks.

"Um. No," I say, my shoulders slumping slightly, a sadness creeping into me. "She's actually never come to visit me." I lay the piece of paper that I'm holding back on the table. "We're . . . not really . . . speaking." I look up into his eyes. "At all."

"What did you do?" Noah asks, more curious than accusing.

"Me?" I ask. "Why do you assume it's me?"

"Okay," he says. "What did she do?"

"Nothing," I say quietly. "She did nothing." Not wanting to rehash the whole pitiful story, not with Noah and not with myself. He thinks she's mad at me. "It's not like that."

Noah looks at me questioningly. "So, what's it like?"

Ugh. Fine. "We don't really see eye to eye on things anymore. She thinks I'm holding on to things that I should have let go of a long time ago."

"And you disagree, so you're not speaking?" he asks.

"No. It's more like, I'm trying to protect her."

"From what?" Noah asks.

From me. But I don't answer him. I think he senses my sadness, anyway.

"Well, you should cut yourself some slack," he says, not knowing what he's talking about at all. "It can be hard—to move forward, you know?" He brushes away the tiny triangles of paper clinging to his palms, like he's brushing away the inconvenient remnants of a former life. "Sometimes we all get stuck."

44

THEN

I KNOW WHAT YOU DID.

Pardon me?

With the bar. I know you bent your knee a little.

I'm sorry, I don't know what you're talking about.

Yes you do. You bent your knee, just a bit, before she screwed on the bar. You're supposed to keep it perfectly straight, but you bent it.

Oh, so what!

So, you won't be happy when your leg turns into a piece of driftwood, and you're hobbling around like Pinocchio.

Shut up. That's not going to happen. I did it one time.

I'm just saying.

I can't breathe, okay? I can't just lie here like a corpse, stiff as a board! I'm a person; I need to move; I need to breathe!

Don't I know it.

I need to sleep! I can't sleep and I can't move and I'm stuck and I'm scared!

Hey, hey, relax. You don't need to convince me. I just thought I'd point it out; you're not fooling anybody.

I can't do this.

I know.

Think Mom knows?

What, that you can't do this or about the bar?

About the bar, I guess.

Sigh. Nah. You're probably fooling her.

45

THE EVENING grows longer and Noah and I find things to keep ourselves busy. I discover another puzzle forgotten in the bottom of the closet, and we sit down together on the floor in front of the fire. "Listen, about earlier," Noah says, dumping the pieces out of the box. "I didn't mean to pry."

"It's okay, you didn't."

We sit silently across from each other, attempting to assemble the border first. We make quick work of it, separating out all the flat-sided pieces, and begin working on our designated corners. Noah peeks at me occasionally from under his eyelashes.

After some time, images start to come together in little pockets of pictures. Colorful islands floating within the sea of my area rug telling pieces of a story. The puzzle, once assembled, is supposed to be a cartoon of penguins on the beach. Noah's focused on a large penguin lounging beneath an umbrella, while I work on where the water meets the sand.

"Too bad we can't swap places," Noah says, glancing from the penguins to the snow outside the window. "Seems like we'd all be happier with a change of scenery."

"Not all of us," I say, searching through the pile for foamy, water's-edge pieces.

"You don't like the beach?" Noah asks, laying a piece with the large penguin's foot into place.

"No, I do. It's fine. I've only been once, actually. But I didn't get to go into the water."

"Only once?"

I shrug. "My mom doesn't like to be windblown."

"I see," Noah smirks. "Well, why didn't you go in?"

Because I had a metal cage strapped to my leg. Because it could have caused infections. Because everyone around me would've stared and been disgusted. But mostly, because I never even made it to the water. "It was the wrong season," I said.

"Family trip?"

"Kind of. We took a drive to the Sleeping Bear Dunes. Have you been?"

Noah smiles a crooked smile. "Oh, that's not a real beach. I meant the ocean."

It sure looked like a beach to me. "Are you suggesting that these penguins are at the coast? How do you know?"

"Well, look at them. The image works because it's supposed to be the opposite of where you'd expect them to be. They're used to an Antarctic tundra, and here they are, in a place that appears to be similar to their home, but is actually totally different, and they're loving it. The tropical greenery, the flip-flops, the suntan lotion, they're emanating the kind of joy that can only be found at a place like . . . Miami."

"Obviously," I say with a roll of my eyes. "Maybe they're faking it."

"Nope. They're not."

I give Noah a challenging look.

"Impossible," he says.

I go back to searching for my pieces.

"I'm a cop. I've received extensive training in things like this. I know when people are lying."

"These aren't people; they're penguins." I know he's just kidding around, but it makes me worried he might try to do some digging on me. I eye him warily.

"Even so," he says. "I can tell. I can tell when somebody's lying, and this penguin is most definitely not. Look at that smile, and the way he's taking his time with that piña colada—there's no way he's faking that."

"You're looking too superficially," I say. "His smile, it's too toothy. I mean, when's the last time you saw a penguin's teeth? Do penguins even have teeth? And look at his foot, the way it's half-buried in the sand. He's hiding something. He's not happy, though he'd like you to think he is. Really, he wants to go back home."

Noah raises his eyebrows at me.

"And he's wearing sunglasses," I add. "I mean, that's a dead give-away. He's clearly trying to conceal something."

"Really? What about all these other penguins?" Noah asks with interest.

"They're probably faking it, too," I say. But then I worry that I *have* inadvertently made Noah suspicious, so I try to keep it light. "I'm really disappointed in your detective work, Sheriff Noah. I expected better."

Noah laughs, and I feel a little relief. He slides the large penguin over to the inside corner of the border and snaps it into place beneath the scalloped hem of a blue umbrella. "I guess there's a little bit of fake in all of us," Noah says.

"Don't I know it," I whisper.

"What do you think the point is, then?" Noah asks.

"What do you mean?"

"I mean if you're right, and nothing is real and everyone's lying . . . well, what's the point?"

"I don't think everyone's lying," I say. "I mean, I don't think everyone *means* to lie. I think the truth is painful, and we all walk around blind to each other's pain because we're so consumed with distracting ourselves from our own."

"What do you mean?" Noah asked.

I pause before responding, not wanting to say too much but feeling like there's a small, hot blister inside me waiting to pop. I sigh. " 'This was one way of knowing people . . . to know the outline, not the detail.' "

Noah gives a small frown. "I don't know," Noah says, searching the floor. "I think people are pretty straightforward when you look close enough." He reaches for a puzzle piece in between my knees. "I think I have a pretty good idea of who you are."

Normally, this is the kind of statement that would panic me—make me feel like I'm being dissected. But right now I just feel sad. "Why is that? Because we've been stuck in a snowstorm together for a few days? Shared a couple of jokes by the light of a fire?" I shake my head. How can I put this so that he'll understand? "People are like Rubik's Cubes. The more time that passes, the more mixed up we get." I blow out a breath. "You can spend a really long time trying to get everything back in order, but very few people actually do. Most straighten out one side just to screw up another."

"But that's the fun, isn't it? I mean, how long can you hold on to a perfect Rubik's Cube without wanting to mess it up a little bit?"

I shake my head again—he's looking at it the wrong way. "No one picks up a Rubik's Cube and doesn't try to get those little squares back in line," I say.

Noah nods and bites at the corner of his lip. "You're saying you don't want me to know how mixed up your squares really are?"

I turn my eyes toward the window and stare back at the dim reflection of myself, wondering how I just let my mouth take a journey without my brain. "Sometimes, I feel desperate for people to know the detail, but all I can bear to show them is the outline."

Noah doesn't say anything. I place the piece I've been playing with and we continue to work on our separate sections. Noah finishes another penguin and moves on to a smaller one in a bikini sharing a bag of chips with a fluffy, gray chick wearing water wings. I do a decent job assembling the water that runs along the bottom edge of the puzzle.

Then out of nowhere Noah says, "Show me something that's real."

Ah, excuse me? I lift my head to meet his eyes. "Is that a come-on?"

"No," he says, affronted.

I immediately feel bad. He was being sincere, and I thought the worst. I exhale, disappointed in myself. "Sorry," I say, bending my head to my lap. I've hurt him. I try to think of a way to make it better.

I set down the puzzle piece in my hand, push myself up off the floor, and slowly walk to the table that holds my TV. I hesitate but then pull out the little hidden drawer. I open the notebook to where the satin bookmark is resting and carry it back to Noah. Hesitantly I reach out to hand it to him. *Just do it. Just do it—what's the worst that can happen?* My outstretched hand shakes a little bit.

"Here," I say finally. "This is real."

He takes the notebook and scooches closer to the fire to read the words in the light.

I dip my toe and hold it there,
A slight chill lingering in the air.
Moss-covered rocks and
  a muddy floor,
Leftovers from the winter before.
      I push in deeper, a little more,
Wading out farther from the shore.
Gauging each ripple,
  deciphering every sound—
While a small voice inside whispers, *Turn back around.*
      I plunge through the swells that glitter like glass
And cut just as deep with each laboring pass.
Splintered pieces worth more
  the more they're worthless—
A currency of tears paid in excess.
      As I near the middle, the bottom gives way;
I release a small cry and then start to pray.
But this was my intention—
  why else brave the tide?
Than to vanish in the vortex of the secrets I hide.
      Somewhere in the distance—a savior!—a sound!
(Or the panic-induced delusions of paradise found?)
But no one speaks up
  so I keep spinning down,
And wonder who might be there watching me drown.

Swirling to the bottom, the fall takes too long
And what I thought would feel right suddenly feels wrong.
Satin promises masked
  this sodden bed of nails,
Framed by fear and futility and bent metal rails.
      Out of nowhere, like a siren in the dead of night—
What the hell are you doing, you idiot? Fight!
The water is lulling,
  the current is strong,
But *this* is the place where you do not belong.
     I claw through the water, fingers like a rake—
No longer asleep, no sooner I wake.
If souls starve without meaning
  like lungs hunger for air,
Now, faced with a famine, I finally care.
     I fracture the surface, ravenous still,
And pray that my limbs hold the weight of my will—
To keep me from the lure
  of the undertow
And places twice as dark as the depths below.

Noah puts the notebook down after he's finished reading. "When did you write this?" he asks.

"Last night," I say. And then I add, "After you left."

"You're right—this isn't fake at all," he says thoughtfully. "This is really, really beautiful."

I smile at the compliment, and I'm immediately glad that I showed it to him. But then he continues, "This is you, Elisabeth," and whatever satisfaction I had just felt vanishes in an instant. I feel like a fraud. I *am* a fraud. My face falls, and I have to look away.

This is not okay.

46

THEN

I SAT BY THE WINDOW, watching the boys across the street shooting baskets, waiting for Mom to bring me my pain medication. I was working on my poem for Ms. Conti. I had an open notebook on my lap, but the only thing on the page was eraser flakes. There are only twenty-six letters in the English alphabet, and only so many ways that you can arrange those letters into words, and those words into sentences. But every time I put them together, I couldn't get them to say what it was I wanted them to say. What was it I wanted them to say?

It was so easy to write a bad poem—why was it so hard to write a good one?

Mom brought me the pills with a little cup of water. "There you are," she said.

I took them from her, placed them on my tongue, and mechanically swallowed them down.

There I am. Here I am. But the real me is not really here at all. I imagined Real Me hiding in the back of my mind somewhere. In a junk drawer. And every day more junk gets thrown into it—spare pennies, some Post-it Notes, a snide comment, a judgmental laugh—shoving Real Me to the back.

It's dark and dusty, and as I crawl into the corner, I step on the crumbs of things that were stuck in here before. I wonder how they might have gotten out, and I look for an escape—but I'm too far away from the small crack of light, and I keep getting shoved farther and farther to the back.

One day something spills in the junk drawer, covering Real Me with a goopy mess. It seeps into my eyes and ears. Everything becomes hazy and muted. I stop looking for a way out. Instead, I settle in.

And there Real Me stays, hidden, forgotten, cowering, and buried beneath layers of something heavy and viscous.

47

NOAH LEAVES in the wee hours of the morning, before either of us falls asleep.

"I'm going to go," he says, unfolding himself from the couch and stepping into his boots. I follow him to the door and cross my arms over my chest.

"Yeah, it's late," I say, checking my wrist and realizing I'm not wearing a watch. "You should go." Those are the words that make their way out of my mouth, but what I find myself really wanting to say is *Don't go. Don't go, don't go, don't go, Noah.* It feels strange.

He opens my door, and a gale of icy air forces its way inside. He steps out over the threshold and into the dark, turning back once before walking away. "Maybe one day you'll ask me to stay."

I close the door once his dark form becomes indistinguishable from the night. The lock, as I turn it, is loud. Dividing.

I retreat back into the blanket pile on the sofa and let the light from the fire warm my face. My skin feels tight and hot. I stare at the half-completed puzzle on the floor. The fire fades and the darkness descends like a curtain—thick around the edges, soft and threadbare in the middle. Eventually, it drags my eyelids down with it, and I fall asleep, stuck somewhere between the push and pull of missing him and feeling relieved that he's gone.

48

THEN

GOING TO THE HOSPITAL for a fixator check was not like going to the pediatrician for a checkup. At the pediatrician's office, a checkup is almost always good news and almost always quick: *Wow, look how much you've grown! Hey, you're in the fiftieth percentile, just perfect! Ears, check. Eyes, check. Check check check—you're doing great!* Fixator checks with Dr. S had no such checks. They were an all-day affair with lots of offices, lots of waiting rooms, lots of waiting, and even more waiting. No one ever said anything lighthearted or encouraging. There were puzzled glances and the occasional questioning frown. And lots and lots of *hmm*s.

But there was something else, too. Something that emanated from the walls of the hospital or, perhaps, emanated from me while I was within the walls of the hospital. Something I tried not to think about too much but that popped unwelcome into my head from time to time—a minor annoyance, a fruit fly. Something to swat at. As scary a place as the hospital can be—the menacing machinery, the endless corridors, the faceless figures in white—there is also, strangely, a comfort in it. The gleaming floors, the smell of antiseptics, the sandpaper gowns and starchy linens. There was a familiarity, a sense of belonging, a sense of being cared for. A sense of being taken care of. Have you ever dreamed of being kidnapped, but not been afraid? There's a lure to being wanted; there's a longing to being rescued. Not everything terrible is a nightmare. Is this how it felt to be loved? Is this how it felt to be cherished? It came close, in a twisted, self-indulgent, masochistic sort of way. I am sick. I am special. I am special here.

By three o'clock I'd already been to the X-ray department, the occupational therapy office, and the lab for bloodwork. After a quick stop in the cafeteria, where I chose a pack of pink coconut snowballs, we sat for an hour in the clinic waiting room before they called us back. Mom walked in front of me, going slowly so I could keep up on my crutches. We passed a group of young doctors in short white coats following the doctors in long white coats around like sheep.

Once in the exam room, it took another half hour before Dr. S came in. Top sheep. He plopped himself onto a little stool and went through the usual review: Bloodwork looks okay; X-rays look fine. How's PT? Keeping up with your exercises? I nodded and said yes to everything, not really listening to him because, to be perfectly honest, he was not really listening to me. Each question was out of his mouth before I finished answering the previous one. And with each pseudo question he asked, and each pseudo answer I gave, the absurdity of it all seemed to matter less and less. He wasn't even looking at me as he spoke.

Dr. S wasn't particularly nice. He wasn't particularly friendly. He wasn't particularly anything, in my opinion, but if you asked Mom her opinion, it would be that he was particularly everything. He was smart. He was brilliant. He won every top doctor award in the country, the world, the universe. God himself raised an eyebrow, impressed. We should bow our heads at the mere mention of his name and curtsy as he entered the room. He was fixing her daughter.

Dr. S wheeled himself like a crab over to the exam table and did the same things he always did: grabbed my foot with his big, meaty hands, rotated it up and down. Then hands at the knee, back and forth, back and forth, range of motion looks good. "Can you walk for me, please?" I got down carefully, headed out into the hall, and used my crutches to swing myself down the hallway and then back into the exam room. He murmured to himself, bent his head low, and wrote a note in my chart. "Looking all right."

I slouched against the exam table until he spoke again.

"Stand straight, please," he said, his face still in my chart.

I rested my crutches against the exam table and used it to steady myself. He placed his hands at my hips. He dug his fingers in and checked to see if they were parallel. He rotated my hips forcibly and then dug his fat fingers in even more.

"Ow, that hurts."

He reared back a little as if he'd just now realized I was here standing in front of him. "Oh. Sorry," he said, and eased up.

Dr. S bit his lip like he was considering something, and then he looked up at Mom. "Well, Mrs. Amos, I think things are looking good overall. Not too much longer now. How often is she taking . . ." And I stopped listening again. He still wasn't looking at me. It was rude that he was asking Mom about my pain and not me. And *I* didn't want to be rude, but it was like I wasn't even in the room at all, like he didn't think I could answer even the simplest of questions. He poked at me with his daggerlike fingers and then asked Mom about my pain? I was tired of being overlooked. I was tired of being ignored. I was tired of him thinking he could pick and choose when my opinion mattered. I did something very unlike myself.

"You know, if you're curious about my pain, you could try asking *me*."

Mom and Dr. S both turned toward me.

I couldn't explain it, but in that second Real Me pushed her way out of the junk drawer and came alive. "You're talking about me like I'm not here. I may be a kid, but that doesn't mean I shouldn't get a say in anything. This is happening to *me*. No one asked me if I wanted this. I'm not dumb. And I can certainly tell you about my own pain."

"I didn't mean to insult you," he said blankly.

"I'm not insulted. It would be nice to be included."

"Okay," he said, looking at me maybe for the first time ever. "Please, tell me about your pain."

When you're in pain, everybody around you tries to label it. Is it shooting, stabbing, aching? Is it constant or does it come and go? How would you rate it on a scale of zero to ten? Is it sort of frowny or a little frowny or really frowny? The pain must be quantified in order to count.

But the thing about pain is that, when it's with you all the time, it starts to lose its meaning. The difference between a three and a six is inconsequential. Stabbing, throbbing, it doesn't matter. All that matters is you can't think clearly. Everything you know is through the fabric of the pain. Music is muffled. Flowers look wilted. Clouds look gray.

And not only for you—the meaning diminishes for everyone around you, too. They get tired of hearing *it hurts*. They get tired of the tears. And so they just stop asking altogether.

The pain is still there, but you can't describe it anymore because it's become the background of your every experience. It's the wind in the trees. The breath in your lungs. The wallpaper in every room.

My eyes started to fill with tears. I wanted to tell him about the pain. Not the pain in my leg, but the other pain, the one that there was no medicine for. The one that had invaded my head and my heart and my soul. I wanted to tell him about how empty and lonely and bitter I'd become. What it felt like to wake up in pain and go to sleep with pain and know that there was no end in sight. I wanted to tell him that laughter and tranquility and sleep eluded me, but fear and dread and shame were ever present. I wanted to tell him about the indignity of being trapped in a body that's betrayed you. That it was too much pressure. That sometimes I felt like I was going crazy. That sometimes I felt like I was losing myself.

I wanted to tell him how it felt to be forced to rely on adults who are sloppy when it comes to how they treat children in their care. That I didn't feel like anyone was really in my corner. I wanted to tell him I felt like I couldn't trust anyone. But because of that, I couldn't trust him. I wanted to tell him that I was scared everyone was going to hurt me. But because I was so scared, I couldn't tell him any of this at all. Because I knew what happened when there was a problem. I knew what happened when *you* were a problem. And the last thing I wanted to do was cause any more problems. The last thing I needed was for him to think there was something else needing to be fixed.

And Real Me, brave as she was only moments ago, cowered back into the drawer.

Instead, I pretended to be exactly who they wanted me to be. I looked at Dr. S and said, "I'm still taking about four Darvocet a day."

I am sick. I am special. I am special here.

49

THE NEXT MORNING, I wake up happy to be alone in my house again. Happy to make tea in my little kitchen, happy to tend to my feeble fire. This is how it should be. This is all I need. This is where I'm comfortable. This is where I am safe.

Reasons to Stay Away from the Sheriff:
He'll only end up hurting me.
I'll only end up hurting him.
Being alone is the only way to stay anonymous.
Being anonymous is the only way to stay safe.

It's around noon when I hear a strange sound echo through the house. It sounds like limbs falling off a tree, and I'm at once afraid. I do a quick search from each of the first-floor windows to see if anything's fallen near the house. The sound continues, but I don't see anything.

I dress for the outdoors and let myself out through the back. The snow has settled a little bit, and each step I take only comes up to my knees. The sound is louder now, reverberating off the nothingness before me. It sounds like it's coming from the direction of Noah's house, and I move carefully, following the noise.

I walk the length of the field, eventually passing the oasis of trees to my right. I slowly approach Noah's property and look for any signs of movement. I can't see anything, but the sound begins to change from a breaking, thwacking echo to a quick, slicing thud. I should turn back. Whatever it is, it's no concern of mine. Noah's probably not even home—he *is* the sheriff, after all—he must be busy. But then I'm reminded of Noah's parents. What if something is wrong at his house, and he has no way of knowing it? I walk a little farther to the opposite side of the property. It won't hurt to just take a look.

As I make my way around the house and behind Noah's driveway, I see the back of a man in a heavy coat, standing, leaning over something, with an axe raised over his shoulder. "Noah?" I call, before realizing perhaps I shouldn't bring attention to myself. He turns around, revealing the huge, round tree trunk partially hidden in the snow. I clench my jaw. Of course he's chopping wood—what else could it have been?

"Hey," he says, a little out of breath. "What are you doing here?"

I shake my head, disparaging myself. "Nothing. I heard a noise—I see you're fine, though." My face heats with embarrassment. "I'm leaving." I turn back in the direction of my house.

"And you thought you'd come see if I was okay?" he calls.

"No. I . . . uh . . . No . . . Oh, shut up."

He laughs and raises his axe again, bringing it down with a speed and force that I find . . . unsettling. But also, impressive.

"I'm surprised to see you dressed up as Paul Bunyan in the middle of the day," I say, referring to his plaid wool coat and heavy workman's gloves. "Don't you have a town to be protecting?"

"There's surprisingly little crime in a town buried in a blizzard," he says.

I laugh then, my teeth chattering a bit. "Surely there's something, somebody out there who needs assistance from you."

"Don't worry," he says, lifting his jacket above his waistband and showing off his police radio. "I'm on call."

I nod and excuse myself again. It's freezing. "Well, I guess I'll go back home, now that I know you're not being murdered or anything."

"Would it bother you if I were? Being murdered, that is."

"Obviously. What would I do for firewood? At least I have your hot plate."

"I appreciate your concern," he says, bringing the axe down swiftly on another section of tree trunk. "But you don't have to go. I've got another axe in the garage."

"Ha!" I say so loud it echoes like the axe off the trees. "I can assure you that's not a good idea."

"It's easy," he says. "Come here, I'll show you."

There is no doubt in my mind this is something I should under no circumstances be doing. But the thought of being that close to him. "Erm, okay . . ."

Hesitantly I walk over toward Noah. *Go home, Justine, go home.* He steps back from the pile of wood. He takes a section that's already been chopped but is still pretty large and places it on a large stump sticking out from the snow in front of me. He hands me the axe, the blade resting on the snow, and stands behind me. He brings his arms around mine and covers my hands with his. His mouth is at my ear, the length of his legs press against mine. "Grip the axe like this," he says, wrapping my hands tightly around the handle, "and bring it up near the side of your head." Noah supports most of the weight of the axe as I bring it up to my shoulder. With him behind me like this, the cold is a bit more bearable.

"Now, keep your eyes on the spot where you want the blade to go. See right there, where there's a knot in the wood?" he says, his face now brushing the side of mine. "Focus on that spot."

I take a breath in, and Noah does the same. I can feel the stubble of his jaw against my cheek, his warm breath mixing with mine.

"Then, just let it go."

I exhale and release the axe, in more of a drop than a launch, and it hits the wood but misses the knot by a few inches. A small piece splinters off. Noah's arms tighten around me, infinitesimally—but I notice, and I feel a warmth spread through me from the inside. We stand still for a long moment. It's like we're waiting for each other to say something important. But neither of us does. Noah clears his throat. "Well, it's not an exact science," he says as I lean the axe onto the wood. "Want to try again?"

"No thanks," I say. "We're not all cut out to be lumberjacks. I'll leave the hatcheting to you." I hear a subtle kind of disappointment lacing my voice, and I pray to God that Noah didn't catch it. I step out of his hold and move a few feet away from him. He pulls his gloves off, revealing hands slightly red from his work. Strong hands. Confident hands. I notice the squareness of his fingernails. I want to touch them. I want to feel them scrape against my skin.

Quickly I move away. It's time to go. But I fear I'm being too obvious, and I don't want to hurt his feelings.

"I should get back," I say, and cock my head in the direction of my cabin.

"Yeah, for sure," he replies. "Gotta get back home . . . to no one . . . and nothing."

"No," I say, a little put off. "It's not nothing."

"Right, right. You and your mementos of your old friend from school. Kacey, was it?"

I pause for sarcastic punctuation. "Yeah, that's right."

"Well, maybe we should get her out here. We could have a snowball fight. I have no doubt I could take the two of you down," he says, picking up some snow and packing it together.

"I don't think so," I say.

"Why not?" Noah asks.

"Because I can't talk to her." I just can't talk to her.

"Why?"

How do I explain that it's not something that I wanted, that it chips away at my soul? Every time I ignore her calls, every time I think about what a terrible friend I am. Every time I think about what I've done. "Because . . . because she's at college—and she's doing great. And she deserves it. Everything amazing and fun and new. And she doesn't need to be . . . burdened . . . by me. I'm doing the right thing. I'm being a good friend."

Noah nods as if he gets it. "But she keeps calling you?"

I sigh. "She wants me to come back."

"And you don't want to?"

"Well," I say thoughtfully, "she was actually the one who talked me into moving away."

"Okay, so what do you think of California?" Kacey said, dog-earing her place in her book and flipping it upside down on the cafeteria table. She

bent into me from across our lunch trays and kept her voice low. The seats were starting to fill up.

"No way." I laughed and shrugged my shoulders. She raised her brows at me. "I'm not really going anywhere, Kacey."

"How about Arizona?" she continued, ignoring me.

I exhaled and humored her. She was on a mission. "Too hot."

"Alaska?"

"Too cold."

"Um, how about . . . Florida, then?"

"Alligators."

"Right. Hmm." She looked deep in thought.

I laughed and began eating my lunch.

Kacey leaned in even closer. "Okay, I'll keep working on it . . . ," she started to say, looking very serious. "Definitely somewhere remote. Somewhere that looks like the cover of a—"

"Kacey," I quickly interrupted. "I was just indulging you. I'm not actually going to like, leave. I mean, I can't . . . right?" I said, shifting my eyes side to side to be sure no one was listening. I wanted to, I wanted to so badly, but let's get serious.

She stared back at me, and I could see the wheels turning in her head. Kacey raised her eyebrows and shrugged her shoulders. She yanked her lollipop out of her mouth, making a resounding pop, and flicked my forehead with it. "I'm just saying," she said.

"I mean, can I?"

"Elisabeth, listen," she said, focused again. "It's your call. It's your life. It just seems everyone else acts like everything is their call, like it's their life. It's like you don't even exist at all. It doesn't seem fair. And I hate seeing you like this. So, I don't want you to go, but I get it if you do, and I think it's *something you should get to decide for yourself. And as your best friend, it's my job to . . . help with that . . . if you want."*

I sat back, too, and bit my lip. "Right," I said. "But, I mean, I would never actually consider something like that."

Kacey leaned all the way back in her chair and smiled. "Of course not."

"Of course not," I repeated, and went back to my lunch. Kacey went back to her lollipop.

Of course not. I would never do something like that. I could never do something like that. But then, then, I started to wonder if maybe I could. I wondered if I could do it. I mean, actually do it. Move away and leave everything behind. A part of my life that I didn't choose. A part of my body that split me in two. Maybe, maybe, maybe, even a part of me.

I'm not really supposed to be here. The thought echoed in my head.

Well, maybe, I didn't actually have to be here.

I let my mind wander. Eternal weekends, silent sunrises and lazy sunsets, salty air, windblown hair, a blanket for one on the beach. Water so still you could mistake it for glass.

The more I thought about it, the more it felt like something had clicked. And not in a pull-me-apart kind of way—but more like something was falling into place. No doctors. No hospitals. No probing fingers. No gawking strangers. No Fear. No Pain.

Just me. Just peace. Solitude. I painted a picture in my head, a breathtaking landscape spanning far and wide. A single silhouette fading into the distance.

Noah pretends not to see the pensive shadow fall across my face. "And now she wants you to come back?" he asks.

"Something like that."

He nods to himself. "Right. So . . ." He draws it out, like he doesn't believe me. "It sounds like it's better this way."

"Yes," I say. "It is. It's better this way."

Noah drops the snowball. His eyes shine brightly with doubt. "Elisabeth, what are you doing?"

I gaze at him. Neither of us moves, yet the distance between us doubles across the snow. "What do you mean?"

"I mean with your life. What are you doing here? How does this all fit into your plan?"

I narrow my eyes. I didn't realize we were in freshman philosophy. Where was this coming from? What makes him think he has any right to question me? It doesn't *fit* into my plan—this *is* my plan.

But I can't tell him that. "Well . . . ," I start to say. But nothing else comes.

Noah looks at me expectantly. "Go on."

"Well, I mean, I'm just . . ." My thoughts begin to jumble. Noah's looking at me like he's expecting some perfect answer. And then the features of his face move like a slide puzzle and a whole new picture appears. One I've never seen on his face before. Something harder but rounded at the edges. Something softly devastating. Pity.

"Yeah?" he says.

"I'm just . . ." I'm flustered and not exactly sure what he wants from me. I feel increasingly uncomfortable. I feel like I'm being dissected. Pulled apart. Examined. And my head can no longer firmly hold on to any thought, let alone my jumbled ones, but instead fills up with a nauseating stream of pulsing beats that sound something like, *Don't look at me, don't look at me, don't look at me.* But he *is* looking at me, he's staring at me with wide brown eyes, and the space behind my eyes becomes a runaway boulder of static. And my chest begs to collapse. And my feet itch to run. Run. Run. Run away. *Be anywhere, Justine, but here.*

Noah assesses me once more. "Hiding," he says, finishing my sentence.

"No," I say. *Stop it, Noah.* Stop trying to figure me out. Stop picking at my peeling, flaking skin—don't you know it's a whole lot uglier beneath the burn?

"Okay, then what? Huh? Please, tell me, Elisabeth."

I don't know what to say. I feel hot and dizzy and my brain seems like it's moving too fast and too slow and has somehow become completely disconnected from my mouth. I can't force anything out. He's trying to expose me for the fraud I am.

"You can't tell me what you want, because you don't even know what it is."

Who does he think he is? A venom seeps into my veins. It congeals and rises to my throat in one sour, pulsating lump, and suddenly my mouth and brain are friends again. "Well, how about you?" I say more spitefully than I intend. "What are you doing here, playing sheriff of this dumpy little town? Are you planning to single-handedly police this shithole for the rest of your life—taping off closed roads, helping old ladies cross the street, and, I don't know, rescuing kittens out of trees, or whatever it is you do?"

I see the hurt in Noah's eyes, and I feel sick to my stomach knowing I put it there.

"Look, you can make fun of me all you like; it doesn't bother me. I know what I'm doing here—I'm giving back; I'm doing good. You . . . ," he says, looking me up and down and shaking his head. "I don't know what you're doing."

The knot in my throat is a cannonball. And even though it hurts to say these things, I can't stop. I just can't. "That's right," I say. "You don't know. You have no idea. So don't act like you know everything. Don't act like you know me."

The seriousness in the set of his jaw starts to look something like regret, and I shrink beneath his stare. I have to look away from him—I have no choice. What just happened? How is this happening? The silence stretching between us—it's unbearable.

Noah can't look at me, either. He lowers his gaze and kicks at the snow in front of him. When he speaks again, his voice is quiet and controlled. "I know if you stay here long enough—cooped up in that house, hiding in the back corners of some dusty souvenir shop—pretty soon you're going to be unrecognizable to anybody who knew you, Elisabeth."

There it is. A hot mixture of righteousness and relief washes through me, and now I can look at him again. Because he doesn't know me. All he knows is the outline. All I've *shown* him is the outline. The pity dripping from his every word isn't pity for me. It's pity for the version of me he wants me to be. And I'm done being what anybody wants me to be. I feel vindicated. I feel justified. I feel safe again.

Because he really doesn't know me at all.

Don't you get it, Noah? Unrecognizable was the plan all along.

50

THEN

TODAY GRETCHEN WAS ABSENT from the Pit of Despair. The people at the check-in desk told me I'd have a substitute therapist. I left my mother to her magazine in the waiting area and shuffled myself to the table in the back while I waited for the sub to help me up.

"Hi, Justine. I'm Justin. I'm filling in for Gretchen today."

Oh my God. Alarm bells went off in my head. What the cute? My mouth was suddenly parched. Or did I just drool?

What was happening here?

Okay, Justin was beyond cute. Tall, molten brown eyes, dimples, messy sandy hair. Look at that smile—did his teeth just twinkle? I had to be dreaming. He could not be my sub.

I think I said hi.

"Justin and Justine, like we were meant to be, huh?" The words tumbled out of his mouth in a cloud of shimmering fairy dust.

"Ha-ha, yeah, erm . . . that's funny." Oh my God, could I be any dumber? I was utterly inarticulate. My breathing had definitely hitched. It was very possible that I might pass out.

"Are you ready to get started, then?" he asked.

"Um . . ." I hesitated, snapping out of my trance. I began to feel a little unsure.

He reached out to help me lift my leg onto the table. "Let's get you up here—"

"No, no!" I quickly interrupted. This could not be happening. Justin was obviously a Greek god disguising himself as a physical therapist in a white lab coat. If I got up on the table, he would want to touch my leg. I couldn't have that—this adorable Adonis touching my gross, ugly, defective leg. "I, uh, I actually forgot to take my pain medication before I came in today. It hurts too much." And I grabbed ahold of my brace and grimaced in fake distress. Because this, of course, was a big fat lie. I would never forget to take my medication before PT. I wouldn't forget to take my medication, period. I needed it.

"Oh, okay." His perfect mouth curved downward into a slight frown. "Well, why don't we head over to the CPM machine?"

I shook my head. "No, I don't think I can do that, either. I'm in a lot of pain." I bent down further and really gave it my all, gritting my teeth and sucking in pained staccato-like breaths. This just wasn't going to work. I couldn't have someone like him helping me. Once I was over the initial shock of Justin's cuteness, embarrassment began to course through me. A new realization set in. Looking at Justin in all his perfection drew a stark contrast to the hideousness that was me. How revolting I was. How unsettling it must have felt to look at me. How grossed out he must've been on the inside. He was Troilus, and I was Richard III— deformed, unfinished, cheated by nature. And suddenly I wasn't lying anymore; I *was* hurting. I was a freak of nature. I was truly desolate. Who would ever look at me with anything other than disgust? I couldn't bear to look at him.

I was crying like a baby now. Drowning in self-pity, choking on my own desperation.

Mom came quickly into the back room. Someone must have told her I was upset.

"I don't know what happened," Justin said, confusion and concern tainting his voice.

"What is it, Justine?" Mom asked as she crouched next to me. She reached out to touch my hair, but I pulled away. I only curled in on myself more. I started crying even harder, hiding my face in my hands, more mortified than I had ever been in my whole life. Finally when I looked up, I thought Mom was eyeing me with exasperation. But then again, maybe she was looking at me with love.

Probably not, though.

But it didn't really matter either way, because it was starting to sink in that maybe no one else ever would. That no one else ever could.

"It hurts, Mom. It just hurts."

51

PRETEND IT DOESN'T HURT. Pretend the pain isn't stretching its jaws wide and swallowing you whole. It's something Kacey taught me to do. *Pretend there's no one else here.*

And I've gotten really good at that. Lying. Pretending. Manipulating perspectives, most notably my own. That pinch isn't a pinch; it's a tickle. That ache isn't an ache; it's a squeeze. That searing agony isn't the unfolding fiery flames of Hades, no, no. It's merely sunstroke on the beach of denial. Anguilla in August. Some other tropical escape. All you need is a tall lemonade and a wide-brimmed hat.

And this regret you're feeling is not regret; it's just boredom. This devastation is not crushing; you're just tired. This chasm that's split the earth beneath your feet and advanced undetected toward the apex of your very soul, nothing to worry about. It's just space. This pain you're feeling, it's not what you think it is. Nothing is what you think it is. Nothing has to be what you think it is. Nothing has to be anything at all.

The most convincing lies are the lies we tell ourselves.

52

THEN

GOD IS PUNISHING ME. This is all a big mistake. I'm not really supposed to be here.

Really? We're still stuck on that?

It seems so.

Hmm. Okay. So, why don't you do something about it?

Like what?

Well . . . there's always . . . you know.

Nope. Not going to do that.

Why not?

If God doesn't want me here on earth, he probably doesn't want me in heaven, either.

What makes you think you'll go to heaven?

What makes you think I'm not already in hell?

Huh. Good point.

53

IN THE EVENING, after spending the day with the all-too-present impression that Noah's absence has left, and after giving my defenses ample time to fall away, I debate heading back over to his house. As much as I try to distort how I'm feeling, I hate how we left things. I hate that he's angry with me. But mostly, I hate that I think he might be right. For so long my sole focus was on getting out, getting away, keeping myself safe. I never really gave much thought to what comes next.

As I walk across the property between us, the trees tower above me and cast long shadows out over the snow pointing back toward my house. I wonder if this is an omen. A sign that I should turn around. Some kind of divine intervention. But as much as I don't want to be, I have to admit I'm drawn to him, and I want to make it right.

At the same time, though, I feel like I'm playing a game I know I'm going to lose. There's no way I could ever be anything special to a guy like Noah. I'm too messed up. And even if he somehow liked that about me in a kind of weird "boy saves girl" fantasy sort of way, I'm too messed up to keep from messing it up. I'm just so . . . and he's just so . . . and that just so wouldn't work. Besides, I could never relax around him enough to let him see the Real Me. I'll always be a fraud. I'll always be untrusting. I'll always do whatever I must to stay safe.

I reach his front door and contemplate turning around. But then it opens before my eyes, before I have the chance to knock, before I have the chance to run, and Noah's standing there with a small kitchen towel folded over an arm bent at the elbow. "Your table is ready, madame," he says as he directs me into the house.

"Madame?" I say, with faux offense.

"My French is shit," he says apologetically. "Mademoiselle?"

"That's better," I say.

"Gracias."

Noah leads me into the kitchen, where he's placed glowing candles randomly around the room. I stop. This is obviously supposed to be romantic. I bite my lip, unsure what to do. He pulls out a chair for me. "Thank you," I say slowly, and hesitantly take a seat.

"You're very welcome."

"Um, what is all this?" I ask, gesturing to the production before me.

"An apology," he says, filling the wineglass at my seat.

"You know I'm underage, right?"

"I won't tell the sheriff if you won't," he says.

"Noah," I say, eager to make things better. "I messed up before. I'm sorry. I never should have yelled at you like that. And I shouldn't have called this town shitty—it's not. I really, really like it here."

"It's okay," he says, now filling his own glass. "There is some truth to what you said."

"No, there's not. And I shouldn't have implied that you're not a good sheriff. You are. At least, when you're not supplying me with alcohol."

"Thank you for the compliment," he says. He draws his brown eyes up to meet mine. They're wide and sincere. "I'm sorry, too. I have no right to judge you." Then he pauses, smiles, and walks over to the oven. "Let me make it better," he says, pulling open the oven door and removing a large, flat box. "With pizza."

"Where'd you get that?" I ask. I thought everything in sight was still buried beneath a mountain of snow.

"Wouldn't you like to know?" he says. "But I'm not going to tell you. You see, I realize the only reason you've been tolerating me for these last few days is because I'm feeding you. If you figure out how to order a pizza by yourself, I fear I'll never see you again."

I clear my throat and focus on Noah. "It's a possibility," I say.

"Exactly. So I've got to keep my methods to myself. You already know about my secret Hungry-Man stash—"

"Campbell's," I interject.

"Agree to disagree," he says, placing the pizza on the table between us. "I hope you like anchovies."

Gross. "Maybe I should be the one judging *you*." I smile as he opens the lid to the plain cheese pizza. "Well, I'm officially impressed. Again. And officially grateful. Thank you," I say again as he places a slice on the plate in front of me.

"As a man of the law, *official* is kind of my thing. And you're welcome. Again."

I look around the room and at all the effort that Noah's put into this. I begin to feel guilty. Why is he doing this? And what does he want from me?

"Noah," I say, clearing my throat again. "This is super nice and everything. I can't believe you went to all this trouble. But . . . I don't want to give you the wrong impression."

"Well, what's the wrong impression?"

"The impression that something could happen between the two of us," I say.

"But something is happening between the two of us."

"Yeah," I say. "That's kind of the problem. It can't."

"Why not?" he asks, now serious.

"As we've already covered—you don't know me, and if you did, you wouldn't want something to be happening between the two of us."

He pauses, taking a taste from his wineglass. "Maybe you could let me decide that for myself," Noah says. Then he smirks.

"It's just—" I say, gently shaking my head. "I can't explain. You don't get it."

"What do you mean, Elisabeth? It's just pizza."

But I'm tired of repeating myself. "It's not just pizza, okay? If I eat your pizza, you'll want to take me out on a date. And then," I say, feeling more than slightly embarrassed but doing my best to push the discomfort down, my effort about as successful as holding a beach ball underwater, "at some point, you'll probably want to make out. And then you'll discover that I'm covered in scars. And then you'll see that I'm not only covered in physical scars, but—surprise, surprise—emotional ones, too." I take a deep breath and look him straight in the eyes. "I'm made of scar tissue."

The shame fights its way to the surface again, but I keep going. "And then you'll understand what I mean when I say you don't really know me, and if you did you'd wish you didn't. And then I'm all alone again. So, let's just skip all of that and let me go back to just being alone. Please."

I take another deep breath. All of this back-and-forth with Noah, this is what it comes down to—me not wanting him to see the Real Me, the rueful, ruined, reprehensible Real Me. This is what it's really all about.

"Look—Elisabeth," Noah stammers, trying to articulate his thoughts. "Life isn't *If You Give a Mouse a Cookie*. You don't know if any of that is actually going to happen. You're just pushing me away. You're just scared."

"Yes, you're right. I'm scared." All the time. Of everyone and everything.

"You're putting too much pressure on yourself, okay? Let's just slow down, here. Let's back up. This is just pizza. Let's just have a totally normal quiet evening . . . eating pizza . . . in my kitchen . . . with wine . . . and surrounded by candlelight." He can't hold back a small, crooked smile. But then he's serious once again. "Can we just do that?"

My brain feels fuzzy. I can't believe I just said all of that. By telling him I can't let him in, I ended up telling him way more than I ever wanted to. Even after hearing it, he still thinks everything is so simple. But I know otherwise. I look up into Noah's reaching, reassuring eyes.

"Nothing bad is going to happen," he says.

54

THEN

"GOD, these appointments take forever!" I whined.

"All things considered, Justine, it's not so bad," Mom said, flipping through a *Vogue*.

"What . . . things . . . considered?" I asked robotically, gently banging my head against the wall behind me, keeping in time with the tiny red second hand on the clock on the wall.

"Please stop that," Mom said, looking at me side-eyed and annoyed. "We're lucky. Think about how many people fly from all over the country to see Dr. S. And he's right in our own backyard."

The platitudes were beyond insufferable, maybe even more so than the monumental unfairness of being stuck in this room. I stretched my good leg out from the exam table and hooked it beneath the thick pad of a small metal stool. I pulled it toward me, then pushed it away, and swung it back and forth and around and around, the worn wheels squeaking in protest against the tacky floor. Mom exhaled loudly and shot me a look.

Ugh. Fine. I kicked the stool away, leaving a dusty footprint right on the seat.

"This is hardly our backyard," I mumbled. I looked around for something else in the exam room to occupy me. I settled for poking holes with my fingernails into the thin paper sheet covering the exam table.

She ignored me and went back to her magazine. "We're very lucky," she said again.

Whatever.

Finally—finally!—we heard a brief knock on the door. A short-white-coat-clad man who I kind of recognized and kind of didn't waltzed into our little room. He was of average height, average build, with average hair, and an average face. I was pretty sure I'd seen this guy at every shopping mall or grocery store I'd ever stepped inside. He was the definition of Average Joe. I looked at the embroidered label on his white coat: DR. JOSEPH MINTZ, MD, RESIDENCY OF ORTHOPEDICS. I laughed to myself. A little sheep.

He plopped down on the footprint I'd left on the stool.

"Who are you?" I asked.

He looked up, caught off guard by my poor manners. "Oh. Um, I'm Dr. Mintz. I'm one of the residents working with Dr. S."

"Isn't he here?"

"Yes, of course. I just come in first."

In all my appointments with Dr. S, and I swear I'd had thousands, I'd never had a resident come in first.

An image came to my mind of Odin's ravens, Hugin and Munin, circling the hapless, stalking the hopeless, and searching far and wide for information to bring back to their master.

I didn't like this. I had a serious medical problem and was in the middle of a serious medical treatment. I didn't need students weighing in. Arrogant young doctors coming and going with no vested interest in me, searching for a dissertation topic or throwing in their two cents in an effort to look smart in front of their supervisor.

"So, Miss Amos, you've had a big surgery, huh?" he asked, without really asking.

"So they tell me," I said, unimpressed.

He laughed a little bit and leafed through my chart. "Nearing the end, huh?"

The end? Now he had my attention. I'd endured months and months of this torment. "Really?" I asked.

"Well, the end of turning the clickers," he corrected.

My face fell, I'm sure, but he wasn't even looking.

"All right," he continued, still thumbing the fat manila folder in his hands. "And was your left leg the only limb that was affected by the polio?"

I quickly looked over to Mom. "The what?"

"Polio?" Mom said. "Justine never had polio."

"Oh." Confusion crept across his face. He bit his lip and began fumbling through the pages once more. "I thought I read that in her chart."

"My daughter never had polio. She's eleven years old! What year do you think this is?"

At that point Dr. Mintz started searching frantically through my file. Stray papers slipped out and fluttered from his lap. He became such a flustered mess he nearly dropped the whole big chart on the floor. I would have laughed if I wasn't so appalled.

"I'm sorry," he said. "I mean, people are still affected by polio. Um, what was it that caused her defect?"

Defect? I looked over toward Mom again. I wondered if Dr. Mintz could see the fury rising in her face, could see her hands turning into tight, white fists at her sides. Her anger was palpable, and it was the first time I'd ever seen her like this. I always just thought she seemed embarrassed. Or at best inconvenienced. But here she was, red as an angry beet. "Her *leg discrepancy*," Mom said between clenched teeth, "was congenital at birth."

That's right, dummy, I was defective from birth.

Dr. Mintz's eyes bounced quickly between Mom and me. A hot flush colored his cheeks. He clearly recognized both of his mistakes. "Okay, yes, I knew that. I think . . . I think I just mixed her up with another patient. I'm so sorry." He cleared his throat, closed my chart, and looked at me with a renewed purpose. "Miss Amos, I think you're just here for new measurements today."

But I wasn't going to let him get away that easily. "Does it say in my chart that I had polio?" I asked.

"No." He shook his head with certainty and bent to collect the papers that had fallen to the floor.

"Are you sure? You didn't look through the whole thing," I said.

"I'll look through it. I'll make sure." Dr. Mintz stood quickly, sending the little stool reeling. He headed straight to the door. "Dr. S will be right in." He could not get out of the room fast enough.

I turned to Mom after he shut the door behind him. "Mom, did I have polio?"

"No, of course not."

"Why did he think that?"

"I don't know!" she said, exasperated.

"I mean, who would have told him that?" I felt a bubble of something troublesome growing inside me.

She took a deep breath. Then another. "People make mistakes. It's fine . . . it's fine."

But it didn't sound fine. I looked at her again, pressing her with my eyes. "Mom?"

"It's fine. Don't worry," she said, looking away from me.

But I couldn't stop worrying. Not because she didn't acknowledge the fear in my voice, but because there was fear in hers, too. Who was on top of things here? Were there things about me in my chart that weren't accurate? And, maybe more importantly, what else could they get wrong?

55

THEN

A FEW WEEKS LATER, another fixator check. It was nearly evening when they finally called my name and directed me and Mom to a room in the back of the clinic. Mom followed behind the nurse, but while turning a corner, I paused as I saw Dr. S. He was talking with a small group of other men in long, white coats. Big sheep. They stood huddled together like bowling pins. I couldn't see their faces, I couldn't hear what they were saying, but one of the unidentified men motioned toward me, and Dr. S turned and pinned me with his eyes. He didn't smile. He didn't wave. After a beat he turned back to his friends and leaned in closer.

"Justine?" Mom called, already in the exam room, her head hanging out of the door. "In here."

My fingers gripped the edge of my seat as I waited for Dr. S to come into the room. But I didn't have to wait too long this time. Dr. S knocked briefly and pushed through the door with someone close behind him. "This is Dr. Mintz," he said. "Not sure if you've met before." How could I forget? I averted my eyes; let's move on.

"So, I want to talk about the X-rays you had taken this morning. The bone here—the femur—is looking good," he says, and points to my thigh. "It's filled in really nicely, and it looks like we've maintained the measurements that we want. The pin sites are looking really good, too." He then grabs ahold of the lower part of my brace. "With the tibia, the new bone has grown in, but . . . the measurements aren't quite what we expected."

I wasn't exactly sure what that meant. These visits had become so routine that I had stopped paying attention other than to fill in the blank with some bogus answer on the off chance that another disingenuous question was directed my way. But now my ears perked up.

Dr. S leaned over the exam table and took my foot in his hands. He moved it back and forth, rotating it at the ankle, and then slid his grip up to my knee. I ignored the way he played with me like an action figure. I ignored his hands, bulky and club-like. I ignored them even though they felt alien. I ignored them even though they felt violating.

"Let's see you walk."

I maneuvered my way down from the table and dragged myself out into the hallway with my crutches. They followed me out to watch. I swung myself down the hall away from the doctors and Mom. I could see it in the distance—the clinic door. A small neon Plexiglas exit sign hanging overhead like a halo. I paused mid-swing with my eyes glued to it. *Keep going, Justine. Just. Keep. Going.*

"You can come back," Dr. S called.

In the exam room once again, Dr. S placed both hands on my hips, digging his fingers in to feel my hip bones like usual, checking to see if they were level. I winced before shuffling back onto the table.

He turned to Mom. "So, like I said, the femur looks good, but the lower part of the leg is not where we want it to be. It could be that she's had a growth spurt, or that we were off in estimating her probable height from the beginning. It could be that the bone isn't growing in exactly as we expected. But, like I said, we're off, and we need to make some changes."

I swallowed against the acid pooling beneath my tongue. "There's something wrong," Dr. S continued.

Red lights flashed like a strobe behind my eyes—something was going south very quickly. I turned to Mom for help. I didn't know what was happening, but I needed her to fix it. Immediately. *FIX IT!* But she kept her eyes locked on Dr. S. It was like I wasn't even there. And then it was like *she* wasn't even there—because she may as well not have been. Mom was close enough that I could smell her soap—but she couldn't have felt farther away.

I couldn't help it—I started to cry.

"You said I was almost done," I pleaded with Dr. S as emotion quickly overcame me. Salty tears fell from my eyes, dripped off my chin, and spattered the flimsy paper between my knees. My voice came from my throat like a zombie clawing its way out of a grave. "You said you would take it off. You said I was almost done!"

Slowly, slowly, Dr. S turned to face me. And as he did, he changed. Gone were the blue scrubs. Gone were the large, alien fingers and the ring of thinning hair. Gone was any trace of an award-winning physician. It all just melted away. It was suddenly blindingly clear to me—he was never a sheep. The whole time, that white lab coat was disguising the wolf underneath.

Something was wrong. Something was very, very wrong—and I was not okay.

I was not safe.

56

BUT YOU SEE, Noah, I know bad things do happen.

I know what it's like to be forgotten.
I know what it's like to be a ghost.
When you peel back the skin to see what's rotten
You uncover the thing you've kept hidden the most.

I know what it's like when a whisper
Resonates far deeper than a scream.
I've watched the world I thought existed
Disintegrate as quickly as a dream.

So where is the harm in keeping secrets
When you're an oyster without a pearl?
There's no point in pointing out the poverty
Of being a forgotten girl.

57

I JOLT AWAKE. The light shines brightly through the window and across the room. It's very cold, and I hesitantly emerge from my blanket cocoon to check on the fire. It's all but out—just a few glowing embers fighting to stay alive. A thick layer of ash sits at the bottom of the grate; a smoky haze curls out from what's left of the burnt logs. I scrape through the soot, and a small dirty cloud rises and tickles my nose. The day feels weird, untethered, like zero gravity in the thin, gritty air. I check the time to give me some sense of purpose, and figure I should get the fire going again. But before I can even light it, there's a loud knock at the door. I stand and wipe my sooty hands across my pants. I check the peephole, though it's fogged up from the cold. Noah told me he was planning to be busy most of the day. It must be Jonathan coming by to check on me again. I pull open the door.

She's standing on the other side, knee-deep in shimmering white snow. *"Mom?"*

"Surprise!"

"What are you doing here?" I ask, barely able to get the words out.

"I was worried about you. I tried calling about a million times. And you didn't write back to any of my emails."

"Um, yeah," I manage, and attempt to pull my thoughts together. "Well, the power's been out because of the storm."

"I know, I figured. But you were here all alone. I was worried." She stands there and waits, an expectant look on her face. "Aren't you going to invite me in?"

Still stunned, I step back and allow her through the door. "Come in," I say quietly. She drags a large suitcase behind her. "How'd you even get here?"

"I flew, once the airport was finally open. And then I rented a car."

I peek around the front of the house and see a silver hatchback parked crookedly in the narrow, snow-lined street. I slowly close the door. "Justine," she says, removing her coat and fluffing her hair. "It doesn't even seem like you're happy to see me." She looks at me accusingly.

"I'm just surprised," I say, avoiding her gaze.

"Well, that was the plan."

We don't embrace. No, never. Rather, she approaches me tentatively. She draws her hands up in front of her, a protective pose—ready to shield or ready to strike—and flaps them light as butterfly wings at the corners of my shoulders. Air-kisses and plaster smiles. I am still as a statue as the air reverberates between us.

Mom makes herself immediately at home. She wanders into the kitchen, glances around.

"Cute. An interesting choice of color for a kitchen, but cute."

She dumps her enormous bag on the table, pulls the zipper wide and begins plucking out the snacks she brought with her from the airport. Soon the table is littered with her stuff—a small bag of popcorn, a sleeve of whole-grain crackers, an open bag of sugar-free hard candy that spills out onto the table, and a half-empty bottle of iced coffee.

"It's freezing in here," she says, dramatically chattering her teeth together and wrapping her arms around herself.

It's then that she finally takes the opportunity to assess *me*. Her eyes scan down, appraising my rumpled hair, my pale complexion, my slept-in clothes with sooty black handprints decorating the front. She can't hide her displeasure; she doesn't really even try.

My mother is a beautiful woman. And what does a beautiful woman want more than a beautiful daughter? The fact that I was born less than perfect is not something we ever talked about. It hurt too much. But it was always there, an unspoken disappointment, a quiet disapproval.

"Sorry," I murmur.

"Show me the rest of the place?"

She's trying to be discreet, but I see her continuing to inspect everything. The mismatched furniture, the worn area rug, the cold hearth smelling of stagnant smoke and ashes. She runs a polished finger along the frayed cording of the love seat. I brace myself for her critique.

"Well, it's certainly *cozy*," she says through gritted teeth.

Somehow, this hurts more. As if it's just what she expected.

She makes her way around the room, picking things up and then setting them back down. She arches an eyebrow at the disarray of blankets hanging off the sofa. She eyes my worn paperback beside the lamp, the paper snowflakes in a heap on the coffee table. "Looks like I got here just in time . . . ," she says to herself.

"How long are you staying, Mom?" I'm beginning to feel claustrophobic. I casually pull my sweater away from my neck.

"Trying to get rid of me already?" she says, the hardness in her voice as unmistakable as caution tape.

Yes. Please leave. I can't have you here.

What is it that she stirs in me? How is it that her very presence stands my hairs on end? The derogatory glances, the subtle but unmistakable air of superiority, the barely restrained criticisms that are ever ready on the tip of her tongue—it's so . . . *cozy*, it's so . . . *cute*. Being near her is like standing beside a beehive—even if you never get stung, the threat is there, constant and buzzing. You can never really relax. Her mere presence is a steady reminder of memories I'd rather forget.

And for a moment I consider saying something. Because surely, she must feel it, too—the tension, the friction. The buzzing. Can't we just be civil? Can't we just be friends? But I don't say anything, I keep it to myself, and I silently wonder if she's wondering the same thing and choosing to keep it to herself, too.

"It's not that," I force out. "It's just"—I say the only thing I can think of—"the power's still out, and I only have the one bedroom, you know. And," I quickly add, "and there's hardly any food in the kitchen."

"It'll be fine. And I'll stay on the couch," she says, glancing distastefully at the nest of blankets there.

"No, Mom. I can't let you do that. It's just . . . there's no fireplace in my bedroom."

"I wouldn't want to put you out in any way, Justine. We can both sleep down here." She runs her finger through the dust on the mantel above the fireplace, bends her head down and peers into the empty, filthy hearth. "You do know how to make a fire, don't you?"

I work on the fire while Mom settles in, determined to build something decent enough for her not to criticize out loud. She's wrapped herself in a long, heavy sweater and replaced her socks with fuzzy slippers. I offer her something to eat from my dwindling supplies in the kitchen, but she declines.

She settles down on the couch and crosses her ankles beneath her. "So, have you thought about filling out any college applications recently?" Mom wonders out loud a little too casually, as if she's asking me for the time.

And there it is. Wow, a whole hour. I'm impressed. "No, Mom."

She nods to herself and doesn't say anything more. Seconds pass. Minutes. I sit down on the hearth and draw squiggles into the ash with the fire poker. I feel her stare, feel her irritation. It's . . . uncomfortable. And then: "What am I supposed to tell people, Justine? It's coming up on a year. Your goofing-around time is going to be up," she huffs, her lips in a thin line.

"I'm not *goofing around*, Mom," I reply. "And you can tell people whatever you want."

"I *don't know* what to tell them, Justine. That's the problem," she says.

But that's not what she means.

We sit on the couch. We watch the fire. We each try not to say anything to offend the other. One more fairly silent hour passes.

"I think I'm going to read." She starts to search through the pockets of her ridiculously large suitcase and comes up empty. "It seems I left my magazine on the plane." She exhales. "Do you have anything I'd like?"

"I can look through my bookcase upstairs. What are you in the mood for?"

"I'll go. I don't want you to go up there—it's too cold."

"It's fine. What do you want?"

"I'll go myself."

I give up and let her go. I adjust a few of the couch pillows and pull another blanket out of the closet for her. I bet she's inspecting my bedroom. After a few minutes she comes back down with John Steinbeck's *East of Eden* and a book of poetry. She holds them both up and looks at me with uncertainty.

Tough call. She'll hate them both.

She holds my gaze impatiently and waves the books at me again.

I point to *East of Eden*.

"Is it good?" she asks.

"It is," I say, and smile to myself. But then I feel bad for silently comparing my mother to Cathy Ames. I mean, I guess Mom's not really *that* bad—I don't think she ever murdered anybody.

I go into the kitchen to fill my teacup, yet again. I take my time, but when I come back into the living room, the Steinbeck is on the end table but Mom is gone. "Mom?" I look out the front window. There she is, staggering along in her slippers to the rental car. I watch her open the passenger-side door, grab something out of the center console, and then slam the door shut. She turns around and slowly makes her way back.

She's covered in snow, her slippers leaving flat, kidney-shaped imprints upon the entryway. "I would've gotten whatever you needed."

"I was just getting my glasses. I left them in the car." She hands me a folded piece of paper. "Here," she says. "This was taped to your door."

I unfold the paper. In messy, quickly scrawled handwriting it says *I see you have a visitor. I guess you're not a hermit, after all. Come by when you can, I'll be home after dark. P.S. Keep the hot plate.*

I try to keep the smile from my face. Mom sees it anyway. "Who's that from?"

"Oh, just my neighbor."

"She could have knocked," Mom says, implying that my neighbor is rude.

"Could have," I agree.

But I'm glad he didn't.

58

"HOPE IS A THING with feathers," Mom says, looking up from her book a little while later.

I smile. I knew she'd hate *East of Eden*—she couldn't get past the second chapter. Instead, she's been flipping through the pages of the poetry book.

"*The,*" I correct her.

"*The* what?"

" 'Hope is *the* thing with feathers,' " I say. "Not *a* thing."

"Oh," she says, and lowers her eyes to the pages again. "Does it make a difference?"

I shrug. "Do you think it does?"

"Not really," she says. "I don't get it. Is she talking about a bird?"

"No, not really," I say. "It's kind of a riddle. Like children's poetry, or a nursery rhyme. You know, it's a lesson."

"About birds?"

I frown. "No, about hope. About persistence in times of turbulence. Do you like it?"

Mom closes the book without reading the rest aloud. "If it's about birds, tell me it's about birds. If it's about hope, tell me it's about hope. Why doesn't she just say what she means?"

I lean forward in my seat. This shouldn't be a mystery to her—Mom's used to putting on appearances. "Because then it wouldn't be poetry," I say.

"I guess that's why I've never really liked it. Things that are vague just for the purpose of being vague," she says. "Is that why *you* write poetry?" she asks, tilting her head to the side. "So you can disguise things? You're still doing that, aren't you? Writing poems?"

"Yes," I say, surprised that she even remembers. "I'm still doing that. And no, that's not why I do it."

Why would she think that? When I write, it's for the exact opposite purpose of wanting to be vague. "I do it . . . to understand things."

Mom puts the book aside and stands. She carries her empty mug to the kitchen and places it in the sink.

I follow her, tentatively. "Do you want a refill?"

She shakes her head, glances casually around the room. She opens a cabinet and peeks inside. Then she heads to the oven and bends her neck to look inside there, too.

"Are you looking for something, Mom?" I narrow my eyes at her back.

"You shouldn't squint like that, Justine. You'll get wrinkles."

I sigh and make my face as smooth as possible for her. I wait for her to check her own reflection in the glass door of the oven, tugging gently on the corners of her eyes.

"Your plant's dying," she says after finally turning around.

"I know," I say.

"Well, why don't you water it?" She gestures to the faucet.

"No, Mom. Don't."

"It looks dry as a bone," she says, as if I'm an idiot.

"No. *It's fine.*"

"It needs water." She rebuffs me and flips up the faucet lever.

"You don't know what it needs."

Mom freezes momentarily, before turning around to face me. I look down immediately. "I'm sorry," I say. "It's just, it doesn't need water. It needs shade. It's getting too much sun sitting near the window like that. This type of ivy grows best in the darkness. Please, just leave it alone," I say, and flick off the faucet.

"Why don't you want to take care of it? You're killing it on purpose?" she asks, like it's the worst crime anyone can commit—neglecting a plant. She reaches toward the little pot to move it out of the sunlight.

"Please don't," I say more forcefully, and I can hear the pain breaking through my voice. I don't want her to take care of my stupid little plant. I keep it there for a reason. I keep it there to remind me that not everything is meant to live in the light. That it can burn you. That sometimes, darkness and quiet and solitude are okay. That's it's okay to want those things. That it's okay to need those things. And the thought of her trying to save it causes a ringing in my ears.

"Fine," she says, exasperated with me. "Just go ahead and neglect it. What do I care if it dies? You know, Justine," she says before walking out of the kitchen, "you might understand Emily Dickinson, but I sure have a lot of trouble understanding you."

59

IT'S EARLY IN THE EVENING, but it's already growing dark. I think about the note Noah left me. Part of me wants to ignore it. I'm breaking my rules with him. I've broken *all* of my rules with him. The whole point of moving to Fish Creek was to be alone. To not get involved. To keep things as simple as possible. Becoming closer with Noah has *complicated* written all over it in permanent marker. Half of my brain is tugging at me. *No no no no no. It's a bad idea. I should just stay here.* But the other half of me kinda wants to go. What to do, what to do? That's when the third half of my brain raises its hand high in the air and reminds me that it's not a good idea to be around Mom too much, either. And now seems like a perfect time to disappear.

"Um, I think I'm going to bring in more firewood, so we don't run low tonight," I say.

Mom waves me away with her hand, her nose curiously back in the book. Maybe she found something she liked after all. Taking advantage of her momentary distraction, I slip on my boots and jacket and open the front door. "I'll be back soon," I say without waiting for her reply, and shut the door behind me.

I use the path Noah dug out a few days ago and walk down to the street where Mom's rental is parked. I turn toward Noah's house, careful not to slip on the packed, plowed snow. When I reach his driveway, I can see the garage door is open, his police car sitting inside. I make my way slowly up the icy pavement and across to his front porch. I knock quietly.

Noah opens the door, wearing his uniform khaki pants and a blue button-down shirt over a white T-shirt. His police jacket is unzipped and hanging open off broad shoulders. His eyes crinkle in the corners as he leans on the door frame. "Can I help you?" he asks with a polite smile on his face, pretending not to know me.

"I got your note," I say.

"Did I leave a note?" he asks with feigned confusion, his smile pulling at his lips.

"You did. You said you missed me," I say boldly, surprising myself.

"Hmm. That does sound like something I'd say," Noah admits, moving away from the door to let me in. "I thought maybe you'd forgotten about me, now that there's a big party at your house and everything."

"A big party? You're quite mistaken. It's my mother."

"Your mother?" he asks, confused. "Were you expecting her?" He closes the door behind me.

"Definitely not. She just showed up. She said she was worried about me."

"Well, I can understand that," Noah says, smirking. "You kind of bring that out in people, you know."

I'm not exactly sure what he means by that, but I don't like it. "Do I?"

"Well, let's take for example exhibit A." And he gestures to himself. "I haven't been able to leave your side since I first found you buried in the snow behind my house."

I laugh. "True," I say. "But I am fully capable of taking care of myself."

"Mm-hmm," he says, mimicking me.

I elbow him gently in the side and take a seat by the fire. Noah follows me and sits so close that our legs are touching. "What are you doing?" I ask.

"I'm not doing anything," he says innocently.

"You're sitting right on top of me," I say, scooting over to put a few inches between us.

"I beg to differ." He winks and smiles a cocky smile.

I shake my head gently, a warning. "I'm not here for that."

"Oh, no? What are you here for?"

A distraction. An escape. "I don't know exactly."

"Sure you do," Noah insists.

"Look, Noah. I like you. A lot. You're funny and sweet, and, strangely, I feel very comfortable with you. And, most importantly, you check off every girl's 'hot young sheriff' fantasy."

"Naturally."

"But," I say, now serious again.

"There don't need to be any buts here," he says, shaking his head.

"But," I continue, looking away from him.

"Hey," he says, drawing my eyes back to him. Noah looks at the space between us and tilts his head to the side. His smile is now gone. He reaches for my hand, and, weirdly, I let him take it. "Who hurt you, Elisabeth?"

Oh please. I pull my hand away and place it in my lap. I fight the tiny urge to roll my eyes. But then I look, truly look, at him. He looks sad and eager and like he's actually waiting for me to answer, like he actually *wants* an answer. The look spurs a little hopscotch to the middle of my chest. And so I give him an answer, a real one, my voice sandpaper across silk. "Lots of people," I whisper.

Noah waits, and as the seconds pass, I think about how many times I've been asked questions that people didn't really want answers to. "You know," he finally says, his eyes thoughtful and calm, "there are good people out there—floating around in this terrible, beautiful world. It is possible, maybe, just maybe, that you've found one."

My hands start to tremble. I know he could be right, but I'm too worried that he's wrong.

"I just want to get to know you," he says.

"Maybe you shouldn't want that," I say, looking at his hands now firmly at his sides, looking at the space I've put between us.

"Why?"

"It's like you said, Noah. There's a little bit of fake in all of us."

"You seem pretty real to me."

I shake my head. "You don't know me," I say. Not the real me. Not the Real Me.

He reaches his hand out to touch my face. I flinch, almost imperceptibly, but Noah feels it.

And so do I.

60

"I CAN'T BELIEVE how long it's taking them to get the power back on," Mom says when I return to the house. "It's like we're living in the Dark Ages."

"It's not so bad," I say. "It's been kind of peaceful, actually. And the fire's nice."

"I suppose," she says, and closes her book in her lap. "I remember your grandmother used to build fires all the time. She used to love the way they crackled. Do you remember?" she asked in a wistful tone.

"I do," I said.

"God, I miss her."

"Do you?" I say without thinking.

She looks at me, stunned. "What does that mean?" she asks. "Yes, I miss my mother!"

"Sorry," I say, contrite. I don't know where that came from. I didn't mean to offend her. It's just that sometimes I wonder if she felt about Nana the way I felt about her.

"Remember the one year we had Thanksgiving at her house?" she asks, her eyes downcast.

"Mm-hmm,"

"I guess you probably don't—it was a long time ago."

"I do."

"I'm sure you don't," she says, shaking her head.

"I remember, Mom," I say.

"All right," she says, dismissing me. "That year was so wonderful, everyone together."

I close my eyes, perplexed. Bewildered. Mystified! That year was so wonderful? Everyone together? Everyone together except for one little girl, sitting off all on her own, drowning in mashed potatoes and misery. Were we talking about the same Thanksgiving? Were we living in the same world? Surely not. I open my eyes again. They meet Mom's, and she looks quickly away from me.

"What do you have planned for dinner?" Mom asks, just as the fire mountain begins to fade from view. She starts searching uselessly through the cabinets.

"Well, we're fairly limited," I say. "I do have some canned soup."

"You mean *this*?" she says, pulling out a can of the stew Noah brought over.

I nod my head.

"No thank you." She returns the can to its shelf.

"What's wrong with it?" I ask.

"Do I really have to answer that question?"

"I know it's nothing fancy, but we are in the middle of a snowstorm here."

"One would think you'd make a visit to the store before the storm, hmm? Your shelves are practically bare, and what you do have can hardly be considered food."

She closes the cabinet door and walks toward the fridge.

"There's nothing in there," I say, "so don't bother." She pauses before reaching the fridge and spins around dramatically toward me. "And I can take care of myself just fine, Mom. I was doing just fine before you got here."

"Okay. Whatever you say." She arches her brow and throws her hands up. "What do you want to eat?"

I rack my brain quickly to come up with something she'd find suitable. "I can make baked potatoes?" I suggest.

"Fine. Whatever." She gives up and shrugs her shoulders.

I take two potatoes from the pantry and wash them in the frigid water, dry them off, and use a fork to pierce them before wrapping them in aluminum foil. I try to ignore Mom watching my every move. I turn on Noah's hot plate and let it warm up, then place the potatoes on the burners.

I let them cook an extra-long time, not wanting Mom's potato to be raw on the inside, and certain they'll come out much better than when I had held them over the fire. We sit down at the kitchen table with a chair, a jar of ranch seasoning, and a decade's worth of unspoken hurts between us.

I don't know why I'm trying so hard. I don't know why I feel the need to prove myself. This is my house, and she chose to come here, without even asking me if I wanted her to.

Mom makes a little choking noise, sets down her fork and knife and takes a sip of her water. She starts coughing, and her face turns pink; her eyes begin to tear. She continues to cough even harder, so I stand up to slap her on the back. Eventually, Mom clears her throat.

"Are you okay?" I ask her.

And for just one moment everything is so silent and still, there is a deep, disturbing sense that there is no quiet here at all, but only the breath between cries.

Then Mom finds her voice. "This potato's overcooked."

61

I CLEAN UP THE KITCHEN. It takes all of thirty seconds.

"Be sure to turn off the hot plate," Mom says.

"I know."

"How've you been dealing with the fire at night?"

"Don't worry—I have it covered. I'll get up in the night to keep it going." *I'm not an idiot, Mom.*

Her eyes bounce around the room as if she's looking for something else to complain about.

"Mom." I try to sound reassuring. "I've got it. Relax."

She props her hip against the counter, stacks her arms across her chest. "Relax?" she says. "Like you? And I see you're still reading that ridiculous book." Mom nods toward *Doctor Faustus* on the end table in the other room. She must have been holding that in since she saw it sitting there when she first arrived. "Haven't you had enough of it already?"

"I like reading it," I say, somewhat dejected. "What's the harm?"

"Isn't it time to expand your horizons a little? I mean, you've been carrying it around since you were a kid."

"It's not like I don't read anything else. I find it comforting. And it changes every time I read it."

"It changes?" she says with blatant sarcasm, insinuating that I'm crazy.

"Not like that." I'm not sure how to explain it to her—I know she won't understand what I mean. "There are so many ways to interpret it. But they're all right, and they all contradict one another. It's a tragedy, but you never really know who to feel bad for. Or if you should feel bad at all."

I pause, wondering if she understands anything that I'm saying. That's the thing with mothers and daughters; you study the language only to discover the locals speak in slang. I try to be a little more clear. "Or maybe it's not the book that changes so much—it's me."

"Exactly in what ways do you change, Justine?" She says it with a dismissive laugh.

I feel so inadequate, so very, very small. The look in Mom's eyes— like I'm crazy, like I'm stupid, like I'm more of a disruption than a daughter. It's a familiar jab. I've never been a person to her—just a problem. It's an old feeling, like a song you know by heart, and no matter how long it's been since you last heard it, it always makes you feel exactly the same way.

Like one time when I was eighteen and about to graduate from high school. I got out of the car and closed the door harder than necessary. It was too hot that day. It had gone from spring to summer in a matter of days, and I did not like it. Mom and I began walking toward the door of the restaurant. I didn't know why I had agreed to go to lunch; it's not like we actually had anything to say to each other. Maybe she was hoping to change my mind about leaving. Whatever. Couldn't wait to stare awkwardly across the booth at each other as we ate our tuna salads and pita.

"Iris?"

Mom squinted, trying to place the woman now dripping in front of her in the parking lot. "Oh. Hi, Sandy," she said, surprised.

The woman gestured toward me, her shoulders and upper lip shiny with sweat. "Is this your daughter? Wait," she said, suddenly remembering something. "The one you needed the baby monitor for?"

What? I felt suddenly ill. My throat became rough and sour, and my eyes began to prick. A sense of shame crashed through me in one forceful, nauseating wave.

"Oh. Yes. Sandy, this is my daughter Justine."

Sandy's narrow eyes swept over me from head to toe, and she raised a sweaty eyebrow. "Well," she said with a loaded air about her, "it looks like you turned out all right."

If I could have melted into the hot, tarry pavement I gladly would have. The way she looked at me—it was intruding; it was intimate. It was wrong. She was a stranger to me, yet it was almost as if she had a magnifying glass to see into my most disgraceful parts. The inadequate parts, the freakish parts. I looked like a normal girl, but I wasn't a normal girl. And she could see what I really was.

It had been years since the fixator was removed, years since I'd seen Dr. S. Yet in front of this woman, and in the five seconds it took for her to assess me, I became eleven years old again.

I'm not all right, they say. There's something wrong, they say. There's something wrong, there's something wrong, there's something wrong with me.

Because what is a fixator if not something that fixes? Something that fixes something needing to be fixed. And if something needs to be fixed, then that something must be broken. And if something is broken, it must be inadequate, deficient. Unsatisfactory. No good.

I wanted to shout at this vile woman, *There's nothing wrong with me!* And yet, deep down, something felt very wrong with me.

"You were very rude outside," Mom said moments later as we slid into our booth in the restaurant.

"What? No I wasn't. I didn't say anything at all." I discreetly swept the nearby tables to be sure the woman hadn't followed us inside.

"Exactly. You could have said hello."

Excuse me? "Are you kidding? She was the rude one. 'Well, it looks like you turned out all right'?" The woman looked at me like I was a sideshow act.

Mom sighed and dismissed the thought with a slight wave of her hand and opened the menu in front of her. "She shouldn't have said that."

"You think?" I scoffed, before putting my eyes in my lap. "It hurts me, Mom."

"Justine. What are you getting so upset about? Who cares what people like her think."

"Uh, you do. Otherwise you would have said something. And people 'like her'? You mean, people who think there's something wrong with me?"

She closed her menu and stared straight into my eyes. "There was something wrong with you." And she doesn't say it, but it seems like she wants to add, *It looks like there still is.*

I searched Mom's eyes as they held mine before she lowered them again. I thought I saw the faintest quiver, the slightest increase in moisture, so brief it must have been something in the air. And I wondered then—what kind of pain might this woman have resurfaced in Mom? What might she have exposed? Maybe Mom had been hiding. Maybe she had been suffering, too. Maybe I had been so overwrought with my own mortification I hadn't stopped to consider hers. And maybe sometimes the only way to deal with that kind of pain was to spread it around.

Eight months later and not much has changed. "Forget it, Mom. You don't get it." You never do.

Just then, the light over the kitchen table flickers on, the refrigerator starts humming, and I hear a faint voice coming from the TV in the living room. "Well, isn't that convenient," Mom says, dusting her hands off over the sink and marching out of the kitchen. "No need for me to stay any longer."

62

"WELL, THIS IS ABSOLUTELY RIDICULOUS!"
Mom nearly growls. "How can all the flights already be booked?"

I come back into the kitchen and find Mom with her fingers gripping the phone. I feel bad about what I said to her.

She's tapping her foot and rubbing her temples. She's clearly agitated. She wants to leave.

"Mom?" I say quietly.

"Can't you see I'm on the phone, Justine," she says curtly, holding her hand over the receiver. I feel like a child.

"Sorry," I whisper.

"Look, whoever you are. I need a flight from Green Bay to O'Hare as soon as possible. Can you help me with that or not?"

She remains quiet while listening to the other end of the line. Then she slams the phone down onto the cradle and throws up her hands. She turns her head around to look at me. "I have to try again in the morning," she says.

"I'm sorry for what I said, Mom. You don't have to leave."

She raises one smug eyebrow, as if to say, *About time you apologized,* but she doesn't give me anything more. She doesn't tell me it's okay. She doesn't tell me she forgives me. She remains quiet and turns her head to gaze out the little kitchen window. She doesn't want to talk to me. She doesn't want to look at me. She just stands there, anger radiating from her body. I wait, watching it slowly evaporate. "It's late," she finally says. She sounds calm again.

"I know."

"You have a pretty view here. The way the light was shining a little earlier"—she motions toward the window—"it looked like a glowing mountain range over the treetops."

I'm stunned. I don't know if it's the gentleness in her tone, or the fact that she sees exactly the same abstract, obscure thing I see out my window, but I have trouble finding my voice. "Yeah," I finally manage to say, "it does."

"Lucky that the phones came back on when the power did."

"Yes," I say.

"I think I'm going to get ready for bed," Mom says, half to herself. She reaches up and fluffs her hair.

"Really? It's not that late. And the hot-water tank hasn't had a chance to warm up again, or the furnace, for that matter. Why don't you wait a while?"

She leans back against the edge of the sink, her arms crossed against her chest. She shakes her head. "It's been a long day. I'm tired. I'm going to wash up."

"Okay," I say, mostly to myself as she passes me on her way out of the kitchen.

Mom climbs the stairs, shoulders square, thumping her suitcase on the edge of every step behind her. I sit on the love seat and wait for her. I hear the door to my bedroom open and then close a few seconds later.

It must be frigid in there. After a few minutes, I hear water groaning through the pipes. The noise doesn't last very long. Then I hear the bedroom door open and close once more, and the abrupt, solid thud of her suitcase on the steps again as she descends.

Mom places her luggage near the storage closet under the stairs and walks to the sofa. She unfolds the blankets I have stacked there and layers two of them across the bottom cushions. She folds my quilt on top of them and begins to fluff the pillow. She's not happy with its level of fluff, so she picks it up and whacks it a few times and makes a show out of fluffing it just right.

She lies down in the bed she's made for herself and pulls the quilt up to her chin. Then she's quiet. We listen to the logs pop and hiss—angry little tantrums, showy but weak. We sit there together for a long while, gazing into the fire, not talking about what we see inside it. Maybe seeing some things different, maybe seeing some things the same.

After a while, it's hard to keep my eyes open, and I feel my head start to droop. I push myself up and go to check that the doors are locked. I don't bother putting another log on the fire since the furnace is up and running again. I'm at the bottom of the stairs, about to go up to change, when I think I hear Mom say something.

I turn to her. She reminds me of Medusa, hair wild around a head seemingly separated from its body. "What was that, Mom?"

And in one swift moment she turns me to stone. "I can see why you like it here, Justine. It's very . . . easy. Simple. I guess that's lucky for somebody like you."

Kacey shook her head and her hair fell into her eyes. "I'm having second thoughts," she said. "I'm having 'lots of time has passed and maybe what seemed like a great and necessary idea then isn't such a great and necessary idea now' kinds of thoughts." She pushed her hair back and met my gaze. "You can't do this. You're not really going to do this, right?"

"What do you mean? This was the plan all along."

"I know, but . . . I think I was wrong," she said, looking up at me with big round eyes.

"You're not wrong—you're the only one who's ever been there for me. You found this perfect little town and everything. You can't turn your back on me now, Kacey."

"I'm not turning my back on you. I'm your friend; I'm trying to help you. You can't just move to the middle of nowhere and hide. We're seniors now. We're almost out! You have to go to college. That's your out."

Kacey was only feeling guilty—she didn't want to leave me behind. But she didn't realize that while she had given up on adolescent fantasies, I still clung to mine. My leg was no longer the only thing that had been stunted and scarred.

Years later and I was still holding on to the hope that I could just disappear. That hope lived in me, a tangible, ubiquitous thing. It was the arm that carried me into my dreams each night. It was the song that rocked me back into consciousness each morning.

It had become more than a dream; it was a lifeline. And I couldn't let go now.

"It's not enough," I said. "At school, my parents are still in charge. They'd be footing the bill; they're getting copies of my class schedules and my grades. They'd select my freaking meal plan. And there'll be too many people around. Don't you understand? I need a clean break. Where I know nobody and can just be . . ."

"Alone?"

I exhaled and looked at Kacey wistfully. "Yes," I admitted. "Alone."

"Alone without me," she said.

My heart squeezed. "That's the worst part of it." I sighed deeply. "This was the plan. Let's just stick to the plan, Kacey. Please?"

Luck? No, chance had nothing to do with it. It was a choice. Now I climb the stairs and choose the frigid room over my mother's icy stare.

63

IN THE MORNING, Mom is up before the sun has the chance to reflect billions of sparkles off the snow. She's already been on the phone with the airlines and has a flight booked for late tonight.

"I guess we'll have to find some way to pass the time," she muses. "Why don't we go into town?"

"I doubt anything's open. The power just came back."

"Well, what else are we going to do around here all day?" she asks.

My stomach feels uneasy when I think about going into town with Mom. But I give in. I convince myself that I should probably check on the store, even if it's just to walk by.

Outside, the sky is a perfect alabaster, like someone took a paintbrush and rolled it in a solid stripe along the horizon. The drive into town takes twice as long as usual. I tighten my seat belt and brace myself as Mom slides on and off the highway shoulder mumbling something about snowplows. Thankfully, we're the only car on the road.

"Maybe we should go back, Mom," I suggest, my hands ready and muscles tensed.

"Don't you want to get out of the house? It's like a mausoleum back there."

"Thanks."

We finally make it to Main Street after a few close calls. The street's been cleared, but it's nearly empty, save for a few brave souls digging out the storefronts and sidewalks.

Mom pulls up to a spot in front of the flower shop and parks awkwardly in between snowbanks. "I don't think anything's open," I say.

"We'll just walk around," she replies.

Curtains of snow swallow the low, sloping rooftops. Gutters bent with weight dangle and sway above frosty storefront windows. The bakery, the flower shop, the galleries and souvenir shops are all dark inside. The only thing open is the market. Ice crunches beneath our boots on the hastily salted curb. A little bell dings as we walk in the door.

Mom lowers her hood and fluffs her hair. "Afternoon," a young man behind a counter greets us. A small number of people are shopping—grabbing produce and toiletries and other staples. They're only taking as much as they can carry, and I realize Mom and I are the only ones who risked the drive.

Mom begins perusing the store. She picks up a box of seasoned rice, reads the ingredients, and then puts it back down. She does the same thing with a bag of flavored pretzel bites and a box of cracked-pepper water crackers. "Aren't you going to pick anything?" I ask.

She makes her way to the spice section and picks up a canister of Simply Savory Spice Mix—the same one I have in my own kitchen. She rotates it in her hand and reads the back, raises her brows in interest, and places it in her basket. "There. I picked something," she says as she walks away toward the produce section.

"Elisabeth?" I look up as Jonathan rounds the aisle in front of me. I quickly look over toward Mom—she's out of earshot, lifting a bunch of bananas to her nose. I whisper a small prayer of thanks.

"Hey, Jonathan."

He transfers his shopping basket to the other arm. "I was actually planning to check in on you after I finished up here."

"Oh, um, thanks," I say.

"Is everything working all right at the house now that the power's back on?" he asks with a look of genuine concern.

I recall what Noah told me about their parents, and my heart tightens a little in my chest. I always thought Jonathan was worried about his house—but now I realize he was probably just worried about me. "Yes," I say, reassuring him, as I glance around to make sure I'm still in the clear. "As far as I know. Everything's in good shape."

"I'm going to grab some instant coffee, Johnny. I hear the snow may be picking up again tonight and—" Mr. Ito appears behind Jonathan, nearly walking into him while juggling a few small packages in his hand. "Oh, Elisabeth," he says, a smile pulling at the corners of his mouth. "So nice to see you. I was hoping you made it through the storm intact."

"Cardinal, I told you Noah said she was okay," Jonathan says to him.

Cardinal? I smile, surprised. I think of the well-loved copies of bird-watching magazines stacked behind the counter at the store. So, *Mr. Ito* is the family friend who stepped in when Noah and Jonathan's parents died. How did I not know that before?

"Thanks for looking out for me, Mr. Ito. Actually, Noah's been helping me out these past few days. With firewood and stuff."

"He finally made it over to your place?" Mr. Ito asks with a grin. "I've been pestering him for months."

"Oh. Well, not exactly. I kind of needed his help. I mean, I didn't *need* his help. There was the snow; it was late at night; it was a thing." Then I stop and shake my head, glad Noah isn't here to hear me. "Never mind."

"No matter how it happened. I'm just glad you made it through the storm," he says, shaking a can of green beans and tossing it into Jonathan's basket.

"I was hoping that you were all right, too," I say a little shyly. "Any idea when the store can open again?"

"Don't worry about that. Johnny's going to shovel me out and make sure everything's in order. No rush to reopen. It's not like anyone needs wind chimes or incense right now."

"Or lavender soap," I say with a smile.

"Or lavender soap," he agrees. "I'll let you know when it's safe to go back in."

That settled, Jonathan says, "In the meantime, I'll come by tomorrow and bring you some more firewood. Noah said you borrowed some from him?"

I nod. "Yeah, I may have had an issue with the tarp in the back," I say, hesitant to admit my blunder.

"Right," Jonathan replies, and an uncharacteristically cocky smile appears on his face. He reaches up and pats Mr. Ito on the shoulder. "We should get going, get back home."

"Okay," I say. "See you soon, Mr. Ito. Jonathan." I smile to myself as I walk away from them.

I find Mom weighing pears in the back corner of the market. "What were you doing?" she asks, not raising her eyes to me.

"Nothing," I say. "Just looking around."

"Who were those people you were talking to?" she asks.

"Tourists, I think."

64

WE ARRIVE BACK HOME before noon. I start cleaning out the hearth, and Mom returns to her spot on the sofa. The fire's not necessary now that the heat is back on, but I've come to enjoy it. Mom has my afghan wrapped around her legs and a cup of English breakfast tea on her lap. "I should probably head to the airport early," she says as dusk approaches. "I can't imagine how long it will take me."

I nod my head. "Okay."

Mom exhales loudly. That was not the response she was looking for. She wants me to say that I wish we had more time together. That I want her to stay.

But I don't, and I won't say it.

She wants me to relent and tell her I've made a terrible mistake by coming here. She wants me to say I'm ready to come home. That I'm miserable. She wants me to ask to go with her.

"If you're that worried, Mom, maybe you should leave now."

That shuts her up. Momentarily.

Mom takes a sip of her tea and sits forward on the couch. She runs a hand through her hair as she considers her next move. "I just worry about you, that's all," she finally says.

"You don't have to. I'm fine."

She sets the teacup on the coffee table a little harder than necessary, fed up that I refuse to play her games. That I refuse to tell her I need her.

"Oh. Okay. I won't worry. As if that were so easy." She raises her arms in resignation and then flops them back to her sides. She wants a reaction—she's *desperate* for a reaction—but I still don't give her one.

So she returns to righteousness. "It's what a mother is supposed to do. There's no such thing as worrying too much about your child," she says, mother of the year. Look at all she has undertaken. Look at all she has endured. She shakes her head and searches her tea, cupping it in her hands. Look how much she's gone through—how much she continues to go through—*for me*.

"Maybe not," I say calmly. "But there is such a thing as worrying about the wrong things, Mom."

Her eyes find mine quickly. "What does *that* mean?"

"You make it seem like everything here is awful, like I'm not able to take care of myself. And that's not true. I think I'm doing a pretty good job."

"Oh, okay. Right. You're doing just fine, sitting here in a freezing log cabin, eating scraps, all by yourself in the middle of a blizzard, waiting to die."

And now, I've had enough. Because there *was* a time when I wanted to die. When death was preferable to agony. When anger and fear melted away and the only thing I desired was an end to the pain, even if that meant an end to everything. But Mom never cared enough to notice.

"Is that why you're here, Mom? Because you were worried about me in the storm? Because you were worried about the sidewalks or the snowplows or the soup in my stupid pantry?" I take a deep breath, feeling the friction in my fingertips. "I don't need your help. I don't *want* your help."

I pause and lock eyes on her. "And for the record, when I did need you, you weren't there."

Her mouth turns into a thin, flat line. I watch her recoil and then recompose. She closes her eyes and then opens them slowly before settling on me once again. Mom knows exactly what I'm talking about. I prepare myself for the barrage of pollution. How she's sacrificed. How she's suffered. How she was the real victim.

But I'm not prepared for the most poisonous thing of all: her denial. "I don't know what you're talking about, Justine." It's half offense—I'm the crazy one. It's half defense—she did nothing wrong. It's wholly brilliant.

And it's all I can do not to lunge at her from across the coffee table.

Mom moves to set down her tea, but she misses the edge, and a pool of pale brown liquid begins to soak into the rug.

She watches it spread, seep in deeper, but doesn't move to clean it up.

Neither do I. Because I feel something begin to spread and seep deeper into me. Slowly, quietly. Almost imperceptibly.

But undeniably.

"I'm just trying to tell you how I feel," I say. "And you've made it nearly impossible. Impossible to tell you anything other than what you want to hear."

This has always been the way with her. If I keep quiet, I lose. If I speak, she wins. It's a trap of a different kind.

"So that's why you came here?" she asks. "To prove to me that you don't need me? That you can do it all on your own?"

"No, Mom," I say with a shake of my head. "I'm not trying to prove anything—that's *you*. I mess up your perfect hair and your perfect family, your perfect picture of your perfect life. I messed it up then and I'm messing it up now. Me, your daughter who is not perfect no matter how much you wish she was, and no matter how much you try to fix her. Do you even love me, or do you just want people to think you do?"

She looks as if I've slapped her. I've given her exactly what she needs—I've proven her right—I am a perfectly terrible child.

I turn and head for the door. No jacket, no gloves, I don't even bother with shoes.

"Don't kid yourself, Justine. Don't act like you know exactly what you're doing. Like you've got it all figured out. You're a scared little girl who runs away from everything. But you know what? I'm not the one you're running away from," she calls after me.

My eyes narrow at her from over my shoulder. She straightens her spine, looks me square in the eye. "The real thing you're just dying to get away from is yourself."

My hand is on the doorknob, my feet are in front of the door. But my mind—my mind is somewhere else entirely.

"I've changed my mind," Kacey said to me. "This is crazy. You can't go. You can't just run away and hide in a Bob Ross painting."

"That's not what I'm doing," I told her.

"Of course it is," she said. "That's exactly what you're doing. But let me tell you something—there's nowhere you can go where anything will be any different. There's nowhere you can hide where you won't think the same thoughts, feel the same fears. They're going to follow you, Elisabeth. Even if you run, even if you're all alone. You cannot escape yourself."

Kacey's voice echoes in my skull, totally devoid of anything else. *"You cannot escape yourself."* As painful as it is to admit it, Kacey was right.

And so is Mom.

A flood of shame and inadequacy crashes over my head. Again. Every wretched thing that I have ever felt about myself rises to the back of my throat. That underlying fear and apprehension I dragged around everywhere. The scarlet letter that had been pinned to my chest since I first heard someone say, "There's something wrong."

There's something wrong. There's something wrong. There's something wrong—with me.

I was inadequate, pathetic, less than.

It became an appendage I carried around with me—even long after the fixator was removed. I couldn't help it. If someone looked at me weird—it was because I am weird. If someone's behavior seemed odd—it was because I am odd. They're not telling the truth. They don't have your best interests at heart. They're lying to you. They're going to hurt you. They want to hurt you. Don't let them hurt you.

It's only paranoia if you're wrong.

I'm not fixed. I am fixated. Isn't that just how they wanted me to be?

Everything is not fine. Everything is not okay.

Everything is not safe.

I turn the doorknob and walk out the door.

65

I DART OUT OF THE HOUSE and under the sunless sky, moving as fast as I can to Noah's, not even bothering to find the path. I sink into the deep snow. I can't feel my feet at all. I keep moving, keep pushing through the denseness, because I think if I stop, I may never move again.

Tears pool in my eyes. But not tears of anger. They're tears of grief. Grief for the things I've lost. Grief for the things taken from me. Grief for the things I have kept from myself.

And as I trudge through the soppy white carpet beneath me, and tremble under the churning gray clouds above, I wonder how it's possible that I've found myself in exactly the same place as all those years ago, even though every day since I've been trying to make sure I'd never be in this place again? I didn't understand it, but somehow, somewhere, everything got turned backward, and my mind became a slave to my body instead of the other way around.

I finally make it to Noah's door. Shivering, I fall against it and bang on the hard wood. "Noah!" I try to shout, but my voice is a pale wisp from the bitter cold. "Noah!"

The door opens and I fall inside; Noah catches me before I hit the floor. "Elisabeth! What's going on, what's wrong?"

"Everything," I manage. "Everything is wrong."

"It's okay," he says. "You're okay."

I look up at him as he pulls me upright. "I am not okay."

It's the first time I've ever said it out loud. The first time I've ever admitted it to myself.

"Noah, you don't understand," I say. "I shouldn't even have come here." I don't know how to explain it. I have no one else to turn to, but I shouldn't be here, either. I don't deserve him, and he deserves more than me.

"I should go—"

"What?" Noah stops me and closes the door behind me. He guides me over to the fire. He snatches a blanket from the couch and wraps it around my shoulders. "Okay. Now tell me: What are you talking about?"

I swallow hard, not knowing where to start. "I just . . . I feel so confused. I left because I had to. I had no choice. It was my plan all along, since I was eleven years old. I couldn't trust anybody—not the doctors, not my mom." I look into his eyes. "Maybe not even myself. I had to go somewhere where I felt safe."

Noah takes my shoulders into his hands and tries to slow me down. "Elisabeth, wait. I don't understand."

"Everything's messed up. My mom is here making me feel worthless again, and everything feels so out of control. And all this time I thought I needed to be alone, but what if I was only making it worse? What if Kacey was right? And you're here—that's a problem, too."

"Why?" he asks. "Why is that a problem?"

"Because I can't trust you. I want to, but I can't trust anybody. Like, literally, physically, I can't do it. I can't ask for help, because when people help me, they end up hurting me. Everyone ends up hurting me, and I don't want that to be you, too, Noah."

I start to cry—big, fat, round tears that feel like they've been fighting to get out forever. Tears that were taking up space inside me, like a living, breathing entity trapped somewhere deep for so long. Now they're breaking loose. Or maybe I'm letting them free. I don't know. Noah sits down across from me, his knees touching my knees, and holds my head to the crook of his shoulder—holds me as I shudder and sob.

Noah and I sit together until I can't remember the last words we spoke. Until my cries quiet and my breathing calms. Until the heat from the fire dissolves my tears, leaving salty stains down my face. I am dimly aware of the minutes ticking by, of the softening of the shadows as they stretch upon the carpeted floor.

After all this time, I think, maybe I've been stretched too far, too.

I hold my breath, not sure whether to force out the words pressing at my lips or gather them safely back inside. "I don't know what's wrong with me," I finally say. Is it an excuse? An apology? Anything to explain myself. "The hurt in my heart just feels too big."

Noah shakes his head, leans into me, and rests his forehead gently against mine. He holds it there, his face so close it no longer looks like a face but a newfound terrain of hills and mountains and valleys. The clear, glossy lagoon of his eyes. The shy slope where the bridge of his nose meets the curve of cheekbone. And then, from the hollow well of his mouth, mere inches away from my own: "Maybe it's just making space for something better."

Noah takes his fingertip and grazes my cheek, tracing the line of a tear slowly down to my chin. I squeeze my eyes closed, just for a second, and hold his words within me. And at this moment I give in. I give in to my body. I let it hijack my mind once more, in a totally different way.

With his forehead still pressed to mine, Noah angles his head up, bringing the very tips of our noses together. His feels cold and smooth and a little bit pointy on mine. He holds it there and slowly raises his eyelids. I stare into his warm brown eyes. And then I fall into them. Tears begin to pool again in mine. I don't know where they come from this time, but suddenly they're right there, exposing me. All of me.

The Real Me.

Noah's hands find mine, and he lays his palms gently on top, his soft fingertips barely touching my skin. He changes the angle of his face once again, and gently, steadily, he closes the feather of space between us and brings our mouths together. Noah's kiss is a pillow—warm, cool, firm, forgiving—all of these things, all at once. The stubble sprinkling his jaw scrapes my chin, and it's like sandpaper soothing a deep barb. He presses his lips to mine, dissolving into me like a sugar cube, as we breathe each other's breath, taste each other's taste. It's new and familiar; it's exciting and comforting. But mostly, it's very, very sweet.

He doesn't push. He doesn't pull. He doesn't ask for anything more. He doesn't ask for anything less. And the whole time I'm thinking, *This is what it is to be touched by someone for no other reason than them wanting to touch you.*

I don't want to move. I don't want to breathe. I want time to stop, and I want to live on Noah's floor in front of the fire with his hands on mine and his lips on mine forever and ever and ever and ever. But I can't. I know it's not wrong, but it's not quite right, either. I pull carefully away from him. "Noah, I'm sorry. I just don't think I can do this right now. It's just too much."

"Don't be sorry," he says, only this time, he says it with a knowing kindness. "I get it. I do. I mean, contrary to popular belief, I haven't always been the picture of perfection sitting before you."

I smile as I lean away even farther. "No?" I ask.

"No," he says, and looks down at his feet. "When we're at our worst, when we're hurting, it touches everything." His eyes then return to mine. "'All places shall be hell that is not heaven,'" he says, quoting my favorite book again.

I think about how long I'd been straddling the line between the old me and the new me, the scared me and the safe me, and how sometimes that line didn't seem like a line at all, but a dream that vanished as soon as you got too close to it. I think about how I came to Fish Creek to leave my old life behind. But the truth is, I left a long time ago. The truth is, I was already gone.

I want to tell Noah that I know what it is to be in pain. When your body and soul are pulled apart and you don't see how they'll ever come together again. That I know how it feels when the world splits in two, when you end up on the wrong side, when you can see everything the way it was supposed to be but can never be. That I know that emptiness, that gap between realities so big it sucks you in like a black hole.

Pain is the divide between what is and what should be.

But I don't know how to say these things. It all feels too big, too intense. So instead, I take a deep breath, steel myself, and I decide to tell him something else. I tell him the story that's written in my scars.

66

NOAH AND I STAY BY THE FIRE for a long time. Long enough for my toes to go from numb to warm to chilly again as the logs snap in a request to be replenished. But eventually his police radio beeps and lights up on his hip.

"I should get back," I say. "You're busy."

He presses a few buttons on the radio before clicking it back onto his belt. "I don't want you to go," he says. Noah stands up and reaches his hand out to me. "Come on," he says. "Let's go for a drive."

He pulls me through the hallway and into the little mudroom by his side door. Digging through the small closet, he finds an old pair of snow boots and helps me on with them. He wraps a winter coat around my shoulders. It feels nice—not just the coat, not just the boots—but him thinking of me. We exit his house and walk around to the garage toward his car. "Get in."

"I don't really think I should leave my mom for too long," I say, not really sure if it's the truth.

"We won't be that long," Noah says, climbing into the driver's seat of his police car.

I tentatively place my hand on the handle of the passenger door. "Are you going to make me sit in the back, like a criminal?"

"No," he says warmly. "Sit up front with me."

"Where are we going?" It's already dark, and the roads are still covered in ice and snow.

Noah wiggles his eyebrows at me. "You'll see."

He backs out of the driveway and starts down our street, then turns right at the light. I haven't been on this stretch of the road since I first moved to Fish Creek. This is the way out, and all I've wanted to do is stay locked in—staying locked in was my way out.

I vaguely recognize a few landmarks. An old barn, a boarded-up fruit stand. A small inn called the Hotel Motel where I stayed when I first got to town.

The fluorescent lights of a run-down gas station flicker against the night. We pass a strip mall flanked by a doughnut shop on one end and a nail salon on the other. Noah turns off the main road and the small-town lights disappear behind us. The moon is absent, the air full of snow dust, and the road is one long stretch in front of us, an icy tunnel to nowhere. There's nothing to see beyond the rush of trees playing hide-and-seek with Noah's high beams. Inside the car it's like time is standing still—a cozy little satellite of him and me.

Despite Noah's promise to not be too long, we drive for what seems like a really long time. Finally, he makes a left turn, and we head downhill and around a curve. Noah rolls down the windows and picks up his speed, and the cold air rushing past us whips my hair around.

We make another sharp turn, this time onto a narrow, barely there road, and something about the air changes. It becomes thinner and it smells alive. The thick white blanket of snow stops just a few dozen feet away from the car, and then there is only blackness. I can't see it, I can't hear it, but I know we are at the water.

Noah brings the car to a stop in the middle of the road. The silence rings all around us. I can't see anything—not a building, not a street-light, not another car in the distance. He comes around and opens my door. "I used to come here a lot, just to get away."

I step out of the car and follow closely behind Noah. The snow here is different, like walking through a pile of confetti, and though it's completely untouched, it's easy to shuffle our way through. "Watch your step," Noah says as he reaches behind him to search for my hand, steadying me as the terrain begins to climb. "Some of these rocks can be loose." I hold tightly to Noah's hand and place each foot carefully as we ascend into the clear, dark night.

"We're here," Noah says after we've gone a short distance, but I see nothing. I take another step, bringing me right to Noah's side. Then, as if appearing out of nowhere at all, an enormous structure takes shape in front of us. I reach out my hand and touch the flat, gravelly surface. I can barely distinguish it from the night sky; it's the same inky blue black. If Noah hadn't said anything, I would've walked face-first into what seems like a solid cement wall.

"What is it?" I ask, but Noah doesn't answer. He pulls me behind him, using his other hand to follow the periphery of the wall, and then stops when he hears the clang of metal on metal. I hear a padlock twist-ing loose and then the swinging of a heavy door, and I'm pulled into a cold, dark, echoing room. It feels small but also enormous, and my mind can't wrap itself around the space. "Noah?" I say slowly, trying to hide the hint of panic.

"I'm right here," he says, his voice reverberating like we're at the bottom of a well. It smells musty, like rotting wood and salt. I hear some shuffling noises and then he clicks on a flashlight. At first, the only things I see in the ring of light are our soggy boots on a damp stone floor. But as Noah redirects the light, more of the room comes into view. It looks like a cellar or a basement of some kind, or maybe even an old shelter, with mud-caked floors and smooth, rock-hard walls. A set of metal, cage-like steps juts out from the wall just beside the door and wraps around the inside of the circular space like a coiled snake rocketing toward the heavens. I look up. It's not a dungeon. It's not a cell. It's a lighthouse.

"What are we doing here?"

"It's just a cool place. The beacon doesn't work anymore, so on a night like this the stars are incredible. I thought you'd like to see."

I plant my feet and shake my head. And just in case he can't sense my determination in the darkness: "I'm not going up there," I say.

"Why not?"

"Well, in case you haven't figured it out yet, Noah, I spend most of my time avoiding dangerous situations."

"This isn't a dangerous situation," he says. "This is a staircase."

I look at the spiral staircase again. It's narrow, and from what I can tell in the soft glow of the flashlight, the corners where each step meets the next are rusted. Some of the bolts look loose, too. The lighthouse whines with the force of the growing wind outside. "Noah, no."

Noah walks to the steps, grabs ahold of the banister, and gives it a shake. The metal moans a little, but it doesn't peel away from the walls and come crashing down to the floor like I expect it to.

"Come on, we'll just go up to the next level."

I don't move at all.

"I'm right here. I promise it'll be fine," Noah says.

I rock on my heels, feeling every hair on the back of my neck bristle, but let Noah slowly lead me up the first few rickety steps in near darkness. "Aren't lighthouses supposed to be, I don't know, light?" I ask.

He laughs. "Well, this one's been abandoned for as long as I can remember. In fact, I used to come out here as a kid—a bunch of us did. You know, just a place to hang out and get into trouble."

"Is that what we're doing here now, getting into trouble?"

Even in the shadows, I can see Noah's teeth behind his wide smile as his eyes slide back to me. We complete one full spiral up and around the small space, marked by a short break in the stairs. Noah motions to the next flight up. It appears even narrower than the last.

"Yeah, that doesn't look like something I'm going to do."

Noah laughs again.

"You said just one level."

He inclines his head toward the top. "I've done it a thousand times."

I reluctantly follow him up the next few steps. The metal winces and creaks beneath our feet, and I can sense the empty, plummeting space below as we climb higher.

"Okay. There. I did it," I say when we reach the second metal landing. "Can we please go back down now?"

"Actually," Noah says, gently pulling me along, "you have to go a little higher to really appreciate the view." Noah tugs on my hand again.

"You know what? I know what stars look like—little twinkle lights in the sky. I think I'll head back—" I start to turn around.

"We're already halfway there," he interrupts, and lurches toward me to rotate my shoulders back in his direction. The staircase grinds in protest of the sudden movement and shifts beneath my feet. I grab onto the railing as the landing tilts and drops a few degrees toward the center of the narrow, but cavernous, room.

"I don't want to," I say like I'm a small child.

Noah doesn't reply, but his nod says *I know*. "It's okay," he says after a few moments. "Not much farther to go."

But I can't go. I'm frozen. I don't know why. It's not the height; it's not the creaking staircase. I glide my hand along the frosty railing, its rigid, unyielding steel meant solely to keep me from harm.

I can't do this. *Why can't I do this?*

I can't breathe. I can't move. My fingers grip the thin metal frame as I simultaneously curse this steel trap and pray for it to protect me, to keep me safe. It feels wrong, and familiar.

"What are you so afraid of, Elisabeth?" Noah asks from somewhere far away.

His question settles into me like a stone settling at the bottom of a lake. And my body, at long last, after years of careful avoidance, caving to the unforgiving metal scoring my palm, takes me to a place where for so long my mind has refused to go.

67

THEN

IT'S COLD. The exam table is hard, and my dishwater-gray gown is scratchy. The ceiling tiles look like Styrofoam. The floor is a speckled terrazzo, gleaming with a recent layer of lemon-scented antiseptic. The walls are white, framed in a warped plastic trim curling up at the corners, but are otherwise bare. It's a small room, nearly empty except for a tiny sink with a few cabinets beneath it, a schoolhouse clock, and an X-ray light box on the far wall. I'm perched in the center of the room on a paper-covered pulpit. Mom sits in a cracked plastic chair, an ancient issue of *Good Housekeeping* in her hands.

The Wolf rises and approaches me with long strides, casually but carefully. Cordial smiles, we're old friends.

Put your legs on the table, please.

He grips my leg in his hairy paws—my foot, my knee, my ankle, he manhandles me back and forth. I plaster my arms to the side of my thighs to keep my gown from riding up.

The Wolf points to one of the X-rays—pictures from this morning. Pins upon pins crisscrossed with other pins, forming *X*s in the middle of the black-and-white image of my bone. Wires. Metal rods. Bicycle spokes. Fifty glinting spears. They enter my skin. They go through the tissue and bone. They come out the other side.

Some of the pins have little beads on them—hard, fixed stones within the regrown bone that keep the pin from shifting. Like the pit of an olive, hidden deep within the flesh.

This pin here—he taps the X-ray with his pen—*it's unnecessary.* Tap, tap, tap. *It should be removed so it doesn't interfere.*

No biggie, we can just pull it out. It doesn't have a bead. We'll cut one end of the pin, then the other.

Does she need to be put under anesthesia for that?

No, we can do it right here in the exam room.

Will it hurt?

He doesn't think so. It should essentially slide right out. A hot knife through butter.

The Wolf leaves the room to gather his supplies. Mom gives a reassuring smile—everything's going to be all right. Nothing to worry about.

The long, thin hands of the clock tick by. Tick, tick, tick. Knock, knock, knock, the Wolf is back and he's returned with his friend. Gadgets weigh down their arms—heavy, silver metal instruments that make a loud thunk as they place them beside me. Bulky things that don't look anything like medical equipment; they look like a handyman's tools. They look like weapons.

I hear the resonant click of the door as it closes behind them. The low whistle of the curtain as it catches in the track. I feel sick. I feel scared.

Lie down, Miss Amos.

And now one of the tools is in the Wolf's paw. A wire cutter. He cuts both ends of the sacrificial pin where it attaches to the perimeter of the brace. I can smell it—the tiny fragments of metal smoke like invisible curls of gas burning my nostrils.

The snip of the pin reverberates through my bone. The pain is both dull and sharp at the same time and it radiates up my leg. A sudden panic grips my throat and my eyes begin to water.

Please stop. I don't want to do this. Please stop.

But he can't stop; he's gone too far. It would be unsafe to leave it now.

Panic coats the walls like paint. I begin to cry harder. But not tears. Rather, a river is born from my eyes. A river to wash away my sins. Mom comes around and leans over my head to try to block my view. The Wolf and his friend stand at my feet. *Hold the brace still. Hold her still.* The Wolf then grips the brace with one paw to support himself, leaning the weight of his body into the frame and digging the brace into the paper-covered padding of the exam table.

And I am trapped.

Don't touch me. Don't touch me. Don't touch me!

The Wolf picks up what looks like an enormous pair of pliers and clamps it down on one end of the cut pin, which now looks like a live wire. And then he starts to pull.

At first, the pin doesn't move, but I can feel the resistance. It feels like a thousand pounds of pressure on a spot the size of a dime. Like a bullet tunneling through my bone. I cry out and immediately cover my mouth with my hands. He stops momentarily and adjusts his grip. *Hold her still. Hold her still.* The Wolf tenses, then starts again. He pulls harder.

Bile rises in the back of my throat and I squeeze my eyes shut. Somehow the tears escape anyway, like they can't stand to be inside my body any longer. And I don't want to be inside my body anymore, either. Because this pain is not pain. It is a splintering of the soul that cannot be contained by words or thoughts. Every time before when I complained that my leg hurt—that was a lie. I didn't know what pain really was. I didn't know what pain could really be.

I focus on the sound. Shrill, like metal being dragged against concrete. The friction of bone and flesh and blood and steel. It feels sticky and hot, like oil on fire. And it spreads—it's not just my leg on fire, but everything within me—every single cell is burning, wailing, weeping. Bright red eyes wink at me from some new place between my brain and my mind.

I'm screaming for him to stop—don't touch me, don't touch me!—but I don't think I am actually screaming at all. Mom is crying—I feel her hot tears spilling into my hair as she leans over me.

It's okay. Be brave. You're fine, you're okay, you're safe.

But I'm not fine. I'm not safe.

The Wolf is pulling and pulling and my whole life is in that little room with him just waiting for him to get that pin out. He keeps pulling and pulling and pulling with what feels like the strength of a bull until finally within the fire I feel something pop. Only it's not a pop; it's the butchering of bone. Shrapnel exploding beneath my skin.

My body is lying on the table, but I can't say how long it's been; the time doesn't move—it laughs. I squeeze my eyes shut and when I open them again, I'm watching my life happen from the bottom of a pool. I've sunken under, yet no one seems to have noticed. The confusion is shapeless, expansive, eternal. It's water in my lungs. It's a static in the air. And then, just when I think I've felt all the things that no human being should ever feel, the sharp, jagged edge of the freshly cut metal pin tears my flesh and scrapes my bone as it's pulled through me. It's one last burn, one final insult, a searing, electric jolt. And the red eyes flash at me again.

I'm crying so hard that it feels like I'm choking and I cannot breathe and I wonder if I'm going to die. And then I do. I die. Right there on the exam table, everything stops moving—my heart, my lungs, the air around me—and I fade into a cloud of darkness that plumes up and over me and sinks into my brain. I can't see anything, I can't hear anything, and I can't feel the pain anymore. All I can feel is the darkness, heavy and thick, as it sweeps through and touches every part of me and whispers from somewhere deep inside. *This is what you get.*

But somehow, somehow I'm back on the exam table and my eyes are open again. Blood covers the lower half of the table, soaking through the paper drape and dripping onto the floor. I feel something in my chest twist and lurch, and out of nowhere, there's vomit, heavy and wet, saturating the front of my gown. It seeps onto the table and mixes with the blood.

Can someone come in here and clean up the mess?

The mess that has become of me.

The mess that has become of me
The less that has become of me
Less of me
Less of me
Nothing left
Left
Gone
Forgone
Forgotten
Forgotten girl

The Wolf wipes the perspiration from his brow.
Hmm. I guess that pin did have a bead on it, after all.

68

THE MEMORY IS SO SHARP I could swear it isn't the metal banister beneath my hand but the metal of my brace. My hand squeezes the jagged, rusty rail under my palm, and it slices my skin, just a little. It slices my skin, and it slices my heart, and it slices my brain into tiny slivers that flicker through my head like a flipbook.

I close my eyes and I see the pages—a thousand shifting images, a thousand memories. A thousand punches to the gut. A thousand times someone told me everything was okay when it wasn't. A thousand times I had to bury my pain so as to not hurt anyone else. A thousand times I had to swallow my screams.

I am unable to answer Noah, because the very thing that hurts inside me is unnameable. It's the deep, bottom-of-my-soul, buried-in-my-brain feeling that something is wrong. That I've been wronged. That *I'm* wrong.

I've spent the last eight years afraid of what will happen if I reopen the door to that exam room. Afraid of what it says about the people who are supposed to protect me. Afraid of what it says about the people I was supposed to trust. But most of all, afraid of what it says about me.

Me, the patient. Me, the problem.

After all this time, I still don't know. I'm still stuck in that cage.

But I'm not caught inside some torture-induced dreamlike reality. I am not lying pinned to an exam table anymore. This cage is not like the one I once knew. It's the cage that I've built around myself.

I close my eyes, and I do the only thing I can do.

I fall.

I fall through the fear. I fall through the pain. I fall through the symphony of sterile instruments, the beep beep beep, the wail wail wail, the click click click. I fall through the morphine, through its luster and its lies. I fall through the loneliness that branched through my veins, the desperation that dug itself into my bones. I fall through what's left when everything else is stripped away. And I fall into a little room, where people treat my body in ways they'd never dream of treating their own. A little room with a cold, hard examination table, the back of my neck slick with sweat and sticking to the roll of waxy butcher paper beneath it, as three adults who I am supposed to trust teach me what it means to be betrayed.

I fall into a place where God is punishing me, a place where everything is all a big mistake, a place where I was never supposed to be.

I fall into it all.

I fall and fall and fall.

And then, in the endless, echoing fall, I find myself in another little room. A room that is full of light but feels immeasurably heavy. A little room where a little girl waits patiently on the side of a borrowed hospital bed. She looks at me with massive eyes and reaches her hand out toward me with massive hope. I take it. I slide my fingers against her small palm and close my hand tenderly around hers. She is both fragile and familiar in the way she grips mine back.

The little girl doesn't speak, but her voice is as clear as church bells. It's a tenor. A vibration. A quiver in the air around me. It's like a resonance floating down from a neighbor in the apartment above. And it feels soft and ethereal like the strum of a harp or a baby's first sigh. Or maybe it's like sinking into a bubble bath, your skin pricking with each inch as the water takes you over, takes you under, every sense filling with a crackling fizz of warmth so impossibly close as the world melts farther and farther away.

And though I have no words, I know exactly what to say—just as I know how to breathe, just as I know how to cry. And they're the easiest words I've ever spoken. They spring forth from my throat pure and smooth, water cascading off the newly baptized. And as I lift her, I know that it is she who is lifting me, out of that little room, away from its secrets, its silence, the anger and agony absorbed into its walls like a sponge, away from the voices that sound so much like my own only they could convince me that they aren't.

And just as I know this little girl has been waiting for me, I know, more, that it's me who's been waiting for her. And I know, too, that it's time to let her go. She does not need to sit here any longer. But before I can release her, before I can turn to her and muster some sort of silent goodbye, it is she who releases me, the distance between our empty palms stretching like a single, solitary note of the piano, until she herself is just a shimmer on the air.

I reach for her, but she is only a memory. I reach for her, and I brush Noah's outstretched hand instead.

69

"ARE YOU WITH ME?" Noah asks quietly, sensing my return.

My eyes fall to our joined hands. I have the weirdest sensation, like doing a handstand in waist-deep water; a part of me feels cushioned and protected while the other half flails around uncontrollably, untethered. I don't respond, but I don't let go, and I follow him as he leads me up the last few iron steps to the landing at the very top. The walls come together at the structure's most narrow point, and finally there is a sense that something solid rests just above our heads.

"Thought I lost you there for a minute," he says.

I shake my head. *No.*

I stand still and slowly, for just a moment, scan the space around me. I know where I am. I know where I've been. I know where I need to go.

I know where I need to go.

Noah shines his flashlight on a peeling, red ladder affixed to the wall with dirty, fraying ropes. I don't know how far we are above the floor, though the echo alone tells me it's a long way down. My heartbeat quickens, but I'm not afraid.

He raises his right foot onto the first rung. I expect it to snap in half, expect him to fall to the platform beneath—but he doesn't. He continues to climb until his head touches the small trapdoor in the ceiling. He places his palms flat on the door and gives it a good push.

A little avalanche of snow tumbles onto Noah's head and down to the base of the ladder. "Come on up," he says as he climbs through the trapdoor and lowers a hand to help me. I draw a breath and wipe the drying tears from my face. I climb the ladder until my head reaches the trapdoor. Then I take Noah's outstretched hand and let him pull me through the little space.

A small accumulation of snow rests at the base of the lantern room, the round, window-lined enclosure surrounding the enormous reflective beacon in the middle. The windows, some ajar, most streaked or cracked with spiderwebbed panes of glass, look out onto an exterior gallery, like a viewing deck. "These should've been closed," Noah says, circling the perimeter and pausing before a narrow glass door.

"Is this it?" I ask, a little disappointed.

"Not quite . . ." Noah smiles, then ducks through the door, and disappears into the darkness that cloaks the balcony wrapping around the top of the tower. I carefully follow him out.

And then everything stops.

Noah and I are suspended in our own little galaxy. The stars surround us in a living, breathing burst of molten light. They glimmer from all directions, above us and behind us, and some even seem to smile up at us from down below. They remind me of Kacey's stars—swirling together in a deep purple sky, shimmering off the spray of the rocky shore below, beacons of hope far brighter than any lighthouse beam could ever wish to be.

Sometimes the universe gives you a gift, and it's up to you to recognize it.

"Pretty cool, huh?" Noah says. Strangely, the wind doesn't feel quite as fierce at this height, like somehow we've climbed above its wrath. The stars provide just enough light to see where it's safe to step. I walk to the railing and carefully lower myself to the floor.

It's hard to tear my eyes away from the immeasurable beauty before me, and it takes me a moment to be able to respond.

"I've never seen anything like it."

"It was worth it, right?" he asks, lowering himself beside me. "Even though you thought you might fall. Even though you were really, really scared. Even though you weren't sure that you could trust me. It was worth it, wasn't it?"

I breathe in the night air, no longer musty or stifling, but clean and calming. He was right.

"Yeah," I say. "It was worth it."

I peek at Noah and wonder if maybe he's worth it, too.

"It usually is," he says, scooching closer to me beneath the glittering sweep of sky. Side by side our breath falls in time to the soft lapping of the waves beneath our feet. We listen to the water stroke the shore and whisper sweet nothings into the ear of the night, and somehow Noah manages to hold me without touching me at all.

I lean onto his shoulder and watch the stars wink at one another. We sit there for a long time, and every once in a while, I think maybe they wink back at me.

"Want to stay out here a little longer?" Noah asks.

I sigh. I could stay here beneath the stars until they decide they're tired of looking at me. But even those stars can't cast the situation with Mom in a better light. And I should go.

But it's just so beautiful. And it took so much to get here. And for one shining moment, with my head on Noah's shoulder and the heavens in my eyes, and the stars blinking yes yes yes, I think I might be exactly where I'm supposed to be.

And a few more minutes won't kill her.

I turn to Noah and smile. "Absolutely."

70

"**ARE YOU SURE** you want to go in there alone?" Noah asks, after driving back into Fish Creek and over to my house. The wind has started to howl again, its temper slowly returning. Snow squalls coat his windshield in a dusting of powdered sugar.

It's nearly eight o'clock, and I know Mom will have to leave for the airport soon. "I'm sure," I say.

"Okay. I'll come over later tonight after she's gone home. After my shift."

I open the front door as I watch Noah pull away from the curb. The fire is still out, and it's dark inside, the only light coming from the lamp on next to the sofa. My high from the lighthouse comes to a puttering halt as the emptiness of the room echoes around me. "Mom?" I call.

No response. I check the bedroom and bathroom upstairs, but she's not there. Back downstairs, passing the empty fireplace, I wonder if she went out back to grab more firewood. I open the back door and do a quick scan of the backyard. Empty. I turn to the door to the basement beneath the stairs—*Maybe something's wrong with one of the appliances,* I think, and I'm suddenly reminded of Noah's parents' accident. But the lights are off, and she doesn't appear to be down there, either.

Then a thought hits me—I wonder if she decided to leave for the airport already. I can't recall if I saw her car parked on the road when Noah dropped me off. Would she have left without saying goodbye? Maybe she did it on purpose—so she wouldn't *have to* say goodbye? I check out the front window. The rental car is still there, gently creaking against the growing wind.

My palms begin to sweat. She's not here, but she didn't leave. Where would she go? Perish the thought of leaving the house in a light drizzle—there's no way she'd choose to go out in this weather at night. "Mom?" I call again, aimlessly sweeping the room as if she'd suddenly appear.

And that's when I see it. The little drawer beneath the TV, the one where I keep my notebook—it's open.

I rush over and find the notebook lying crookedly in the drawer.

I pick it up and quickly flip through it. What did she see? The poem I let Noah read by the fire? The anxiety? The memories? The panic? The pain?

I don't know what to do or what to think. Where could she possibly have wandered off to? Did she just run out into the woods? It's dark, and she doesn't know where she's going. Should I wait for her to come back? I chew on my thumb while I contemplate the options.

Then something catches my eye out the window. It's started snowing again. Only it's not a few delicate snowflakes fluttering gently to the ground. The sky has opened up and released the mother of all snowfalls—a thick, heavy mix of snow and sleet and ice plunging out of the heavens.

I hurry into the kitchen, pick up the phone, and dial 911. "It's my mother. I think she's lost out in the snowstorm," I say to the operator. I give her my name and address before I hang up. I then hurry to my closet, kick off Noah's boots, and tug on my own. I throw on gloves and a jacket and grab a flashlight. I nearly fly out of the front door.

The sharp, icy mixture cuts across my face as soon as I'm out from under the pergola. It feels like a thousand tiny arrows piercing my skin. I scan the snow-covered ground and find a path of footprints leading from the front porch to the side of the house. They're quickly becoming obscured by the new downfall of snow, but they look fresh.

I follow the footprints, sleet stinging my eyes, my legs sinking into the snow up to my knees with every step. I use my flashlight to follow her path, but then it seems to split. One line of disturbed snow points to the untrodden woods, while the other disappears around the back of the house.

"Mom!" I shout into the dense night. I don't know which path to follow, so I choose the one that would get her into the most trouble. I make my way to the tree line, a collection of indistinguishable shapes and shadows rising up before me. There is no moon, and the forest is dark, darker than I thought it would be, given the porcelain carpet upon its floor. The snow shimmers and sparkles in the glow from the flashlight, but the space around it is a black expanse. The trees loom tall and menacing above me, haunting in their stillness. Outside the beam of the light, everything is just nothing.

Carefully, I step into the forest. I know I shouldn't. I know it's stupid. But guilt propels me forward. Or maybe it's fear? "Mom," I call again, hoping to hear anything back. But all I hear is the wind whipping through the trees and knocking the branches above me. Not the low call of an owl, not the scratching of a squirrel shimmying up a tree—all of nature's creatures have hidden themselves from the storm. All but me, surrounded by the hollow tapping of snow on snow, ice on ice. I trudge through the woods, growing more tired and weak with each step, sweeping the light back and forth across the forest's floor, hoping to see anything other than the endless, ubiquitous white.

I'm shivering and I'm scared and I start to wonder if I'll ever find her. And then I stop for a moment, as a horrible part of me wonders if I truly *want* to find her. When we were talking about Dr. Faustus, Noah asked me which was worse, being deceived by others or deceiving ourselves? I hear Mom's voice from so long ago, telling me to put on a brave face, telling me everything is okay, when nothing could have been further from okay—and I'm not so sure.

Don't cry.

You're fine.

You're okay.

You're safe.

My searching turns to wandering, and I wander until I can no longer feel my feet. Then, finally, a light other than my own catches my eye. "Mom!" I shout again, so loudly that it echoes in my head. I try to run in the direction of the light, but the snow is so heavy. "Mom!"

"Elisabeth?" someone shouts. It's not Mom, of course—she would call me Justine. It's Noah, the light from his flashlight blinding as a strobe as he moves quickly toward mine.

"Noah, what are you doing here?" I ask, almost panting.

"You called 911. Who did you think would show up?"

A gust of wind blows through the trees, and they shake and bend like the weight of the world is upon them. And I feel the weight of the world upon me. "We have to find her," I say to Noah, resolutely. I am thankful that he's here.

Noah shines the light in every direction as we move even deeper into the woods. The sleet is blinding as it comes at us nearly sideways. Small trees, collapsed by the weight of the snow, litter the ground, like decomposing soldiers.

We keep searching, hand in hand. Flashlights side by side. We keep calling for her. The ground angles up a little, and the climb becomes slippery. We come to what appears to be the top of a berm, and the vast expanse of snow dips down a few feet in front of us. The wind rustles the treetops above us—the branches knock together as they sway.

"She's not here," I say. "Let's go back."

"Wait," Noah says. "She was probably looking for you, and if she was, she'd go to the nearest house—that's mine." He turns abruptly and starts heading out of the woods toward the tree line. I remember the second path of footprints disappearing around the back of the house. I follow closely behind, trying to match my steps with the deep prints he leaves in the snow. I'm beyond exhausted—my legs fossilized chopsticks beneath me—I don't know how I keep up. Noah heads toward the island of trees in between our two houses and sweeps his flashlight across the thick tangle of brush at the ground.

"Mom?" I whip my head from left to right, searching for any sign of her. But I see nothing.

Then, for a split second, the light of Noah's flashlight catches on something shiny and metallic—a zipper. And I hear a faint voice on the fraying edges of the wind.

"Mom!" I follow the direction of her voice. Noah and I both move our lights frantically, trying to locate her. The zipper catches the light again, and as the breadth of the light expands, her body comes into view, the broken pieces of a large jagged branch by her side. For a brief moment I'm taken back to the day when I first met Noah. The day when a fallen limb led me to climb into the back of his car. The day when I wished I had turned around and walked back on my own. Did I wish that still?

"Mom," I call, coming back to the present. "Are you okay?" I rush to her side.

"I'm okay," she says weakly. "It didn't hit me when it fell, just some of the debris."

A large gash hovers above her right eye. "Don't move," I say, using one glove to put pressure on the wound and the other to try to keep the blood away from her eye. Noah calls for assistance on his radio. "Mom, what were you doing?"

She turns her head away from me. "I don't know. I was worried, Justine."

"Justine?" Noah says, clipping his radio back on his belt and kneeling down by Mom's side. He glances questioningly toward me.

But I don't clarify. I can't—not right now. I avoid his gaze and turn back to Mom.

"Why would you come out in this storm?" I asked again.

"We've got to get her out of the snow." Noah interrupts me. "Paramedics are on the way."

"I don't need an ambulance," Mom says to him.

"Someone should look at your eye. It'll be the quickest way to the hospital in the storm."

Noah reaches down and pulls Mom's arm up and around his shoulder. They tromp back to my house through the dense snow and I follow in their trail.

"Keep applying pressure," Noah says as we reach the porch. "I'll be right back." Then he disappears into the darkness.

I open the front door and help Mom over to the couch. She falls into it while I get a towel from the kitchen and run it under cool water. I bring it back to her and hold it to her head.

"I found your journal," she says, a strange mix of sadness and guilt on her face.

"I know," I reply, avoiding her eyes. With my other hand, I dab a few flecks of blood off her cheek.

"I didn't mean to, and I know I shouldn't have opened it. But what you wrote, Justine . . . your poetry? It's horrible. I mean, it's beautiful, but it's so horrible." She shakes her head before continuing. "I never really knew how horrible it was for you. I mean, I knew—I knew. But I couldn't really let myself know. You know?"

I'm not really sure what to say. Mom and I stand in a graveyard of hurt, surrounded by ghosts, terrified to take another step. I breathe out one shaky, tear-laced sigh. "Why, Mom?"

She's quiet for a few moments. She then places her hand over mine, takes the towel from my grip, and holds it herself. I watch as fresh blood starts to seep through and turn the white cloth red. "Because there was nothing I could do."

I sit beside her and let it all come back to me. I allow it to. The memories I've swatted at like flies. Memories I shoved to the back of the junk drawer, tried to bury, tried to hide. I let them return to me, slowly but clearly, like a photograph emerging in a darkroom. Like it had happened just yesterday.

I remember the X-ray. I remember the pin.

I remember the fear.

The blood.

The pain.

I was not fine. I was not okay.

I was not safe.

I remember the one resounding emotion that had plagued me in the days following that visit. I felt numb. Desensitized, diminished, drugged. I was all of these things and none of these things. I spoke, but I was mute. I moved, but I was still. I was awake, but asleep.

All Dr. S had ever done was lie to me. Lie to me and hurt me. When he ripped that pin out, he took more than just the pin. He ripped out everything in me that was good and pure and trusting and secure, and left me weak and withered. I felt as if something had been stolen from me. Is that what he wanted the whole time? Not a patient but a rag doll—a limp body on a paper-covered exam table with which he could do whatever he wanted. Something close to a cadaver, quiet but with all the important parts still in there, able and willing to react to painful stimuli. Someone he could wear down, layer by layer, pin by pin, until almost nothing remained. Did stealing my humanity make him feel like a god? I was only Justine A., after all.

My mother was not my mother anymore; she was the physical embodiment of betrayal. My father—who I knew had been given a graphic account of the event but chose not to bring it up in my presence—was no longer my father; he was an accomplice. And I was no longer me; I was just a weak, stupid little girl deserving of pain, degradation, and lies. I was a fool to believe anyone was ever really on my side.

The sense of brutality only grew bigger; the fear went deeper. I was left to feel hollow and alien. I wasn't a person at all. It was an emptiness that seemed to stretch for miles all around me. But even as I stewed in it, breathed it in, soaked it up, I did not want to give in to it. I did not want to give up. I had been wronged, and I was angry. Dr. S might have stolen something from me, but I wanted it back. I wasn't going to just lie down and play the cadaver.

A week later, when Mom and I drove to the hospital for a checkup, I was prepared. No way was I letting him get his paws on me again. I sat in the exam room with only one thing on my mind. I was ready for him. I had nothing to lose.

"So, Miss Amos, how've you been doing since I last saw you?" he asked, in his usual asking-but-not-asking way.

"Since you last saw me?" I said. "Oh, you mean when you physically tortured me? When you decided to experiment on me in your little white room? When you ripped a metal fucking pin from my bone?!"

Dr. S's eyes flashed to mine, cold and steely. "Oh, well, that shouldn't have happened. That pin had a bead on it, and even if there hadn't been, I shouldn't have just pulled it out like that. At the very minimum we should have used a local anesthetic. I, uh . . . it was a mistake."

A mistake? "A mistake?"

"Miss Amos—" he said softly.

"No," I interrupted, unable to contain my rancor, my indignation. "You listen to me. You call yourself a doctor? What ever happened to 'do no harm'? You yanked a titanium spoke through my bone! Didn't you hear me screaming? Didn't the whole world hear me screaming? Didn't you think you should stop?"

"Justine . . ."

"You are a horrible, evil monster of a man. I should report you. You shouldn't be allowed to do this to anybody else ever again. Do they know? Do they know how many mistakes you've made? Do the other doctors know what you did? Do you even know? Do you know what you've taken away from me?"

My screams were so loud I was positive everyone else in the clinic could hear me. I was hot and sweaty and I wanted to jump up and shake him. Someone was going to rush in any second now wondering what was wrong. I looked at Mom, expecting outrage on her face. Outrage for me or because of me, I'm not sure. But when I turned to her, she wasn't outraged at all. She just sat there in her plastic chair, hands folded atop the magazine in her lap, face calm and composed. She hadn't moved, hadn't reacted to my outburst or accusations in any way.

And then I realized, I was only screaming in my head.

And so, because I was only eleven, and because I was nothing but a coward, and because it was clear everybody else had decided to pretend it never even happened, I didn't say anything at all.

Nobody ever said anything at all.

71

WHEN I WAS LITTLE, when Mom and Dad first noticed there was something wrong, one of the first things the doctors did was take X-rays of my legs. The bigger bone in the lower part of my left leg—the tibia—was shorter than in the right. And the smaller bone beside it—the fibula—didn't appear normal at all. The top half of the bone was completely missing. Imagine taking a toothpick and snapping it in half with your fingers. The break wouldn't be clean across—it would be jagged, splintered. That's exactly what my bone looked like. At the ankle it appeared normal, just like it was supposed to. But then, moving up toward the knee, it disintegrated and disappeared. It crumbled away. My bone just . . . vanished.

When Dr. S pulled that pin out, when everyone decided it was no big deal—that's exactly what happened to me. Whatever was left of me at that point, I splintered.

And I was gone.

72

I FEEL TIRED. I feel sore. I feel like my body is no longer a body, just a giant purple pulsating bruise. Not from searching for Mom out in the storm, but from hiding for so long from something else. From keeping a part of myself buried.

I stand and take the towel from Mom and carry it into the kitchen. I run it under the faucet, rinsing the deep red stains out of the soft white cotton. I watch as the pink water splashes against the steel sink and makes its way down the drain, and I can't help but close my eyes because I, too, feel drained—I feel spent, wasted, and hopeless. I feel like I've been barely hanging on. With my eyes still closed, I grip the towel and wring it out as firmly as I can—I twist and squeeze until I feel the cotton crack beneath my palms.

When I open my eyes again, the red in the sink is gone. I see only crystal-clear water spiraling down, down, down toward its escape. And, for no reason at all, I feel something unexpected within me find its way up. Something that's been hiding for too long. A need. A voice. The Real Me. She missed her chance with Dr. S; she abandoned me when I needed her most. But here she is again, giving me the go-ahead. Giving me her blessing. Attempting to pull herself out of the drawer and into the light.

Now is my chance. This is my chance to say something. To say anything. To say everything—everything I've ever wanted to say. Everything I couldn't say. Everything that she never let me say before.

I carry the clean towel back to Mom and sit on the couch beside her. *What is it, Justine? What is it you want to say?*

"How could you let them do that to me, Mom?" I look right at her, but I don't see her sitting here beside me. I see her leaning over me, trying to cover my view, stroking my hair, telling me to be brave, telling me everything is okay.

She inhales one shallow, shaky breath. Though we've never spoken about it, she knows exactly what I'm asking. "Can't you just let it go, Justine? You're not in pain anymore."

I am in pain, Mom. Just a different kind.

"Do you know what that felt like? You let him brutalize me. And then you pretended it never happened. And, Mom, somehow, that hurt even more."

I expect anger. I expect denial. That's all she's ever given me before. But something's different now. Her face changes. Softens. Not out of understanding—more like, she's just given up. Like she wants to be done with this. Her face becomes trounced and tired. "I didn't *let* him, Justine."

My brows draw together. I don't understand. It's like there's her world and there's my world, and there's an entire galaxy stretching between them. And somewhere in that distance lies a painful hypothesis. "I was just as much a victim as you were," she says.

My heart sinks as her words take up space in my head, because although I wasn't sure exactly what I was hoping for, I know that this is not it. But maybe that's part of the problem. Is there anything she can say that would make this better? Is there anything she can say that would change what happened?

I don't know if things could have been different if my mother had been different. I don't know if my mother was really a victim.

What I do know is that *I* don't want to be a victim any longer.

My chest feels tight as my lungs attempt to expand within it. Suffocation—it's a funny word. Too much of one thing, too little of another. I feel it now like I felt it back then.

"Why can't we talk about this?" I ask her.

"A part of me had hoped you'd forgotten about it."

"Would that make things easier for you?"

"Wouldn't it make things easier for you?" she asks.

I shake my head. "It's a part of me, Mom, all of it, from the first moment they put it on. I can't forget it. I wish the whole thing never happened."

"I wish it never happened, too," she says.

"I know you do," I sigh. "But it did happen. And, Mom," I continue, looking her in the eyes as if I could see into the past. "I thought I deserved it. You made me *feel* like I deserved it. You made me feel like there was something wrong with me. Not just my leg, but me. Inside. Like I wasn't good enough. Like I was nothing more than a disappointment. Like I needed to be fixed. You made me believe it. And I've believed it every day since. I try not to, I try to bury it, but all I want is to be alone so that no one ever looks at me the way you looked at me. So that no one ever treats me the way you treated me. So that no one ever makes me feel the way you made me feel." I exhale shakily and unburden my lungs of my enduring injustices. "But the truth is, that horrible, shameful part of me—it isn't even true. There was never anything wrong with *me*."

My throat burns as the words escape me. It was a bitter ball of poison that I had been swallowing for so long. I didn't want to confront my mother. I didn't want to be a problem. But I have no choice—there's no more room left inside me to hold it.

"Mom, every time you told me everything was okay, every time I've ever told *myself* everything was okay—*nothing* was okay. Just because you say it doesn't make it true."

Mom's eyes begin to fill with tears. She turns away from me, like she can't stand to look at me, like it hurts too much. And I want to tell her again that I'm sorry. That I'm sorry I made it so difficult, that I'm sorry I wasn't what she wanted me to be. That I'm sorry I wasn't what she needed me to be. And that I'm sorry I was hurting her all over again now.

It's on the very tip of my tongue. *Just say it. Just say it!* But I can't. Because I know I'm not the one hurting her. I know that her pain, just like mine now, it's coming from inside.

"I was there for you the whole time," she says.

I shake my head slowly, because I know I'm about to make it worse. "No, Mom," I say. "You were just *there*."

She slides her fingers along the couch cushion and tentatively covers my hand with hers. Tears begin to slide down my face without my permission. I try to hold them in, but I can't. I don't want to feel bad for Mom, because she contributed to so much of my pain—but I can't help it. It's like Dr. Faustus—I don't know who to feel bad for—or if I should even feel bad at all.

Mom nods her head and pats my hand. And I know that's her way of saying *enough*. She doesn't want to talk about this anymore. That's it. That's all she'll give me.

In this moment it becomes very clear to me—Mom could never have saved me, because she had been lost, too. Maybe she still was.

The truth is I should have died on that bloody exam table. Death by betrayal. But I didn't. Instead of ceasing to exist, I was refabricated. My lungs took new breath; my heart beat a new rhythm; my eyes saw through a sharpened lens. A lens that focused on the dangers all around me. That's what trauma does—it bookends the chapters of your life. It perforates your story with pauses. It demarcates the Before and the After. Part One and Part Two.

I should have died, but I went on living. It was a deathless death.

A trauma like that is not something you can carry around with you forever—it's too heavy. You have to put it away, somewhere locked up in the back of your mind, where it's invisible, where it's weightless. You must. Only when you dare to peek inside does it take shape and form again and threaten to claw its way out.

I put my trauma in the junk drawer and kept it there for a long, long time.

Maybe it's selfish of Mom to deny me answers to my questions. But maybe it's selfish of me to expect her not to. I guess it doesn't really matter. Because when it comes down to it, this isn't really about Mom. Maybe it used to be; maybe there was a moment in time when she could have made things better. But that moment has long passed.

She was half right when she told me I was running from myself. What I had really been running from was the girl she had taught me to be—fearful, weak, and silent. To whisper when I should have been wailing, to be permissive when I should have protested. To be servile in the midst of suffering. I had learned to hold myself accountable for the actions of others, and when others should have been accountable to me, I learned only to question myself.

I wonder if that's what kept me coming back to Dr. Faustus. I was always searching for answers, hidden meaning in the text, some clue as to who was really to blame when everything literally went to hell.

But maybe it's not about blame. Maybe I'd been fixated on the wrong thing all along.

Maybe it was never me that was broken.

Maybe some things are simply beyond repair.

And maybe, just maybe, that's okay.

73

I WAIT OUTSIDE ALONE, the snow falling like red confetti as it reflects the blinding glare of the oversized, glowing ER sign. I listen to the soft mechanical whir of the automatic doors sliding open and shut as people scurry in and out of the building, shoulders curled against the biting wind.

I turn my head up toward the sky. I see no stars, but I know they're there. It makes me think about the things we can't see, even when they're right in front of us, and the things we can see but choose not to. I think about the times I've prayed for the stars to stop moving, and how sometimes I wished they'd move just for me. I think about how sometimes the sky looks so close you could poke it with your fingertip, and sometimes it looks so impossibly far away it's hard to imagine there's a god behind it.

The motion-sensitive doors slide open again, but no one passes through them. I chalk it up to the wind and resist the urge to peek inside. Noah followed the EMTs in to make sure Mom would be well taken care of. I declined. I chose to decline. It was a big deal—to me. Not because I didn't want to make sure Mom was okay—I did. And not because I was being a brat and was trying to prove a point—I wasn't.

But because after all that had happened, after all that had been said and all that had not been said, this time, finally, I felt that something might be different.

But to walk into that ER beside Mom, to be the dutiful daughter, to pretend everything was fine, to hold her hand and shed a tear and tap my foot anxiously against the hollow gurney as I sat by her head waiting for some doctor to tell me she was perfectly okay, when all I wanted for so long was for someone to tell me that *I* was perfectly okay, well, that might have somehow washed this new change all away. And I didn't want to lose it. I wanted to hold on to it and protect it and rub it all over me. I wanted to saturate myself with it, this thing that wasn't simply the end of something but rather the beginning of something better. And I decided I would cry no more tears here tonight.

If I could have counted each one of my tears as they fell over the years, they would have added up to this very moment. This moment when I decided enough was enough. This moment when I decided *I* was enough.

Sometimes it felt very important to cry. Sometimes it felt important not to.

74

NOAH MAKES A PREDICTION that night after emerging from the ER. We stand face-to-face as he slips his hands around my waist and into my back pockets. I do the same, and we are locked together like two sides of a zipper.

"You're going to go, aren't you?" he asks. But it's more of a conclusion than a question.

I shrug and lean my face onto his chest. "You can't save everybody, Sheriff."

"I know." He nods, slipping his hand out of my pocket to tuck a piece of hair behind my ear, then sliding it back in again. "You wouldn't let me, anyway."

It occurs to me that Noah might not be able to leave this town any more than I can stay. At least not right now. "You're going to stay."

Noah doesn't say anything, but rests his chin on the top of my head.

"Sometimes it takes courage to stay, and sometimes it takes courage to go."

I look up at him, and he smiles a smile of recognition, lowers his head, and kisses me softly. "You're so very, very wise," he says, pulling back. "Almost as if you're meant for something bigger and better."

"Bigger and better than Sheriff Noah? Does such a thing exist?"

Noah laughs, and the movement shakes my body. "I don't know, but if it does, I have no doubt you'll find it."

I shiver a little from the cold and let Noah pull me in tighter. I rest my cheek on the silver star embroidered on his jacket, but what touches me is the heart of gold beneath it. I smile. "And *I'll* know just where to find *you.*"

75

HE WAS RIGHT, the know-it-all. I decided to say goodbye to my little cabin in the woods. I said goodbye to my mint-green kitchen and my fire mountain. I said goodbye to empty afternoons in The Treasure Box and nameless faces on sidewalks. I said goodbye to my little cocoon. I said goodbye to what I'd thought I'd needed in exchange for something I knew I wanted—a new beginning.

Well, another new beginning.

I'm trying to make different choices now, too. Not choices out of fear, but out of faith. It's not always easy. There are days I still find myself stuck in the junk drawer, still find it calling to me. It creeps in—that old viscosity—heavy and thick, and lingers for a while. Light becomes softer; voices become muffled. Everything seems grainy and worn. It's not a comfortable place to be, but it's familiar. Sometimes the thickness threatens to pull me to the back, back into the shadows—that rectangle of light getting smaller and smaller as the drawer starts to close. But I haven't sealed myself in just yet.

Most of the time the junk drawer is just something I carry around inside me. A place to keep all my secrets. A place to keep all the hurtful things people have said and done to me, and the hurtful things I say and do to myself. A place to keep all the fears and insecurities. Sometimes I wonder just how big the drawer is, how much it can hold. Sometimes it feels like it's about to burst wide open, and those are the days I worry about falling in.

But the more time that passes, the more I realize what I can change and what I can't. I can't change what happened to me. I can't change the memories. I can't erase the scars. I can't empty all the pain and anguish from the drawer. I can't yank it out of me and turn it upside down over a trash bin and start fresh. Because as much as I hate it, it's still a part of me, the Real Me. Without it, there'd just be a big hole.

So maybe instead of looking at the junk drawer as this hidden, disgraceful part of me, instead of fearing it as something that can take me over, maybe I can think of it as something that I overcame. Something that I conquered. Something that I'm proud of. Something that I own.

Not something that nearly destroyed the Real Me, but something that helped to build it.

And maybe I should just shut the fucking drawer.

Because nothing is predestined if I don't want it to be. I get to choose. I get to make good choices and bad choices and live with the consequences of all of them.

But at least they'll be mine.

76

DEAR KACEY,

When the day turned to night,
You stayed by my side;
When it all became too much,
You helped me to hide.
When I was drowning in self pity,
You never let me sink;
When I took you to the edge,
You pulled me from the brink.
You're the angel on my shoulder;
You're the wind in my sail;
You're my road to redemption
When it all goes to hell.
You stitch everything together
When the whole world pulls apart.
You're the North Star in my sky;
You're the compass in my heart.

I won't ask for your forgiveness—
It's been way too long.
I won't ask for a second chance
When the first went so wrong.
I won't ask to hear your voice again
On my answering machine—
I know I've been a nightmare;
I can't ask for a dream.
I won't ask you for understanding
This time around;
I won't ask you to believe
My feet are firmly on the ground.
I won't ask you for anything
When you've given more than I could ever repay,
But I hope you'll still give it all to me, anyway.

Love,
Elisabeth

77

"**DID YOU MAKE IT** there okay?" Jonathan asks.

"Yep, walking in right now," I say. I slide my key card into the reader and yank on the heavy double doors. I prop them open with my over-stuffed duffel bag and remove my sunglasses. My shadow stretches out far and long against the concrete entryway in the late-afternoon sun.

"It feels kind of empty without you here. I hope you don't mind if I call to check in every once in a while?"

"Not at all," I say, dragging a few cardboard boxes behind me and letting the door fall closed. "How's your new tenant?"

Jonathan exhales, and I can hear his smile. "Old and crotchety."

"Really? He never seemed crotchety to me."

"That's because he likes you," Jonathan says, a wink in his voice. "Plus, he's not nearly as neat as you were, and he's got so many wind chimes hung up around the place it sounds like a symphony anytime anyone sneezes. But at least this way I can keep an eye on him."

I picture Mr. Ito in my little cabin, reading his newspaper in the kitchen, daydreaming in the orange glow of the fire mountain at sunset. There are places that are easy to leave behind, and there are places that you take with you no matter how far away you go.

"That's great," I say, slinging my bags across my chest and stuffing everything into the elevator.

"I think he's finally warming up again to his new neighbor, too. Although, I agree with him, Noah's *incessant whining*," Jonathan shouts away from the phone, "about you leaving is taking its toll on us both."

"Please come back, Elisabeth!" I hear Noah's voice in the background. "I was wrong. A college education is highly overrated. There's nothing wrong with organizing soaps and dusting dream catchers for the rest of your life—just ask Cardinal. You'll never want for anything . . . ," he moans.

"He's still at it?" I ask Jonathan.

"He hasn't let up since you left."

I hear Noah again, groaning dramatically in the background.

"Please come back soon," Jonathan murmurs.

"Mm-hmm," I say as I weave my way through the crowded corridor, sidestepping an overzealous game of table tennis spilling out of a common room stuffed with tattered sofas and a blaring TV. I stop at the last door at the end of the hall. Then I turn the key, push open the door, and take in my little room.

"You know, Jonathan, I actually think things worked out pretty okay."

He's quiet for a moment, and I wonder if the call dropped, but then he says, "Yeah, me too."

I let my bags fall to the floor and take a deep breath. New paint, old mattresses, the raw anticipation seeping from all corners of the campus.

I'm about to let Jonathan go when he says, "Cardinal would like to say hi."

"Okay," I reply, surprised.

I hear the shuffling of the phone and then a raspy voice. "Elisabeth?"

"Hi, Mr. Ito. I hope you're managing all right at the store without me."

"Oh, yes, everything's just fine. We just got a new shipment of soaps in—sandalwood, or something like that. I think the local gals will like it. Anyway. You know, I never really did need much help. Not enough customers to really warrant an extra pair of hands."

"Oh," I say, feeling slightly guilty. "Well, um, why did you hire me then, Mr. Ito?"

He wavers but then takes a breath and continues. "As a favor to my wife's niece. She said you needed looking out for." He clears his throat and chuckles softly, "You take care, all right?" before turning the phone back over to Jonathan.

I furrow my brow, worried that Mr. Ito might be confused. "Jonathan, is Mr. Ito okay?" I ask.

"Sharp as a whip," he says. "You better get going."

"Yeah," I reply, deciding to let it go—he's got Jonathan and Noah there now. "Tell Noah I'll call him later?"

"I will. Don't be a stranger, okay?"

"I won't be," I promise as I hang up the phone.

It's the end of August, and the late-summer breeze blows another type of promise through my open fourth-floor window—the promise of possibility. It ruffles the dingy curtains hanging crookedly against the wall. The rest of the room is pretty barren, and I want to get started right away making it feel like my own. I shake out my bedsheets and smooth them until they're perfect, lay my comforter squarely on top. I organize my clothes in the narrow closet by color and season. But just as I peel the tape back from one of my large boxes of books, I hear a heavy fist rattle the door. Then a thin pile of rubber-banded papers appears beneath it.

It's mostly junk—a couple of advertisements for nearby pubs and late-night pizza joints, a flyer advertising different clubs operating within the dorm. But at the bottom of the pile I find a small eggshell envelope with my name on it.

I recognize the handwriting immediately. It's addressed with my mother's perfect scrolling print. I haven't seen her since she was discharged from the Fish Creek ER almost seven months ago, but I did send her my new address when I got my housing assignment. I wonder how long this letter's been waiting for me. I hesitate with my thumb beneath the flap of the envelope, not really wanting to read whatever it is Mom feels like she has to say. But if I try to ignore it, I know I won't be able to think of anything else. I open the envelope and inside find another sealed envelope with a sticky note stuck to it. *This came in the mail for you. Love, Mom.* Now even more curious, I remove the sticky note, open the second envelope, and unfold the pretty floral stationery. It smells faintly of strawberries and is dated almost exactly one year ago.

Dear Justine,

Please accept my warmest congratulations on your recent high school graduation. Now that you're officially kind of an adult, I thought I'd take this opportunity to remind you of the child I knew, an exception only in that you were exceptional. I've kept the enclosed paper tacked above the desk in my home office since the day you wrote it in the sixth grade. I thought you might like it back. I hope one day to see it in print.

With gratitude,
Antonia Conti

Folded within the stationery is a worn piece of notebook paper.

Fixated

by Justine Elisabeth Amos

We live together but we are not friends.

I stand determined, you waver and bend.

I crave control while you fumble about;

I keep it all in, you let it all out.

I've got my fists up while you're down in a crawl;

I hang on by my pinkies when you're ready to fall.

I don't like you and you don't like me—

Side by side in a discordant harmony.

I hide in the tolerant, sheltering night,

You're caught in the cruel, unrelenting light.

I'm scared to trust while you have no choice;

I'm silenced by the sovereignty of your stronger voice.

Your cries are loud, but what isn't spoken

Is, I am the plight—I am what's broken.

I am a storm cloud swollen with rage;

I play the hostage—but I am the cage.

Still, you take the blame for all of my lies

And for that, I do apologize.

You are my body and I am your mind—

Since we're stuck with each other, let's just be kind.

I'll ignore you and you ignore me—

We'll go on with our lives, separately,

With a clear understanding of what each other intends.

We live together but we are not friends.

My heart squeezes as I fold the poem and slip it into the envelope with Ms. Conti's letter. I hesitate for a second, but then I stick it in between the pages of my yellow notebook and drop it into my bottom desk drawer along with my worn paperback with the orange cover.

I shut the drawer—and I smile to myself.

Another loud knock rumbles the door. I narrow my eyes with annoyance, expecting the mail boy again, and yank the door open to a chaotic scene. The hallway is teeming with kids running up and down the crowded space. Parents are lugging boxes, diligently checking room numbers. Dorm staff stand at every hallway intersection with whistles around their necks, shouting instructions over all the noise.

But I don't hear any of it. I don't see any of it. All I can make sense of is the person standing right in front of me.

Kacey fills the doorway, her long black hair gleaming beneath the fluorescent hallway lights. She has a gigantic worn duffel bag thrown over her shoulder. A crinkled, handwritten poem on a sheet of notebook paper in one hand, a silver glittery Fish Creek snow globe encasing a butter yellow rose in the other.

"I'll always be here. I promise."

Kacey had been looking out for me the whole time. Of course she had.

"All right, freshman," she teases, looking me up and down. Her eyes giddy and swimming with emotion, her smile warm and stretching widely across her face. "You ready to do this?"

This is where I belong. This is where I'm supposed to be. I am fine. I am okay. I am safe.

"Mm-hmm," I say. "I'm ready."

I am ready.

ACKNOWLEDGMENTS

Dear Reader,

As someone who always reads a book's acknowledgments section before anything else, I've taken great delight in the crafting of my own. It is true that no (wo)man is an island, and neither is any book. I cannot overstate the influence of the colleagues and collaborators, family and friends who helped to shape *I Am the Cage* into the novel it is today.

To begin with, I am unequivocally indebted to my agent, Richard Pine, who truly propelled what might have been merely a dream floating around in my head into a novel with two little words: *keep writing*. Thank you, Richard, for your patience, your advocacy, and your wisdom. Thank you for never forgetting to say, "and I'm Allison's agent, too." But mostly, thank you for believing in Justine and her story, and in turn, believing in me. Every chapter, every page, every poem exists because you told me it could.

To my editor and publisher, Julie Strauss-Gabel, thank you for taking a chance on me. Thank you for seeing something in these pages that others did not, something in my story that others did not. The time that you dedicated to these characters will not soon be forgotten, nor will the immense knowledge I have gained from your partnership. Working with you has become the stuff of legend in my home: "Stop everything! Julie has written!" In every way, it's been a dream. The truth is, I still can't believe you picked me.

My appreciation in spades to everyone at InkWell Management for your commitment and enthusiasm. Thank you to the talented teams at Dutton Children's Books and Penguin Random House for your hard work and for giving *I Am the Cage* such a warm and welcoming home. Tremendous thanks to the sales, marketing, and publicity teams at Penguin Young Readers, especially Elyse Marshall and Marisa Russell, for going to bat for me and this book. I have great admiration for the entire crew at Listening Library and want to thank you for your creativity and diligence. I'd also like to recognize jacket designer Theresa Evangelista and interior designer Anna Booth for their elegant vision, as well as artist Erin Cone for permitting the use of her gripping work, *Unfolding*, for the cover image.

My most sincere thanks to those who read early drafts: Laura Boroughf, Kate Bowler, Glennon Doyle, Sarah Hurwitz, Amy Neeran-Steinman, Nancy Rothbard, and Nancy Xiao—I am overwhelmed by your kindness and support. Thank you to Susan Grant, for your editorial contributions and endless cheerleading. Foophratootaloofra (fancy thanks) to Marissa Solomon Shandell, who donated her time and insight selflessly, and with equal parts passion and gentleness. An enormous thank you to John Green, who unknowingly kept me from highlighting it all and hitting DELETE.

Thank you to Stacy Brand and Julie Bagley, for being there from beginning to end, and for all the muck and magic in the middle. To Susanna Choo, for being the kind of friend I didn't know grown-ups could have. To Laura Beauchamp, whose generosity knows no bounds—you are truly a force of nature. And to Liad Pernock, for your wonderful feedback, wonderful friendship, and all-around universal wonderfulness.

A very special thank you to LC, SP, and JJ, who each, in their own unique ways, contributed to the evolution of this book. To SG, for giving me the courage to trust it. To SD, for gifting me the time to write it. And to SS, for your grace and guidance in the aftermath of it all.

Thank you to Mom and Dad, for making hard decisions so that I might have easier ones. To Ian, for reminding me we all face an important choice in life between preserving relationships and playing Trivial Pursuit. And to Eric, for everything and then some—you're the family I'd choose even if we weren't family.

My heartfelt thanks and gratitude to my devoted husband Adam, for your unwavering encouragement and for convincing me that maybe I had something sort of important to say. Thank you for the countless rereads, the countless rereads, and the countless rereads, for your spelling expertise, and for acquiescing that sometimes, yes, it is okay, and perhaps even advisable, to use a run-on sentence. There's no one I'd rather be in an alliance with than you.

To Joanna, Elena, and Henry, thank you for allowing me to be your momma—it is far and away the greatest thing I'll ever get to do.

Lastly, I'd like to say thank you to *you* for picking up this book. It means the world to me for you to be holding it in your hands. While you may be touching a smooth, shiny jacket (or tapping at the shadowy page-turns of a e-reader, or perhaps listening to my own shaky voice as I read my own shaky words), *I Am the Cage* started with just one word pressed into the top margin of a piece of loose-leaf paper in dusty, cursive pencil: *Justine*. She is as much a part of me as anyone who is not me can be—but she is not me. Though the facets of our experiences may feel familiar, they are not one and the same. She lives between these pages and nowhere else.

From the bottom of my heart, thank you for reading.

Allison